The Ravens of the Moon

CHARLES L. GRANT

DOUBLEDAY & COMPANY, INC.
GARDEN CITY, NEW YORK
1978

All of the characters in this book
are fictitious, and any resemblance
to actual persons, living or dead,
is purely coincidental.

Library of Congress Cataloging in Publication Data

Grant, Charles L.
The ravens of the moon.

I. Title.
PZ4.G7714Rav [PS3557.R265] 813'.5'4
ISBN: 0-385-12969-6
Library of Congress Catalog Card Number 77-82758

Printed in the United States of America
First Edition

Author's Dedication

When all is said and done . . . and done,
When all the letters and calls are passed,
There's still that bottle on my cabinet file

For Tom

And Nat

And Damon, their son

The

Ravens of the Moon

One

At the Fringe Kilometer, on one darkened street, the temperature too slow in its falling made the local Blues surly. They had arrived just before sunset to raise the electrified meshnet to the level of the rooftops, had inserted the Gateways to admit those foolish enough to have forgotten the time. Now they waited, motionless, for something to happen. Some praying nothing would because it was much too hot to do more than try to think, others hoping something would just to relieve the duty's standard boredom. They checked their uniforms, their stunton sticks, their projectile ammunition, their fingernails. No one looked at the bulky cases sitting unopened against one of the buildings.

A sergeant walked up to the mesh. Delan Caine. He reached into his pocket and pulled out a slip of paper, balled it up in his palms and tossed it. The paper flared a bright white, faded to yellow and sparked its ashes onto the street. He nodded, adjusted the black helmet, heavy on his head, and turned to inspect his twenty charges. Perspiration ran down his sides. Formed droplets at the tip of a thrice-broken nose. One more night and he would be off the Fringe, back in City Prime where the lights and the pedestrians clashed in their colors. He had started his career as a Denver cop, moved to Washington to live with his sister when her husband died. In the war. In the desert. She had hoped his duty on the Denver Fringe would exempt him from similar work in the Noram Capital; but experience was his traitor, and though he hadn't argued, he felt as she did, that surely they could have chosen someone else. Someone younger. He shrugged. One more night.

But the ratgangs had learned, and he wasn't worried. They had learned far too well for the tempers of some, and they stayed in the suburbs with the shadows of deserted houses, prowling the empty streets, picking at the long-ago looted stores and small offices. When winter arrived some would surrender invisibly, infiltrating the city and finding employment, discarding their past like discolored snakeskin. The rest would drift south and harass the Fringes of Houston and Mobile.

A WatchDog buzzed suddenly over the border of the Fringe, its spiderleg lights pinning the Blues to their stations. Caine watched as it vanished, an alien thing, then frowned when he saw a starflare pop noiselessly and float on the currents to the ground. He wondered if it had been a signal that a ratgang was moving in his platoon's direction, but a check with the radio micbut on his chest told him otherwise. A greenie, then, he decided, spooked by the shadows that his machine created.

He grinned and rejoined his men, who were gathered around the tank that squatted in the center of the road. They greeted him, included him, and they told each other lies to pass the night to dawn. Ignoring the heat. Ignoring the silence.

In City Prime, however, there was no quiet.

Advocs enticed with regulated lies from hidden grilles over shopfront doors, complimenting the ladies and luring the men while carefully timed windowscreens flashed the night's first sales. A theater colonnade spun rainbows around its shimmering pillars; a joyhall vented loud musical snares that were scented with the essence of the games therein. The citybred paid little attention to the aural assault–it was merely background noise that faded into distance as they spilled from the sidewalks into the vehicle-banned streets.

And then the venners came to meet the peak of the crowds.

There was little that the merchants could do about their arrival. Legal procedures had ended months before when the Noram High Court Star reasserted the rights of free competition; besides, the majority opinion scolded in carefully couched phrases, the venners sell far too little to be a serious threat to an established, well-run firm–leave them alone and they'll soon go away. Unsatisfied, some businessmen tried the physical approach; but after a brief concerted effort to drive the venners out, there were fires. Timid fires. Scarcely extensive enough to char a wall or damage a shelf of flammable stock. The hints, however, were taken, then used as an incentive for a tacit truce uneasily arranged, begrudgingly maintained.

And the venners came out to meet the peak of the crowds.

In front of a restaurant with a mirrored gleaming front, then, a stall had its fans cut and it settled awkwardly at the edge of the curb. It was a meter-and-a-half cube with its streetside glowing in black-and-green swirls, its pedside opened down to display on stepshelves handcraft figurines. There were no advocs or music, no neon, no banners. The shelves weren't velvet, the prices not in view. Only hand-high carvings of gods long dead: Zeus, Ares, Marduk, Isis—tiny gods for the nervous, demigods for the proud; talismans against the coming of the war, amulets in place of churches. Primitive. Appealing. Silently staring.

The venner, standing alongside his stall, was a small man, slender, his flat black hair cropped close to his ears. Dark eyes were shadows beneath the ledge of his brow, a blunted nose, thin lips, a jaw line that paused only momentarily to form a cleft chin. His long-fingered hands reached up to straighten the folds of the cowl draped behind his neck, to brush at the sweep of the fitted brown robe. Around his waist was a broad red belt to carry his creds and his cards, and it gathered the robe in unequal folds, incongruously revealing below the red-trimmed hem a pair of sturdily built dark boots. A quick appraising glance into the mouth of the stall, and he adjusted a Wotan into profile before turning his smile to the passing citybred.

He could sense, then, their discomfort at the heat. They would wonder why he chose to wear such a confining garment. They would stop, stare, perhaps buy after his tricks. But he was, he acknowledged with a rueful grin, known mainly for his tricks, and so the tricks he would do.

He lifted his hands palm out, pushed back with his wrists the sleeves puffed to give him some size and plucked from the air a meager bouquet of moist orange roses without a word. He threw the bouquet to a young woman who laughed and touched self-consciously at the nest of ruffles at her breasts. As she walked away, giggling to her companion, he watched the play of muscles on her bare back, the deceptive sweep of unrecognizable black material that draped from her waist. What a shame, he thought, to hide such hips. But black was the wrong color for a night like this. If it got any hotter . . . and he shook his head, grinning, and wove from the air a trail of bright ribbons.

A woman, alone, in a high-necked white suit, stopped as he did, her frown fading as he piled the ribbons into her hands. "I don't know if I can coin any of that," she said sadly, nodding toward the stall.

He bowed, swept his arm toward the figures on his shelves and with his free hand carefully cupped her elbow. Drew her closer. Away from the flow that threatened to pull her on.

"We'll see," he said politely. "Shanlon Raille at your service, Mistress. And these ugly things here are my friends for tonight."

The restaurant's streetface was mirrored and narrow, the only opening a clear circular window barely large enough to frame a small boy's face. The menu was a discreet whisper over the bronze-edged door, the foyer a small room paneled in walnut, dimly lit. No chairs. No lounging bench. No frames on the walls.

Ty Yenkin, co-Host for the night, fingered the simulbrass chain that was linked boldly around his neck. The metal was cool in his hand, cooler by far than the tight gold tunic and black trousers he wore. He squinted through the window, shook his head and straightened with one hand on his hip to massage a dull cramp.

"He makes me hot just looking at him."

A similarly dressed man, shorter and stout, moved next to him and nodded as he mopped nonexistent perspiration from his forehead. He pulled, then, at his tunic's braided hem, trying to hide the paunch that threatened to part the bulging seam. "Bastard thing this is," he muttered. "Over at the Ambassador their Hosts wear kilts on nights like this. Silk, I think. Damned cool, anyway."

"You haven't got the legs for it, Haward," Yenkin said. "If you ever decide to lose a few kilos, maybe then I'll agree."

Haward snorted, jerked a thumb toward the window and raised his eyebrows.

"Statues and things," Yenkin answered. He pulled at the thin stub that passed for his nose. "At least this one isn't pushing food. For a change."

"He's bad enough, take my word. People see the stupid little window, they see the stall right out there and they'll hit the stall every damn time." He rubbed his fleshy hands together, transferred the massage to the sides of his neck. "We shouldn't allow it, you know. I don't care what the law says, we shouldn't allow it. We ought . . . we ought to get someone who knows someone who knows someone in a ratgang. Smuggle him in. Maybe push this guy to a more favorable location. Favorable for his health, that is." And his laugh was a wheeze.

Yenkin glanced outside again. "Those tricks he does aren't half bad, you know. Better than that singer guy we had last week. Remember him? I wish I knew how many creds that sobitch cost us."

"One is too many."

He watched as a woman in white accepted a price for a tiny laughing Loki, decided that the tricks saved that venner a lot of wasted time haggling and compromising. Clever, he thought, and moved away abruptly when the venner pointed at the window. A moment later the woman came through the door, smiling, holding the godlet in her hand as if it was an offering to the chef. Haward greeted her, accompanied her down the short corridor into the dining room. When he returned a few minutes later he was frowning.

"I don't get it," he said, resuming his post. "She told me that shagger out there recommended the place."

"Well, thank his small gods for small favors, idiot, and stop worrying."

"How can I? See, how can he recommend a place he's never been in?"

"How do you know he's never been in here?"

"Hey, come on, Ty. Take a look at him, will you? There isn't a chance he can afford this place on his best day."

Yenkin stared out for a third time. The venner's robe wasn't all that ancient, nor did he seem as generally unkempt as most of the others set up along the street. If he lived close enough to the Fringe, his profit might be rather sizable, depending upon how much he paid for the wood. Assuming it was wood. Assuming he paid for it.

The door slid open and Haward jabbed at his ribs. He stiffened, bowed to the murmurs of a trio of Highmen, and preceded them into the restaurant proper. Without asking their pleasure, he led them by the exposed front tables, the gilted arch to the liklounge, brought them directly to a string of privbooths set along the rear wall. They said nothing as he pulled aside the shimmering black curtain, and he noted as they slid in that they carried tension with them like a hulking fourth partner. Smiling apologetically, then, he reached over the polished, light-grained table and coded menu, music, lights and privacy into the canted panel on the wall.

As he did so, he felt a feather-light touch at his hip from the man on the right.

The roaring intensified. Echoes against the rubble of buildings, the reclamation of forests beyond the boundary of the Fringe. Caine swore. A ratgang evidently had discovered a cache of gasoline and an automobile to drink it. The two-score police shifted into a ragged line behind the tank and waited. More than likely it would be a short-lived game of charge and run, the 'gang spilling out of the car before it slammed sparking into the mesh. He ordered fire equipment to be readied on the sidelines. Shook his head when the tank crew asked if they should mount.

Lights, then, in the Keylofts bordering the street. Heads poked out, elbows rested on the sills. Another show for the masses, Caine thought sourly, and he wondered what made people take Keys so close to the edge. Hoping, perhaps, there'll be a time when the suburbs would be readily accessible again and they wouldn't have to live so close to their jobs. There were still small towns scattered between the cities, but they regulated their sizes and encouraged no more than sustenance business. Hoping, then, but a false hope at that, he thought. The retreat had begun after the first Oil War, culminated after the second, and dreams of turning the migration around were abundant and vocal, and lacking foundation. The hovercats were still too clumsy and uncomfortable for extensive traveling, the lectrics too limited and expensive for other than local or transystem use. No, he thought as he spun his stunton to midstrength, they were stuck in the city with the rest of the country. Even cleaned up and modernized, luxuries and gadgets and reasonably adequate housing, it was still the city. They were all still the city.

"Sergeant Caine?"

There was a time when he visited a town on the other side of the mountains. To see his nephew and learn how the Blues outside the city had handled the ratgangs forays and raids.

"Hey, Sarge!"

So much space. Trees. Not nearly as clean—

He blinked when a fist jabbed at his shoulder.

There was a shape in the outer darkness.

He snapped an order and the snub-barreled turret cranked round to face it.

A laughing jibe from above about the weapon's reputation for accuracy. He ignored it. Without the Blues and the 'Dogs and the clumsy-looking tank, the people in the Fringe would be helpless to constant attack. Ratgangs weren't larks; they were definitely aptly named. And Caine knew, then, what his worth was, and prided it silently.

If the car smashed the barrier, they'd be screaming for blood.

Yenkin slipped unnoticed into the employees' lavroom and looked at the coin that had been dropped into his pocket. He whistled silently and rubbed a slow hand over his jaw. It was without a doubt a payment for a sudden and convenient attack of amnesia. And the donor had been Helman Talle, a Usam Senator for whom Yenkin had worked for several years when the Senator had been an aspiring candidate for the slot of Premier. That had been nearly twenty years ago, and a period of service he regretted leaving. But Talle had been buried in the primaries by a Cenam Consul whose name no one remembered. Not being one who fought windmills with knives, Talle contented himself with Congress, eventually rising to the leadership of a persistent Opposition. Yenkin, who missed the excitement, took what creds he had saved and traveled around the country, had returned to Washington only two years before when the jobs and the money and the women ran out.

Being a Host wasn't all that bad, he told himself as he patted his still-black hair back into place. The hours are good, and I still get to see old friends. Once in a while. When they remember. When they care to acknowledge a faintly familiar face.

He sighed, grinned sadly and glanced at the privbooth. The two Consuls, however, he did not place. One, by his winter-pale skin and thinning light hair, he decided was from Canam, perhaps Montreal; the other's complexion wasn't dark enough to be from Cenam, so he had to be one of the two Consuls from Usam.

He laughed aloud suddenly, covered his mouth with a quieting hand. Canam, Usam, Cenam Consuls; Senators from states and Reps from districts–how the hell they got anything done was more than he could understand, even after having worked within the circles they formed. Still . . . well, they did keep things moving after a fashion.

He patted the slight bulge caused by the coin and hurried back to Haward to tell him he'd be taking a double shift that night.

"You're a craze, you know that."

"I can't tell you how much I agree. But there's the creds, you know. If I'm heading up north or going back to the other coast I have to get the creds. Travel still ain't free, no matter what they say."

"And what are you going to do, Ty? Host in another eatin? The wages are the same all over. It's ridiculous to leave."

"Climate, then," Yenkin grinned. "I need a change of climate."

"Oh sure," Haward said. "You need a change of climate like I need a new wife."

"Ah, don't be so bitter. If you're smiling when the Highmen come out, they might give you a little something on the side. You know what I mean—a tip on the elections, things like that."

"No chance," the stout man said. "I'm off in two hours, and heading right for my Key and a lastmeal that will make me sleep for a week."

"You don't need it," Yenkin laughed, poking at Haward's stomach.

Haward shoved the hand away, pulled at his tunic, brushed idly at his chest. "You should have stayed with that Senator, Ty. Being servant to a Highman isn't all that bad, you know. At least you'd end up with a pension instead of a stupid-looking uniform."

Helman Talle double-checked the Host's setting of the curtain, puzzled that such a faceless man should seem so familiar. Certain of his privacy, then, he relaxed, settled back to allow the booth to massage his spine and drain the tension that had been with him most of the day. His eyes closed momentarily, opened only when a frosted glass drifted onto the slide beneath the wall's slim console. He tried not to snatch at it, sipped politely the cool dark green liquid before someone launched into a time-consuming toast. His companions retrieved their own tall drinks as soon as they arrived, and neither of them noticed, or were too polite to mention, that Talle's hands were trembling.

A finger lifted to touch-dry his lips, his head tilted slightly to the right. "All right, Faux," he said to the younger, Canam Consul, "what foul thing have I done this time that you have to play spanker for the Premier?"

Faux winced theatrically at the question. A hand reached up to tug at a curl bothering his right ear. It was an affectation Talle knew well: everything the Montrealer said from now on would only be half the truth, and that would be suspect as well.

"Helman, you seem unusually paranoid today. Why can't we share a friendly drink before lastmeal without having to bring up nonsense like business?"

Talle laughed without parting his lips, shook his head and looked to Sandar Bendal on Faux's left. "Would you tell this man here, Sandy, that we're both too old to be playing at diplomatic courtesies? He drags me away from a perfectly acceptable evening with my wife and daughter, makes dark and ominous hints about the coming of the storm, and then when he's got me here tingling like copper in lightning, he has to get up on a carousel and let me run along beside him."

Bendal only smiled. Weakly. He offered nothing.

"Come on, Faux, what's the matter with you two?" He frowned and folded his hands around his glass. "Never mind. The Premier has heard from Meditcom. The Community won't listen, is that right?"

Faux looked to be searching for another topic, then—reluctantly—nodded and discovered the fascination in the table's grain design. "The pouch arrived early this morning. We," and he nodded to Bendal, "were told not two hours ago in the Premier's office. It wasn't much of a discussion, actually. We'd been planning our reaction for some time. What the other Consuls have to know they'll be told tomorrow in Session."

"And what about the Congress?" Talle snapped. "Do we get around to learning about the war sometime? I certainly hope it's before the Service sends the troops out again. It would be nice to let our people know, you know. A gesture from the top, so to speak. A sign of their confidence in our ability to keep fighting the same damned war all over again."

Faux stared at a thumbnail.

"Quiet, Helman," Bendal said softly. While his own frail gray matched Talle's, his face was doubly lined, doubly chalked. Wattles sagged over the tight collar of his office's somber jacket, and he swallowed constantly as if gulping for air. He had less than a year before he rotated into Senate Emeritus and Cabinet Adviser, but there were few politicians in Noram who believed he would live that long. "We can understand and appreciate your bitterness at the system, but none of us were around when it all changed,

Helman, so do us the respect of office and keep your bile to yourself while you hear us out." He cleared his throat, sipped at his glass. "To be honest, I don't know if we can completely avoid involvement in the new war. But I do know there's a way we've worked out with the Premier that might be able to keep the Noram Confederation from falling apart while we're about it."

"Now that's fantastic," Talle said, his sarcasm uncharacteristically heavy. There was a time once, he thought before speaking again, when a Premier's policy wouldn't have been made without his participation from the outset. A time once . . . apparently no more. "What will it be this time? Save the Colonies from starvation again? Increase planetside production so we can siphon off the excess profits and pay for the ships that will keep the Martians from dying? Or will it be Luna this time around?" He raised a hand to block Faux's impatience. "Let's see . . . if only one of the domes has been left unbreached by some dreadful natural disaster, it will be up to us to stick together and marshal our resources to repair and rebuild. Throw in a few grandiose promises about sending up more from the worst Fringes, and couple them with an equal amount of recruiting campaigns that will end with all but a handful of the public washed out because they're not quite right for the long trip Out. No. Wait a second. There's something better. We've discovered an alien–"

"You know, Helman," Faux interrupted, "you're a damned relic when you want to be! Why don't you come back from the–"

"What?" Talle said, his eyes wide and incredulous. "Are you denying, Consul, that those things never happened? Are you saying for the record that we've never pulled one of those stunts to keep the Noram myth going?"

"I never said that, Helman."

"For that I thank you, Consul."

"And Noram's not a myth, either. You're living in it, aren't you? It thrives, doesn't it?"

"That depends upon your definition."

"Helman," Bendal said finally, "Helman, shut up for a minute and listen to me. Hear me, Senator, when I tell you there's going to be a revolution."

She flounced, jerking her head angrily away from the girl walking beside her. It was too hot to argue. She was getting a headache with no poppers to help her. And she didn't know why she just didn't drop the whole thing and find something more pleasant to talk about. But Delia persisted, and she couldn't help responding. "I don't care what you say! I say he's cute. Not handsome, you understand. A little too tiny, a little too . . . thin. But he is still cute. For someone who doesn't work for a living."

"Hah! You're a snob, Caro, you know that? And I won't be surprised if the day after tomorrow you drag me and him down to the Hall to sign up for a pact. And not just a temporary. Oh no, nothing like that. This one will be for the life of the parties."

"You don't think I mean it, do you? I say he's really cute!"

"Caro," Delia said solemnly, "if every man on this planet was lined up from here to Luna, you couldn't find an ugly among them. Not a shagging one. You're just not capable of it. I swear it, if your father wasn't one—"

Caro looked back at the venner in front of the restaurant, then to the slender oriental fan he had caressed from behind her ear. It seemed to have been fashioned somehow from wafered leaded glass, translucent, shimmering hypnotically in the lights that they passed. It was an item she couldn't have ordinarily afforded, not without help, yet he had refused her return when she told him she didn't want to buy one of his gods. Refused her with a smile that seemed almost shy, then forestalled Delia's added protests by teasing a green flower from under her chin.

"Caro!"

She blinked, realized she was standing stupidly still while the hovbus drifted to its stop, its hurricane winds blocked by the low glastic partition that protected the lines waiting for its coming. It was black trimmed in white, sleek, staring.

"Well, Caro? Are you going to come on or do I have to leave without you?"

Caro drew the fan lightly over her palm.

"Blesséd priest, Caro, you can follow if you want!"

But she hesitated without knowing why. Already the line was too long for her to locate a comfortable seat within. If she boarded now she would be bruised from elbow to hip before reaching home. She shrugged. Delia took a step forward, looked back and slapped her thigh angrily before darting through the door as it readied to close her out.

I'll see you tomorrow, Caro mouthed to a shadow of a face that glared through a port as the hov coughed, lifted, drifted, plunged down its ramp into the old subway tubes. A whale, a beetle, a dozen like images. *Bye,* she said as the brief hurricane died, and she took her place at the head of the new line. A half hour wait now. She would be late for lastmeal. Again. Again. If her father came home for a pleasant change, her mother would be furious and pout all night if Caro didn't show up. But she told herself she needed some time to think more about the fan. No one, not even a venner more prosperous than most, gave away merchandise like that with no hopes for return. That he was setting himself for her was a faint possibility, though hardly probable. She knew what she looked like, and she didn't like what she saw: hair too red, skin too pale, the angles of her thin frame too underweight sharp despite the softening of flowing white ruffles at her neck and breasts, the puffs of cream at her blouse's shoulders, the effect of dawn clouds her brightly dyed slacks gave. Earlier, she had laughed with Delia at a woman who'd been wearing little more than the obligatory ruffles; and Caro had wished her father be something less than he was—though she was of age and more, the restraints of being public too often shackled her like a child of ten. A man thumped into her back, breaking her thoughts, and she nearly spilled over the barrier. She turned as he muttered an insincere apology and cursed fluently at him in a forgotten Cenam dialect, grinned broadly at the scowl on his perspiring face. Not all men are cute, Delia dear, she thought; nukes sure weren't, and neither were fat men.

Delia, however, consistently feigned discrimination despite the hard evidence that she charged with anyone who asked. Delia claimed she was only being patriotic and loved only soldiers, but there weren't many left who weren't soldiers these days. Another war was brewing, had been since the last uneasy truce, not to mention the Fringe riots and the university skirmishes and the seemingly weekly threats on the old Premier's life. Everywhere you turned there was a uniform of some kind, all from the Service, all topped with the featureless silvered masks that denied the wearer's humanity from forehead to chin. Her father had opposed the adornment, calling it nothing more than sculptured anonymity. She thought it true. And they were especially unnerving at night when they reflected the city lights, kaleidoscope masks with no eyes behind them.

Face it, Caro, you're bored.

Maybe, then, it was time to join another Cause. There were several currently vying for newspace these days. But they were all old and had lost whatever glamor their origins had provided. The worst in terms of appeal potential was the EcGroup—and Delia didn't help by being a fervent, though possibly temporary, disciple. She was always battering Caro's ears about the preservation of the environment, the air, the earth, the need to move back into the suburbs in force, with troops if necessary, and reclaim for pleasure what had been once used in rape. Caro didn't much care. There was no gasoline for popular consumption, not even for the airliners that rusted on tarmac fields; what landcars were left had been reserved to the Government and the Service and the few long-distance transports that flowed like segmented snakes between the continent's cities—with everyone cuddled within the urban womb once again, who needed it? Solar, fission, hydroelectric, wind—with luxuries rationed for so long few people missed them, and with the city air clean and the sky always sharp blue, who worried about the gray-yellow clouds that hovered over Lima or Rio or Capetown, ABS?

Delia did, a dozen times a day.

Caro decided that if a Cause was needed to fill her freetime constructively, she would probably join the Luxes. They were the logical opposition to rationing that, they claimed, long since had lost its urgency, the semihistorians who claimed the cities could still have the luxuries even the ordinary man had Way Back When. She grinned to herself. They wouldn't be too bad, the Luxes wouldn't. Her father didn't actively disapprove of them, and at least they gave parties now and then; the EcG was too damned serious.

The man behind her sneezed, and she hunched her shoulders.

She looked, then, at the fan. She lifted it, spread it carefully as if it might shatter if she breathed, moved, blinked too rapidly. It had been etched and tinted. White, and on the white a sketch of a hillside brush-stroked so fragilely a wind could have made it powder. To the left of the hill a misshapen tree, and beneath its branches a man sitting with knees drawn to his chest and his face hidden by a fall of thin leaves; to the right the suggestion of a plain, and above it a moon that was bloated, pocked, a background globe for a flight of dark birds.

She closed the fan partway. The hillside collapsed, the man and the tree and the moon vanished into the folds of frail glass. Only the birds remained. Gliding.

There were four in the group, in blue nearly black, ribboned and medaled without pretension. Staring at the storefronts, listening to the advocs, pausing without pattern at the stalls closest to them. Buying nothing. Whispering and laughing. No one spoke to them, yet no one ignored them.

Shanlon saw them approaching his stall and immediately stepped into the street to keep the cube in front of him. They weren't green, he thought; there was no arrogance in their walk, no self-imposed class that lifted them above the level of the civilians. A slight disappointment, but he wouldn't be able to bait them; they would be too knowledgeable to take it even if it were offered. If he was lucky, then, they would pass him by with only a glance at his goods and spare him the temptation. His hand settled briefly on the belt at his waist, on the pouch at the belt, and he squeezed it. It was thin tonight, and so was his remaining supply of tricks. He sucked in his lips and bit down gently. He nodded, once and slowly, and knew then that they would indeed stop. That's the way it had been tonight. The woman in white took that one small Loki, and that had been that. The soldiers would stop all right. That's the way his luck had been running—all in the other direction.

They stopped. He smiled politely. A trick would be wasted on soldiers just strolling.

Three of them, and he noticed they were all officers, moved to walk away. The fourth, heavy-set and obviously uncomfortable beneath his Service mask, stayed them with a short gesture and reached to a shelf to pick up a Zeus.

"Five creds, Captain," Shanlon said. "A bargain at any price, and especially at that one. Put him in your sack and you'll sleep better at night, wake up with a smile and a love for your command."

"Is that a guarantee, venner?" The voice was partially muffled, seemingly seeping from the man's broad chest. "Suppose, for example, I take this to Barracks tonight and I end up with some insomnia. What do I do then? I wouldn't be able to find you again, would I? What would I do?"

"Swear a lot," Shanlon grinned.

"Shanlon," the captain said, shaking his head, "you'll never make a million that way. Despite yourself, you're too damned honest."

Shanlon leaned forward, his hands gripping the edge of the stall. It tilted, threatened to slip off the curb, and he released it and stepped quickly to one side. Staring. Trying to force his vision through the mask to the face beyond. Quickly he rummaged through a list of his friends who had opted for Service, but they were all too young to have reached officer rank so swiftly. He shook his head, cocked it and waited.

The captain laughed, half-turning to his friends, who only looked at each other and shrugged. "Shanlon," he said, "you never could tell anything about a man in uniform, could you?"

"You have me, Captain. I don't follow."

"Well, do you remember the day your father brought you up to New York? You came directly to my Key and I was waiting outside for you. I was on leave, if I recall, and when you met me you thought I was a Blue. You said all the uniforms looked alike to you, and you were disappointed that I was a soldier, and not police."

Shanlon reached out a hand to grip the stall.

"How old are you now, Shan? I imagine you've tipped over the never-return thirty mark sometime soon back. Am I right, or am I talking to one of your statues?"

"No," Shanlon said, "it isn't possible." He stepped onto the curb, ducking as if he could see under the mask, then threw his arms wide and accepted the captain into his embrace. Laughing. Hands pounding backs. Heads tilted back, twisting, shaking in disbelief.

"I was right, wasn't I?" he said, pushing the other back without releasing his shoulders. "It isn't you, is it? But of course it is! Damned if it isn't! Blesséd priest, I can't believe it is!" He turned, then, to the others and held up a hand to keep them from knocking him down. Turned again and addressed his figurines. "My friends, and you too, officers, sirs, I want you to meet a young uncle of mine, the last mistake I believe my paternal grandmother made. His name is James Thrush, as prosaic a cognomen as his strutting profession." He dropped his hands, nodded and poked at the heavy man's chest. "It is you, isn't it, James? Isn't it? Blesséd priest, how did you find me?"

"Bad luck," the captain said. The grin was hidden behind the lipless silver, but the voice carried it just the same. "I came here with the annual movement of my brigade. Washington is my bane, as usual."

"Captain," one of his friends began tentatively, but James waved him away impatiently.

"Go on ahead, gentlemen. I'll catch up with you before you've gone too far."

The faceless eyes stared at Raille, uneasy, doubtful, but deferring to the older man.

And when they were alone while the crowds flowed noisily by, Shanlon closed up his stall and leaned an elbow on it, scratching at his chin. "I don't believe in coincidences, James. This city's too big, and so is the world. And if you don't mind me asking, do you have to wear that stupid thing?" He flicked a forefinger at the mask, and his uncle flinched back. "Sorry, James, I didn't know it was cursed."

Captain Thrush stared at the restaurant, shifted his gaze to the filling theaters across the street. Shanlon thought he was looking for someone, but he said nothing, only waited until James had had his fill of the neighborhood.

"You know, Shan," the captain said, "I would have thought that by now you'd be in something better than this. I really never expected to find you a venner, of all things. If your father had lived to see it, he would have died."

Shanlon smiled, barely. "Don't be so disillusioned that you get nightmares, good Uncle. This stall here isn't my principal source, if that's what you're worried about. Assuming you didn't know it already–and remember what I said about coincidences–I happen to be a registered EcG lobbyist. A local leader, no less, with his face in the news once in a half moon. When the sun comes up I race out to tackle Highmen on the noble Hill, and rant and foam and generally raise hell. No one listens, but then I don't expect them to. The ranting is expected of me. And it pays."

"You amaze me," Thrush said with a quick shake of his head. "I didn't think you were the protester type. No," he said before Raille could answer, "I take that back. You are the type, if you haven't changed much. Especially, as you say, if it pays. But why not the Luxes or the Abors or something like that? At least they get a bill through once in a while."

Shanlon shrugged. "Frankly, EcG pays better, for one thing. Also, they've somehow convinced me that they do have a telling point once in a while. They're right about the war, for example. We don't use any more Mediterranean Community oil, so why bother to fight over it? When the starship's been completed, when the spacefacs have been set up and, hopefully, working, what do we gain by nuking a bunch of sand dunes?"

"If we didn't, I'd be out of a job, for one thing."

"James, you're not serious!"

"No, as a matter of fact, I'm not. It's the same old story, you know—I just do what I'm told."

"Well, whatever."

"But you, a lobbyist?"

Shanlon shrugged. "It's easy work, James, and like I said, good pay. I don't work hard and I haven't changed that much—I like the smooth way. But you . . . talk, James, please! It's damned good to see you again."

Thrush tilted his head back to follow a 'Dog racing over the buildings. "Shan, I didn't walk all this way to talk about me." He took a deep breath, released it slowly. "Shan, you're right about coincidences. I don't believe in them, either."

Delia nudged her way to a seat near the back of the 'bus and sat angrily, ignoring the stares of those around her. Caro was impossible! Worse, she was heading for one of those lifer contracts if she didn't watch closely the man she was chasing.

She pushed at her hair, sniffed, and wondered if she should have told her about that venner. No matter the kind of clothes he wore on the streets or the tricks he did, she knew him right away. And for some inexplicable reason, she was glad he did not admit that he knew her, too.

Shanlon Raille.

She shook her head and wondered why the rest of EcG just didn't hold a caucus and throw him out. It wasn't that he was the most effective man on the Hill—there were at least half a dozen others she could think of who did more for the lobby than that little priest. In fact, if she tried, she knew she could come up with a score of names, maybe two score if she really put her mind to it. From the first time she had met him, too many years ago, she knew he was not serious about much of anything, especially EcG;

and his mocking smile, the way he tilted his head whenever some-one cornered him with a new approach to a Consul . . . it in-furiated her.

And then, from nowhere and not welcome: Delia dear, are you sure you're not just a little bit jealous? It was a nice fan, you know.

Lights. A pale white. Dim. Two. Slowly advancing behind the sputtering roar of a combustion engine. The Blues on the left of the street inched forward despite their orders. They were curious, and slightly puzzled. Ratgangs did not make passes; they attacked fully, forceably, and retreated if they could in the wake of liquored laughter. Caine noticed the pull on his men, cleared his throat and ordered them back into line. He frowned when they hesitated be-fore obeying, but his eyes didn't leave the track of the approaching lights.

Something new has been added, he thought, and wondered if the shagging bastards, the scum sobitches, would actually try to break into the city in force. There was no sense in it and he dismissed it instantly. All they would gain would be newspace and gravespace, and of the latter not a hell of a lot if they really thought they could run the tank.

A young Blue leaning against the right-hand Keyloft looked up and winked at a girl who was whispering down to him.

The roaring steadied.

Caine snapped at the man, and the girl lifted her middle finger and flicked it against her teeth.

Somewhere within the tank metal rubbed harshly against metal.

The roaring grew.

Talle heard them out, trying to suspend immediate judgment, wrestling to avoid believing what he knew would be true; what he knew would be true as far as these two Consuls were concerned. And as he listened, his right hand fell absently into his lap, drifted to his sidepurse lying cocked at his hip. He caressed it. Within was a priority passage card, a granted privilege never used even in dreams to take his family to one of the Colonies if he decided that the earth no longer fell within his definition of dedication.

His attention divided further. Listening, thinking: the Colonies had become an unhealed sore, a bleeding wound. They were scarcely two centuries old by the reckoning of those who had landed first and survived, thriving as best they could under uncertain circumstances which forced them into wormlike existences beneath the surfaces of the bodies they tried to occupy. Yet, in spite of the deaths and the crises and the toll of human souls, they remained front-and-center objects of mooning idolatry for all the romantics who sprang up with each generation. There was something about the words *star* and *planet* and, lately, *starship* that dredged up the dreamers, rousted out the word-rousers who demanded reasons why the poor and the struggling couldn't look for a second beginning on an airless frontier. They could not, or refused to understand the prerequisite skills, chose to ignore the economics behind the refusals. They saw creds pouring into the Service and would not see the intricate financial limitations on even the shuttles to the Hubstations drifting beneath the moon. They were told that to make a difference in the groundling population would require a move of millions of bodies, millions upon millions over a space of years in order to close the gap with the newborn and the long-lived. They were told, but they didn't listen.

It worked in their dreams, and the reality awakened only anger. Testers like the EcG, which based its own dreams on earth itself, lobbied for ways to dampen the dreams, and Talle had worked with them; to promise the bread as others had done and hold out only the stale crust was a vile way to run a world, and he wanted it stopped.

But now, as he listened, things were different. A fear that had lurked starving in some shadowed recess had found the light, and it was growing.

Meditcom and Eurepac were once again gnashing their blunted teeth. The oil confederation, in anticipation of the spacefacs, had doubled their prices again; Eurepac, despite the frantic export of Noram technology and the financial base on which it could spread, still relied heavily on the Meditcom's raw fuel. There was the panic of dwindling time in the pronouncements from London and Cairo; and like scavengers anticipating a slaughter of titans the Russchin Alliance squatted sedately on the sidelines waiting to see what pieces would be left to swallow without risking a man though they had millions to spare; and Africa Below the Sahara mobilized carefully and quietly, wanting neither Russchin or Eurepac to swim in the dying Mediterranean.

More pouches were exchanged.

More maneuvers were plotted and discarded and attempted and denied.

While neutral, and huddling, Australia provided the tables around which the scowling and shouting and grumbling could be vented unheard.

"But, Helman, it's all falling apart faster than we can pull it back together," Bendal was saying. "Scanda will leave Eurepac as soon as war comes, and what's left of the Continent will need our assistance or splinter even further. And there is simply, realistically, no more room on this damned earth for an unconfederated country."

"That much I can agree with, Sandy, but—"

"No. If there is a war then Meditcom will win. That much is foregone. And if they do, the ABS will take the desert countries with hardly a deep breath. It doesn't take much imagination to see that when that happens, Russchin will belch and we'll be alone."

"My people," Talle said slowly, "they'll not care, you know. They see things over here running relatively smoothly without the blessings of a Meditcom fuel. I think . . . in fact, I know I can speak for the rest of the Senators and Reps when I say that few people at all care! Not enough to make the supreme effort, anyway. Even the Service isn't entirely satisfied, you know."

Faux downed his third glass, slapped at the console for another. Talle frowned, unsure why the Consul was struggling for control; if he didn't know Faux better, he'd swear the Cenam was fighting against fear.

"Helman," Faux said finally, "either you're playing the advocate badly for our amusement, or you're not all there."

"Now wait a damned—"

"Stop it, both of you!" Bendal snapped, his first drink untouched and warming. "There's no time for this, Faux, damnit, and you know it! Talle, listen to me and try to accept what I am telling you. If we don't send Service aid to Eurepac, they won't fight. They can't. There's every chance, then, they'll negotiate properly without resorting to . . . whatever. And we know that Meditcom can't call its people into a third war without using Noram as the basic threat. They'll have to negotiate too. If they do, Russchin and ABS will sit tight and watch. If either of them think of trying anything on their own—and there's absolutely no reason to believe they'd try something together–Medit and Eure would be reluctant allies before the first missile coughs. Damnit, Helman, can't you see the potential for disaster we have here?"

Someone passing the booth ruffled the curtain, and they quieted, each staring at the table, hands folded around their glasses.

"All I see," Talle said, "is that if we do not fight or ship over massive aids, then there will be no war. But by the same token, you can't simply abandon all our interests without an explanation. We can't just tell them we're not going to fight and we're awfully damned sorry about it."

Faux smiled, and his face became disturbingly foxlike. "You are as astute as ever, Helman. You're right, of course. We cannot tell our allies we won't send in the Service as we have in the past. That being the case, it's obvious we have to buy some time. Time enough, obviously, to get the facs working so energy will no longer be a case, a reason . . . a spark, if you will."

"A diversion," Talle agreed.

"A revolution," Bendal corrected.

"Damnit, where?"

"I thought that was clear. Here."

Talle sat back suddenly, looked at the two Consuls and let his confusion be unmasked. "Who with? We haven't had enough serious dissidents in the past forty years to fill up a park."

"There are the ratgangs, Helman. Don't underestimate them."

"Nonsense. They're not organized into any sort of network. They're in a constant state of fluctuation when it comes to their personnel. Most of them give up on the point of starvation. It's ridiculous to consider them seriously. In fact, if I remember them correctly, the largest known band was reputed to have only five hundred members and most of them were women and children. If you're serious about this nonsense, you can forget about the ratgangs."

"If we have a revolution," Bendal persisted, "we can truly plead cause and stay out of the threat. Helman, if we go in . . . we can't."

There were voices behind the roaring. Caine could see nothing. But the voices added to the din, and the people in the 'lofts were making his men nervous. He sent one into a building to get at the roof, check the defenses that protected the Fringe and return with a count.

Voices.

The Blue returned. The defenses were functioning; the streets would still be the only access to the city. But it was dark, and he heard only the engine, and the roaring of voices.

"James, I do this because I enjoy thinking up tricks. I'm not pro enough to make the theaters or trivids, so I do it for nothing on the streets. No one knows me, so I don't compromise my supposed dignified position on the Hill. It's fun, James. It's a nice way not to make enemies."

Talle stared at Bendal. Incredulous. Not at all positive this was the same man with whom he had shared a lastmeal the night before.

"We've spoken with the Premier, Helman," Faux said. "It began a long time ago. He agrees. In principle, he agrees."

Talle shook his head.

"It will give us an opportunity to clear out things beyond the Fringes, Helman. Think of it. Free travel between cities and towns again. It's not nearly as bad as it used to be, of course, but now it will be even better. Safer. When the facs begin operation, we can even restructure the suburbs again."

Talle slid closer to the curtain.

"There will be a leader, naturally," Faux said matter-of-factly. "It's all arranged, though he doesn't know it yet. We've set plants with the newses. At the word, there'll be special editions of the faxes and break-in broadcasts. Of course they don't know it's arranged. That part the Premier had to handle himself."

"You said 'we' spoke," Helman whispered.

"Devereaux," Faux said. "But he started to get nervous."

"Devereaux," Talle repeated, despairing.

Faux shrugged; Bendal found interesting the whirls in the ceiling.

"They don't happen, you know," Talle said, more to himself than the watching Consuls. "Things like this don't happen." He tried a weak smile. "We are dreaming, aren't we? I am not here listening to this talk, am I? I am home. I am in bed with my wife and my child is in the next room. I am dreaming that we are planning a false revolution to convince our allies that we can't help them fight so they'll convince each other there's no need to fight so we can have the time we need to turn on the facs and send them down the sun so there's nothing left to fight over."

Through the walls of the restaurant, then, the faint sounds of thunder.

"I am dreaming. I am."

"Helman–"

"–and then we turn our resources to the resurrection of the planet, the completion of the starship and the salvation of the Colonies."

Faux glanced at Bendal.

"And what if they fight anyway?"

"They won't," Bendal said. "I told you this was working for a long time. We have people, now, to see that they don't."

Talle set his palms on the table as if ready to rise and leave them. But his arms gave him little support and he sagged instead, his head bowing so his chin brushed at his chest.

"Why me?" he said, the words weary with resignation. "If this is such a terrible secret that you had to . . . that Devereaux . . . why are you telling me any of this, Sandy?"

"Because you are who you are," Faux said quickly. "You are known internationally. There are few knowledgeable ones left in the world who do not respect you, Helman."

"You mean I would have seen through the sham and exposed you all."

"I mean we realized–Sandy, the Premier and myself–that you must not be excluded from such a serious undertaking. We felt you had to know the truth, all of it, before the revolution begins."

Thunder.

"Begins? He lifted his head, his eyes wide and ready to tear. He wondered, then, how much more of this he could take before he could no longer stop himself from screaming.

Bendal stared at his timepiece. "Begins," he said.

"And Devereaux the first martyr for what will be known as our side?"

"He doubted," Faux said simply.

"No. No one will believe it's a real revolution, even if Devereaux was killed. Assassinated." Suddenly he was sure the men he faced were mad, insane, more than long dead. "I'm sorry, but they won't believe it."

"Take our word for it, Helman," Bendal said. "Take my word for it. They will believe it."

Shanlon glanced down the street. The three officers were waiting in front of a joyhall screen, not watching the writhing figures, awkward in their attempts to appear interested in what they were not seeing. He looked back to his uncle, frowning, inexplicably nervous. There was thunder in the air of an unusual kind; yet he had noticed no clouds, had heard no reports of storms moving up the coast.

"I've heard talk," the captain said. "Rumors sneaking around the barracks. There's going to be trouble of some kind. I don't know why, but the word is that the EcGs are behind it."

"Then that's exactly what they are–rumors," Shanlon said. "The last time we got into any trouble at all was when someone forgot to file with the taxers. Two or three years ago. We were stunned with a fine and a scolding. We're clear, James. There isn't going to be any trouble from us, you can believe that."

"I don't know," James said. "But damnit, Shan, there is definitely something in the air. I told you about the troops, right? Well, there's no reason for this brigade maneuver. There's no reason why we should be massing. And we're not the only ones. And we are. All over the place."

Shan laughed shortly. "Since when does the Service ever give you a reason for shunting you around? I don't know, maybe it's the war. You want to hear talk, I've got some–"

"No," the captain said. "Look . . . for the past year I've been assigned to the Service Liaison Team on the Hill. Everything was calm until a few weeks ago when we were swamped with questions about the ratgangs and EcG–"

"You people have to be out of your minds!"

"–and then, suddenly, everyone shuts. Nothing. Not a word. Devereaux gets himself wiped in the New York Fringe, the Premier swings back from the Westhouse without telling anyone and before you know it the troops are on the damned move." He shook his head slowly. "Shan, I even heard your name once. It was by accident when I was . . . never mind! I heard your name, that's all. Take one of your gods, Shan, and swear to me you're not up to anything."

Shanlon wanted to laugh again, but couldn't. He sensed that a denial would only increase Thrush's evident disbelief in his total innocence. "Maybe they want to give me one of these little gems," and he fingered a triangular gold medal on James's chest.

"Maybe," the captain said, "but damnit, Shan . . . hell, I don't know. It's just a feeling. I just think that there's going to be trouble. I only wanted to tell you."

A group of teeners swaggered past, cloaks wide to scoop at slow-stepping peds, voices loud to drown out the advocs.

"Thank you, James," he said. "Now tell me something else: how did you know where to find me?"

The officer backed away, stepped onto the sidewalk stiffly. "The Service knows everything, Shan," and the voice was only partially jesting.

Shanlon decided to say nothing more. It was all too conveniently melodramatic. Talking with a faceless soldier he knew to be an uncle not much older than he, listening to talk about some sort of nebulous trouble for . . . for a venner who masqueraded as an EcG lobbyist. It was so patently unbelievable it had to be someone's poorly contrived fabrication. He couldn't take it seriously, even if James did. Word of such potential danger with the High Courts or the Congress would have reached him long before his uncle had stumbled into the vine. And he wasn't even a Highman within the organization, only a district speaker who yelled louder than most.

Thrush, realizing the little impact his warning had had, turned to go.

"James, wait a minute!"

"I have to go, Shan. I have to get back to the Team before I'm missed too much. Back to the front and all that, wherever the shagging hell the front is going to be. Take care of yourself, and your friends. Let's try not to have another decade go by without speaking."

Shanlon lifted a hand to mock salute him, dropped it when the captain about-faced sharply and strode toward his companions. They grouped around him, hovering, their questions almost visible in the air over their heads. Thrush said something and they all looked back at him, then marched off briskly to the nearest hover-queue.

Thunder again.

A WatchDog buzzed overhead, circled, vanished.

The restaurant door opened, and Shanlon moved to uncover his gods.

Caine shaded his eyes unnecessarily and peered intently through the meshwall, trying to estimate the size of the 'gang crouched behind the dull black car. Spotlights from the tank swept over the road, illuminating the rubble of the buildings that had once been neighbors to the Fringe, pausing long enough to give the sergeant glimpses of faces only, dirt-streaked, hair caked, rags and tatters and shards of costumes and clothes. Impossible to tell if there were women among them. Poised a hundred meters beyond the barrier. Stretching past the hazed farthest reach of the constantly moving lights.

He sniffed and rubbed a finger under his nose. Watched a Blue sway on his feet. Heat. He'd forgotten how hot it had been. His sides were wet, and his chest and back. Again he wiped at his nose, then flicked on the micbut at his lapel and whispered into the Headquarters link. He requested reinforcements, was told his sector wasn't the only one that was threatened.

One more night, he thought.

Angrily he ordered his men to put up their 'tons. Cautiously they backed toward the large boxes sitting alone. Caine stared at the iron bands, then negated their stricture and one by one he personally handed out the bulky ML-9s.

"He didn't look like ex-Service. Is he an old friend, Captain?"

Thrush turned to look at the speaker. To look at all of them standing around him. All captains, all at least a decade younger and wondering why the old man hadn't advanced any more than he had with his years in the Service. Not that it made a hell of a lot of difference. When the war came they were all sure to be majors, equal in time and grade and he wouldn't be able to push them around. They hated him; and he knew it. There had been a time when he cared.

The question came again and he waved it away. A muffled roaring of fans and the hovbus rose from its tunnel, secure behind the barrier that looped round the openings to form a large paddock. He moved forward, pushing the civilians to one side gently, flashing his red card to no answering arguments until he reached the head of the line.

A redheaded girl standing by the gate watching the debarking passengers put a shoulder to him, kept him from passing. "Hey," she said when he insisted with a not-so-gentle push, "come on! Service, can't you see that thing is nearly full? I've been waiting here for almost–"

"Sorry, Mistress," he said, holding the gate open for his companions to pass. When he released it, it slid shut with a rattling click, and he leaned on the barrier's narrow shelftop. She struck him lightly on the shoulder with something he didn't recognize, and pouted. He wished, then, she could see that he was grinning. "I'm sorry again," he said, "but we're going to route this one anyway since it doesn't go toward the Hill. You wouldn't get home for a long time if you got on."

"I'm not sure you're welcome," she said, but the pout faded. He bowed. She opened the gadget and he saw it was a fan she settled in front of her face. He laughed at the feigned coy stare and swung himself into the bus. The passengers groaned when they saw him, but he only shrugged and tapped the driver's battered cap. When the man looked up, he held the red card to his eyes and pointed east with his thumb. The driver swore as a matter of course.

"They ain't going to like this, General," he said, pulling down his mike from its niche over the windshield. "It's shagging hot enough in here without we got to make a detour up there. You guys are officers, right? Why don't you get yourselves a 'cat or something? Steal a landie from a Rep. Blesséd priest, it's a shagging waste of–"

"So write your Senator," Thrush said lightly.

"Sure, sure. And a Blue comes to the 'loft and wants to know why I'm bothering the Highmen. Shag, General, it's been a rotten day."

Yenkin stood almost at attention, and felt ridiculous doing it. His back held the restaurant door open while Haward brushed frantically at the Highmen's clothes, his smile a twist too obsequious. Yenkin watched the fat man's moves and wasn't surprised when neither the Consuls nor the Senator returned the smile. They were silent, oddly so after all the drinks they had consumed, and Yenkin wondered what governmental policies had been argued about this time, and who had lost the argument. Talle, by the look of it, and it was unusual. He had never known the aging politician to lose anything in his life, much less a debate with the likes of the Consuls. But he was determined not to stare at the trio to glean more clues for speculation, just as determined not to sweat in the streetheat that mixed with the cool air spilling from the foyer.

Behind him he could hear the blast of a 'bus descending into the tunnel, and he wished he was on it, heading for home. The creds be damned; he was suddenly tired and he wanted some sleep.

The Canam Consul left first, stood in front of him to wait for the others. A clenched fist at his side betrayed his impatience.

"Gentlemen, we haven't much time," he said stiffly.

"Relax, Consul," the fleshy one said. He reached into his sidepurse and drew out a coin. He considered its value as Haward worked hurriedly on the Senator, then replaced it and drew out a smaller denomination.

Yenkin tried not to grin.

"Consul, please! There are people gathering around out here. We'll have a crowd if you don't hurry up."

"Of all the damned shagging luck," one of the younger Blues said. He hefted the ML to his shoulder and thumbed the warming plate until he was satisfied. The laser, primed, would have to be fired soon, and yesterday was not soon enough for him. "Shagging rats ought to be terminated."

"You'll get enough of that by the looks of it," his partner said. They pressed against the side of the building on the right, one kneeling at the other's toes. There was a warning whine within the bowels of the tank, and the barrel leveled, rose, leveled once again.

Caine watched as his men placed themselves and thought of the WatchDog flare. It must have gotten the rats mad, he thought. It had to be. What they're trying is goddamned suicide.

The *whump!* then, and the blast of furnaced air and the screeching tear of an explosion as a rocket exploded on the front plates of the tank. Flames stretched their arms, and there was screaming.

The watchers in the windows vanished as glass shattered and blood stained the sills. The lights went out. The tank served as torch.

There was no need for Caine to give the order. His men were already firing, ignoring the incineration of the Blues in and near the tank. The mesh sparked. Flared. And from behind the car the thundering advance of a reinforced truck.

Another rocket, and Caine was slammed hard against the corner of the building. Air deserted his lungs. Light fled from his eyes. He lay, paralyzed, listening to the slaughter of the Blues while his throat worked to scream.

Caro glared angrily at the hovbus' descent, her hands gripping her hips. She nodded once when the fat man behind her let loose a stream of curses. A woman's voice asked if anyone had heard an explosion.

No such luck, she thought; that 'bus will be on the Hill in less than five minutes. If only she had thought to tell that insufferable Serviceman who her father was; that would have stopped him from taking her place.

She looked up, then, and her gaze stopped at the venner who had given her the fan. He was standing by his stall, and there was a small crowd gathered around him. She wondered what trick he was doing for them, then saw the three Highmen waiting for something in front of the restaurant. She squinted, but her vision didn't clear and she recognized none of them. She shrugged, stared when the crowd suddenly broke and the venner was standing alone.

The three stood as if posing, the Senator in the middle.

A few hands applauded, and they nodded. Smiling.

"Let's get on with it," Talle muttered. "Get me home, now! I'll need time to–"

"Remember the revolution," Bendal whispered in his ear, and turned the man to face him.

"Not here!" Talle hissed, thinking his friend had lost what sanity he had left. He yanked the Consul's hand from his arm and stepped back. He turned, then, and saw the faces before him, smiling, grinning, all of them knowing who he was and how he cared. What he never saw was the upraised hand. Felt, only, the flame, the searing, and had no time at all to gasp out a warning before the darkness blotted out the city, the crowd, the venner with the bouquet in his hand . . .

Statues.

People. Running.

People. Screaming.

Faux shook off the feeling of terror while Bendal carefully lowered the Senator's body to the sidewalk. He swallowed, ordering himself to stick to the plan, and pointed a trembling finger at the openmouthed venner.

"That man!" he shouted to those who hadn't fled. "I saw him! Get him! He's assassinated your Senator!"

Two

The Hill. A carry-over euphemism apt only in terms of its relationship to the Noram Capital that surrounded it. Taller, more ornate, capped by a stylized dome of hexagon glastic panes that caught firstlight and last, blue sky and black clouds in a constant display of none-too-subtle symbolism that none but the blind were able to miss. Above the plant-strewn, building-wide foyer the guards called the jungle, the first double-dozen levels housed all Reps and Sens and minor cabinet officials—controlled pandemonium when the Government was in session, birthplace of echoes when the holidays sounded. The public was invited, and the public came in, and newseyes hovered at every corridor, turning like monocled cats crouched for their prey. Another foyer, then, controlled with a variety of passes that provided access to the next five stories where the Prime Cabinet and Advisers hid behind walnut doors; more quiet, more sedate, the careful air of dignity slightly stained by the Servicemen stationed at lift/drops and emergency outs. There was no free movement here, nor on the three floors following where the Consulates reigned over their preconfederation loyalties: Cenam the first, then Canam, with the last being Usam in case the others had forgotten who had invited the merger. Silence was the order, and it was enforced by twice the number Servicemen higher in rank.

Four stories more enclosed the chambers of Congress and the High Court Star.

Floor Forty-three had no interior walls. A massive white marble plain treed with black polished pillars thick at the base. A full company of armed men, mixed Blues and Service, inhabited the plain in four-hour rotations to screen the users of the lifttubes. Those who were acknowledged were marched to a central gilted pillar into which the final lift/drop had been inserted.

Mordan Alton, twice elected Premier, waited then beneath the stylized glastic dome.

He was battling his way to a retirement seventy, panting while most men coasted, taking deep breaths while most men felt nothing. Tall once and thick-waisted, he had years ago fallen into a comfortable slouch to carry the weight more easily; and when the weight had deserted him shortly after his first five years, he slouched to carry the yoke of his age. His hair had turned to a tired yellow-gray, was brushed back impatiently behind his ears. His rounded face had more lines than planes, more purpled shadows than the suntan he'd been after at his Westhouse stay. His eyes, when he thought no one was looking, wandered as if seeking ghosts in the corners of his office; his lips, when it was silent, moved in inaudible whispers as if there had been a creed he had known and was trying to regain. He was seated. Stiffly. His arms were long, his hands wide and they settled now on his knees as he watched the banks of comunit screens on the wall behind his desk. A map of the Confederation had been drawn up into the ceiling to reveal the vision of the scanners' lenses, flickering dimly, too many to follow simultaneously. But the scattered mosaic of harshly tinted images made him frown, sigh, resign himself to the steps he had been convinced he should make.

The windowed wall to his left was dark, brightening only once to a rocket's red announcement.

Finally, he blanked out all tiers but one and watched as the Fringe Blues gave slow way to the advancing ratgangs. There were casualties, too many, far too many, more than he wanted. He watched the Blues die and the ratgangs swarm over them. He stared at them, leaned forward and urged them to fight. Grunting. Saw one small group repel a still smaller. Grunting. And he swiveled around, flicked at the array of toggles on the desk's comunit master and ordered his guards to send in the first flight of panicked birds.

The idea, he thought as he pulled his dark shirt from his trousers and loosened his belt, was so complicated it was simple. But when the worst was over–Faux had assured him a week at the most–he would have a quiet word with the Canam Consul. A very quiet word. A long quiet word that would send the pompous toad packing back to his mansion on the shores of Hudson Bay.

The Liaison Team entered first, maskless in his presence. They arranged themselves from general to captain in front of the desk, standing, ignoring the chairs that slid out for their use. With a wearied gesture he blanked out the final screens. The general saluted. Alton nodded.

It was late. He was tired.

"General Manquila," he said, his voice lacking the timbre of his authority, "if you tell me 'I told you so,' I'll have you shipped to the Arctic."

"I wouldn't think of it, sir," the dark-faced general said. "But I did, you know."

"Well . . . for the record, if you want it that way, you were right and I was wrong. Are all your men still at the ready?"

"There are a few still not quite in position. I'm told, however, that they should be within the hour."

Alton pushed back from the desk, propped his heels up on its edge. The Team stared steadily over his head.

"An hour, within or without, General, may be too late. You've seen yourself, I assume, the trouble we're in already." He raised a palm quickly, dropped it to his knee. "I know, I know, I should have listened a long time ago. But rumors don't help me, General. I can't properly handle a situation like this unless I have verifiable facts, none of which your men were able to give me. If you remember." He shook his head slowly. "In a hundred years I couldn't have imagined those 'gangs could have been so remarkably organized."

The general glanced at the colonel, the major, the captain beside him. "Sir, if I may . . . time is not on our side in this thing. The word is already out, and those rumors you refused to listen to will spread worse news throughout the city in a matter of minutes. The population will panic, sir, unless you give us the order to move now. As it is, it's going to take a long time to clear out the 'gangs' nests they've established. A long time."

Alton looked at the others; their faces were carefully blank.

"It definitely will take a long time, General. I'm afraid we won't be able to stop at the Fringes this time. We'll have to pursue. All the way."

"I think we're aware of that, sir. It has been discussed by the Chiefs. Several times, in fact."

"Are you also aware . . . are the Chiefs also aware that I am ordering casualties on both sides to be kept to an absolute minimum?"

The general blinked. "Sir?"

"General Manquila, these are Noram citizens we are dealing with here. Not the most desirable, to be sure, and especially not now. But they are our own, and there's no getting around it." He dropped his feet back to the floor and pointed sharply at the world map on the wall opposite the windows. "Politics as well as Service, General; there's no way we can avoid it. So. I do not want your relaying of this order to in any way imply that the 'gangs are to be wiped. They are, instead, to be contained in such a way that their unconditional surrender can be effected as soon as possible. Then we can deal with them in a manner chosen by the High Court and Congress. No tacnukes, General. No implications of a slaughter. Are you clear on that, General?"

Manquila chanced another glance at his subordinates.

"Yes, sir, I am clear on that."

"Fine," Alton said, smiling for the first time since the Team had entered. "Then please take the order and your men and get the thing moving. I would like to grab a little sleep before long, secure with the news that the city will not fall down around my ears while I'm snoring. Captain Thrush!" and the captain started in spite of himself. "Captain, I'd like you to stay with me, if you will. He is available to me, isn't he, General? You can get someone to handle his normal battle duties?"

"There will be no problems, sir. Captain Thrush will stay as long as you require him."

Alton nodded. "Excellent, excellent. All right, General, you can go now."

The general and the colonel and the major saluted and slipped out, their masks readied for donning as soon as they stepped through the door. When the room was sealed again, cutting off the brief explosions of angered fear from the antechamber, the Premier gestured the captain to take a seat. Thrush hesitated, but moved quickly when Alton's hand became a quick fist.

"Captain Thrush. I do have the name correct, don't I?"

Thrush nodded. The weight he carried below his shoulders curiously did not reflect in his face. He was smooth-lined, with a long angled jaw that reminded Alton of Faux. Without, he corrected himself, that constantly calculating expression the Consul never changed. He stood, then, and walked slowly around to the front of the desk, perched on its edge and scratched at his chest. He stared briefly at the ceiling, at the windows, at the soft curve of his boots.

"Captain Thrush, I've been told that you spoke, and spoke at length with the venner who assassinated Senator Talle this evening. Just before it happened, in fact. Why?"

He saw the perspiration on the captain's forehead, the tightening of the fingers on the rim of his mask.

"You didn't by chance have prior information of the killing, did you, Thrush? That conversation didn't happen to include a warning, or a signal, or something like that, did it?"

"Sir," the captain said steadily, "if you're asking me by those questions if I had knowledge of or was a part of the assassin's plot, the answer is no. Emphatically no!"

"Oh, I know that," Alton said, smiling again. "But I would like to know what you two talked about."

"He was a venner, sir. He performed tricks and things. Magic tricks. I wanted to know how he did it. The secrets of the trade."

"Your fellow officers were under the distinct impression that you knew him. Rather well, I'm told. He threw his arms around you, one of them said."

"Sir, I'm afraid–"

Alton slapped at his thighs and jerked a thumb at the blank screens behind him. "Captain Thrush, we're wasting valuable time here! And under the circumstances, I haven't got that time to waste. The country is spilling into a revolution that will surely fail if only because of our numerical superiority. But it is a revolution nevertheless, and a damned awkward political situation as well. I'll have a dozen ambassadors in here in a few minutes screaming about what this is going to do to the Meditcom situation, and our part in it. I'm going to have to tell them things they won't like hearing. I'm going to have to juggle this damned planet before it drops into a nuclear bath. I haven't the time to waste on folk like you, Captain. So do me a favor and stop your lying!

"Venner, he was? His name is Shanlon Raille. He is, or was, a registered lobbyist for the EcGroup, indistinguishable from all the others except that he spends his spare time selling carved statues and doing magic tricks. He also happens to be your nephew. I expect that you told him that there have been rumors lately of trouble for the EcG, though the rumors had no specifics. You were probably trying to learn if they were true, and if this Raille had anything to do with anything that's involved. What I want to know is what he said to you."

He glared, softened, reached into his breast pocket and pulled out two nics. Handing one to the obviously shaken soldier, he thumbed his lit and drew slowly on the treated smoke, blew a gray cloud to the ceiling's exhausts. Thrush only rolled the tobac cylinder between his fingers and thumb. A man in fear of a not-too-successful career, he thought; pity.

"Captain Thrush?" he prompted.

"Well, sir . . . he told me that they–the rumors–weren't true. He said it was ridiculous. There was nothing to them. I . . . at the time, I believed him."

The Premier watched a curl of smoke twist away from his face. "I see. What you're saying is, then–and please correct me if I assume too much–you no longer believe that he was telling you all the truth. That he was, probably, hiding something from you."

"Well, how can I take his word now, sir? I mean, after all that's happened in the past couple of hours, how can I believe him?"

There was a quiet knock at the door. Alton ignored it.

"Captain Thrush, you've been kept at your present rank longer than most men your age, with your time in Service, because you have an annoying habit of telling your superiors what you think of them and their ideas. No," and he grinned at the captain's stiffening, "don't bother to deny it. I know it's true. It is true. I make a point, Captain, to study all the men I use on the Team, just as you would go over the men you need for a special command position. I know you, Thrush, better than you think; perhaps even better than you'd like to know yourself. It's no coincidence I ask for your opinion more than that bloated major who tails along after you and the general. And I won't bother to comment on the colonel.

"So. Tell me again, Captain Thrush: do you think Raille has had a part in the Senator's assassination, or that of Consul Devereaux? Or in this incredibly stupid revolution? Or both? A straight answer, by the way, Captain Thrush. I'm not in the mood for word fencing, if you don't mind."

In the following silence, Alton moved back to his chair and waited for the captain to realize that, innocent or no, his career was at an end. It was a sad thing to do, and he wished it could have been done another way. But there was a slowly growing fear at the back of his mind that all the plans he had made were beginning to show signs of early wear. The poor captain just happened to have turned up along the seam.

"No. To all the questions: no." And he dropped the mask.

"Leave it be!" Alton snapped when Thrush bent to retrieve it.

"No, sir, I do not think Shan had anything to do with it. Any of it. He's too much the thinker, not the doer. I haven't seen him for quite a while–ten years or so, by accident when his parents were killed–but from what I can tell, he hasn't changed all that much. His father used to call him a glider, moving along the lines of least resistance, and least exertion."

"Consul Faux, you would not have known, saw him fire that handgun. A military one, Captain, stolen from the Service."

"If I may, sir, there were a number of people there. The Consul, respectfully, could very easily have been mistaken. It happens at times like that. As I'm sure you know. Sir."

Alton nodded, wiped at his face to hide a grin of admiration, a grimace of mild despair. As he had feared, he thought as he stubbed out the nic. Already the fabric was fraying. He looked at the middle-aged officer and tried not to allow his gloom to affect his expression.

"Captain Thrush . . . damnit, let me call you James, all right? I don't have the time to be formal, either. James, then, you have a command that's not at present in the city proper, is that right?"

"I do, sir. All the Team members do, in one way or another. In an emergency, like this one, we're supposed to move out with the rest of the troops. The Service Chiefs will take our place after any briefing that's necessary."

"I know all that," Alton said, instantly regretting his tone. "Look, James, the Chiefs are anxious for a lot of things, one of them being the clearing of the outland of the ratgangs. And I mean clearing in the deadliest sense. But those hunting days have been gone for over a century." He smiled, ruefully, and pointed at the captain's shoulders. "You're not long for the Service, you know, James. I'm sure other eyes besides mine have seen that report of your meeting with and your relationship to Raille. I'm afraid, too, suspicions will be raised."

Thrush did nothing more than nod.

"In that case, I meant quite literally what I said to General

Manquila. I want you to stay here. With me." He smiled, now, with open friendliness. "If nothing else, James, it will be a shagging lot more safe for you. For the time being."

He brushed aside the captain's flustered protests and spoke quickly into the comunit grille. Then he sat back, waved Thrush to a position standing behind him and watched as the first of the handwashing Reps and Sens, the white-faced Cabinet officers swept noisily into the room, each seemingly waving a sheath of white position papers. Sleep, he thought as he rose to greet them. Damn, but I'm tired.

A young man not yet marked for Serviceterm crept from his bedroom to the front window of the topfloor Key. All the lights had been extinguished, and his parents were huddled against the wall, a handful of bottles lying between their legs. They grinned stupidly as he stepped over them, tugged weakly at his shirt while he threw up the window and leaned out.

The street lamps were still on, and he could see a silent black mob moving purposefully toward City Prime. From their rags he recognized them. Twenty, maybe thirty. Armed. Battling, the comunit news said, against the monolith Hill.

He pulled thoughtfully on a black curl over his forehead. If he could join them . . . if his friends would join them and use the potential he could see immediately, perhaps one of their demands would include Cenam independence. No more displacement. No cultural disintegration.

He slipped into a jacket and hurried out the door, ignored the l/d for the stairs and ran panting into the street. Calling out. Waving a small handgun he'd bought in a joyhall. The ratgang moved on. He caught up to their tail and had one moment to protest before a blade slit his stomach.

A rookie Blue saw them first and alerted his partner, who in turn called out to the sergeant, who was playing cards with a tankman. Before anyone had moved the fight had begun, and the rookie Blue noticed the scarred faces of several nukes in the midst of the attackers. He wondered, as he turned his ML-9 on the advancing 'gang, why an ex-soldier would lower himself to join up with a ratnest. Traitors they were, no more than that; and he grinned when the meshnet collapsed and he burned his first rat. Waving when a newseye swooped low to record the blood of the skirmish. Groaning when the first wave of Servicemen crashed into the fighting.

Damn, he thought, still waving at the eye, there goes my medal and that girl's probably watching. I'll never get her now. And he kicked angrily at a head that rolled to his feet.

He was alone. The peds who had gathered quicker than his magic had scattered instantly. The long-faced Consul had accused him without hesitation, and there was no sense in believing he would be given the opportunity to deny it. No matter that he had not done it, had not fired the shot—he was an assassin at the end of a pointing finger. Quickly, not thinking past the moment, he snapped on the stall's fans and set its forward motion as high as it would go. He aimed, shoved the cube into a group of five recovered sufficiently to attempt to take him. Most scrambled out of the way; the others were pinned against the restaurant, screaming, twisting, until the glass shattered inward and they were spilled into the foyer.

He ran. Seeing paled faces follow him blankly, not yet comprehending the shouts in his wake. One woman reached out hesitantly and he slapped her hand aside, snarled and angled across the street. But a crowd had formed, was waiting, and he swerved back, nearly tripping over a small boy crying for attention. They were all following him now, and the voices raised were charged with the hysteria of bloodlust and vengeance. Someone fired a shot that felled a man readying to tackle him. He cut to one side, moving further down the street until he saw the hovbus barrier blocking his direct return to the sidewalk. There were people jammed against the far side, pointing, shouting, and he skidded to a brief stop, saw the pursuit at his shadow and leaped the low wall and darted into the mouth of the tunnel.

Downward. Blinking rapidly to adjust to the gloom.

There would be light; he knew that much from his transystem use, more than enough to keep him in the center of the tunnel cleared by the hovbus fans. Debris, damp and rotting, was thrust against the inward sloping walls of gleaming black grime. He saw none of it, listening instead over the echoes of his boots to the cries of pursuit reluctantly following. Reluctantly because they would be afraid of meeting a 'bus. Why a WatchDog hadn't appeared on the scene more swiftly he didn't bother to think about—someone would get in touch with the Blues soon enough and their subground patrols would move to the exits, flow into the sunless warren and slowly, methodically, sever the arteries of his attempted escape.

He slipped in sludge, rolled, ran.

The pursuit faded, and there was only the sound of his breathing, his boots, the constant crystal dripping of condensation from the curved ceiling: the entrapped heat that encouraged the heavy stench of lingering fumes, putrefying garbage, the stale dead air. In the distance, the reverberations of a 'bus on the move.

Running, releasing the conscious control of his legs, allowing himself time to work at preventing his mind from racing in tight panicked circles. Steadily, then; falling into a deadening constant rhythm, his lungs close to aching, his mouth slackly open.

To return to his Key was out of the question, a flicker of fantasy caught at and discarded. Had the incident been pure accident he might have found a valuable short respite there; but the smell of plot was too thick, too urgent to pass over. They knew who he was. The Senator's death at that particular time at that particular place was no more a coincidence than the daily rising of the sun. The Consul's accusation had been immediate and unerring, and the man hadn't even been looking at him.

Captain of the Service James Thrush, brother to his mother and an uncle in name only. In on it—yes or no? Yes, if his sudden appearance had been due to driving conscience, a last second wavering and a chance to remove him from the area before the plot could be culminated; no, if what James had said had been literally true, and he was merely acting on those rumors he had heard. Yes. No. Shanlon passed, with a marked reserve.

A light, bobbing in front of a thunderous roaring. He stopped, arms wide in indecision, then held up a hand to clear his vision and saw the branching. He raced to his left and was in twilight again while the hovbus hurtled by and the faces in the oval windows were blurs of white. Fading. Two pricks of red. Merging. One. Gone.

Running to a stumbling trot. The sudden need to see the sky, then, and a claustrophobic reaction that broke a sob from his throat. Past a tunnel ramp, a glance up and back, and he calmed himself, cursed himself for not watching what lay ahead–the next ramp he passed might be swarming with Blues.

He found himself succumbing to a pattern. Left branch, right branch. Right branch, left. They would be expecting him to head for a prearranged place of relative safety. His Keyloft first, the offices of the EcG next, and then the acquaintances that passed for friends. There were no relatives, he thought thankfully; not here, not anyplace except with the dead. He concentrated on breaking the pattern. They wouldn't be able to cover all the city transystem exits, nor would they pour men in without first being sure. They would be searching for him for days, otherwise, and he could be halfway across the country before they realized it. They might commandeer a newseye or two to handle the remotest ramps or the Fringes but, strangely, none had appeared and he didn't think the Blues were so thickheaded that they wouldn't have already considered their use.

Running. Slower. Falling to his knees in ankle-deep dark water. Tripping over something he didn't dare touch.

Resting unwillingly. Leaning against a clear space on the wall and feeling the trembling of the masonry as the 'buses passed on the other side. A tremulous smile. As a child he had wanted to be one of the drivers, to hoist the tons of metal with the power of his hands and thrust the sharp-nosed vehicles in and out of the barriered holes in the streets. His father, a merchant of games and toys and simple magic tricks, had despaired and blustered; but the dreamphase ended when schooling began in earnest and Shanlon decided that law would be the answer. His parents approved, and he approved, and he had pictured himself taking the Hill with his idyllic rhetoric, charming the public with his one-sided smile, raising his arms to the tune of his swift victories. And victories. And victories that would lead him unfailing to the desk of the Premier. But he was good. Not great. Too often peeling aside the façades of the universe to make a successful politician. He abdicated his dreams, then, and rationalized his studies into the offices of the EcGroup, marking slow time with an eye toward the day when the Colonies would no longer require the specific skills of the craftsman, the scientist mind, and would take just plain people interested in the divine art of living.

Mars it would have been had he been more careful. Had the wars not been. Had the Consul not chosen to . . .

He shoved himself off the wall and began running again. Blindly now. Heedless of direction. The only conscious effort the avoidance when he could of the upward sloping ramps.

Good. Not great. Something had taken the impetus of his trying. Running.

In New York it was. His father and mother had taken him to see the Fringe, to learn what it was like to live in squalid dreaming. To watch the Blues erect the meshnets, to hear stories of the monsters who lived in the outlands. There had been a power failure just as they were leaving. A ratgang looking for winter supplies had thrashed through to raid some small shops. There was screaming. There was blood. And the ratgang passed, and his parents passed, and his schooling thereafter was something less than it should have been.

Good. But not great.

He dropped. In the center of the tunnel. Beneath a dim green light that hid the walls, the refuse, all shadows but his own. He waited for the city to catch up with him. To snare him. Cage him. Perhaps lynch him, though more likely to drag him by the heels to the High Court Star where the somber-faced judges would cheerfully order a public execution.

His legs suddenly cramped, and he screamed a climbing wail, rolled onto his back and clawed at his thighs in helpless, useless massage. His head jerked up, back, and cracked against the tunnel floor. Firelights danced and sucked the air from his lungs. A fist slammed down by his side and the skin split, bled, and the pain was less than the tears molding salted mud through the dirt streaked across his face.

Gasping.

An image of the redheaded girl detached itself from the haze of the overhead green light. She was smiling, shyly, and he knew then as he had known on the long-ago street that she thought herself plain. Hid the self-deprecation behind a coquette's titter. But her hair was sunrise soft, her skin a perfect match. And her eyes–he struggled for their color . . . and suddenly they widened in fear-recognition, and he saw her standing in the hoverqueue, gaping for a shout when he vaulted the barrier and ran past her into the tunnel.

"Girl," he said aloud.

Saw the eyes the green of the light.

"Girl," he said, an incantation.

Calming.

Stretching out on the cold damp floor and squeezing his eyes shut until the image passed and the screams gasps sobs faded and there was nothing but the rapid pumping of his lungs.

Frowning.

Sitting up and grasping his knees. Lifting a hand to suck absently on the slow bleeding wound.

Silence.

No 'buses, no footsteps, no triumphant shouts of discovery.

His nostrils flared. The stench had become a bearable piece of the tunnel's puzzle.

He rocked thoughtfully on his buttocks, then crawled to the wall and used it as a brace to regain his feet. The light flickered, extinguished, relit dimmer than before, and he hurried away. There was no telling how much time had died since he had first gone belowground, but in the dark, beneath the city, he knew he would quickly lose hold of his reason. He stumbled, walked, broke into a ten-pace trot before walking again. To get out before the tunnel shrank around him. Searching for the nearest exit ramp. Wondering where he could have run to that the 'buses didn't run.

Babbling ghouls. Clawed scavengers. The stuffings of an all-too-real Hell spewed mewing into the streets. The crowd became a mob.

Yenkin fought to grab at the reins that would re-establish his mind's control before fear quartered him and rendered him useless. His back was still holding the restaurant door open. The Senator's head was cradled in the Canam Consul's arms and a dozen newseyes spun into the air to float overhead, bobbing for the best angles of attack like bloated flies over carrion. One settled close to Yenkin's chest and he slapped at it angrily to shove it away, cursed when a mild electric charge tightened his palm. He turned away from the assassination scene. Heard instead the pulsating agony of men trapped beneath the dead weight of the stall, which had struck the foyer's far wall. It had burst into flame, was quenched almost immediately by a quick second's flood. He had seen only a glimpse, but sufficient to know that Haward had been swiped by a corner of the gaily painted cube and his face slashed open from temple to temple. A curtain of patrons from the inner dining room blocked further vision and he allowed himself, stunned, to be finally pushed back away from the door, away from the restaurant, until he grabbed at a joyhall's adpillar and clung to it desperately. A warset flashed by, swirling promises of action and gore. He closed his eyes.

He was crying. Telling himself there was no need, no cause, to grope for a better reaction. He had not seen the Senator in several years, had not worked for him for several years more. He sobbed at the age he was denying. He hardly knew the old man any more. But he was crying. Silently.

While WatchDogs let loose their banshee sirens and scattered the aimlessly wandering mobs. A fleet of half a dozen settled black and gold onto the street and spilled their contingents of helmeted Blues with stuntons raised. There should have been quiet then, a routine matter of containment, but a newshawk clambered to the narrow top of the hovbus barrier and switched on the amplifier that bulged at his chest. He waved the sheath of glittering newsheets and blared out the headline that the city was under attack by vast armies of ratgangs. A Blue, more alert than the others, plunged stiff-armed through the crowd around the barrier and grabbed at the man's legs. The newshawk protested, his voice covering the street, but a quick jab of the 'ton felled him, jerking, and the newsheets scattered in a slow rising wind. His voice replaced by screams of emptying buildings, protests, cries of mindless revenge.

An elbow thudded into Yenkin's ribs and he gasped, loosened his grip on the pillar and was swept away to be pushed, pinned against a darkened shopface. Still crying. Suddenly wanting to reach the Senator's side and keep the people from trampling the body, tearing off bits of clothing, threads of hair, for souvenirs and banners. He reached out to snatch at a shoulder and his wrist was grabbed, twisted, and he bent reluctantly to his knees.

"Old man," a voice told him, "get out of here before you're killed. Don't you listen? Don't you know there's a war on?"

The hand freed him. He stood, turned and looked at his reflection in the shopface. Hair still black, but only because of the coloring he used; the lines that were erased only when he saw them . . . Haward, the poor shagging bastard, had thought him merely overworked. Yenkin had almost convinced himself it was in fact true. Almost told the mirrors he used that age had nothing to do with the face that peered out, myopic and melancoly.

Almost.

A boot came down on his ankle. He sucked in air noisily, crouched to rub at the injury and was knocked to the ground by a sudden surge of faceless men and women. His arms crossed immediately in front of his face and his knees hunched to his chest. Buffeted, then. Tipped. Feeling a tear split the spine of his tunic. A heel into the small of his back. He rolled and scrambled to his feet, wiped once at his face and staggered away from the shops to catch himself on the edge of the hovqueue barrier. Again he brushed a hand to his face and a Blue touched his shoulder gently. Yenkin stared at the young eyes beneath the black helmet, saw the question and nodded his okay. The Blue searched his own eyes before hurrying back to the line being drawn to link the 'Dogs. Yenkin's smile stiffened. The Blue was frightened.

He sagged and noticed there was no one near him. A window shattered. Another. A 'Dog positioned in front of the restaurant deafened with its siren. Yenkin spun around and spotted a small knot of men moving away from the building. In the center were the Consuls with the dead man in their arms. They vanished into the 'Dog despite the attempts of several women to stop them; and the vehicle rose, screaming, scattering, streaking overhead and vanishing in the direction of the Hill.

People began running.

Another newshawk blaring.

A hovbus rose from its tunnel and the people nearest it charged over the barrier, scrambling at the doors the driver would not open. Yenkin could see his face through the darkglass shield—white and glistening, lips drawn back to bare his teeth. The 'bus didn't stop. It dove again, carrying with it a score of clawing men and women, who were smashed against the tunnel's sides, dragged from their perches when the vehicle swayed and bumped against its barrier.

More screaming.

This time ignored.

Yenkin hunched away from the blast of the powerful fans, and was forced to grab tightly to the barrier when the crowd around him suddenly joined the others in their running. The streets, he saw then, were emptying slowly as the realization of war sent lofters home and officials back to their offices. He considered making his own move toward the safety of his home when a young man in red leaped the barrier clumsily and a knee caught Yenkin's side. They fell, spinning, entangled, struggling until they separated themselves and the man dashed on while Yenkin lay propped against the low weakened wall.

Die here, die home. What's the difference, he thought; I'm too damned tired to get up again.

He listened with eyes closed as several of the WatchDogs rose and fled, listened with chin on his chest to the faint sounds of thunder.

Heard a footstep. Opened his eyes to better protest he had nothing left worth stealing except the coin in his pocket the Senator had slipped him. And there was a face there, framed by the still flashing lights of the nearby joyhall. It was pale, trembling, framed in glittering red.

"Are you all right? I saw that man and he . . . are you sure you're all right?"

He thought about nodding, shrugged instead.

"Here, please," and hands took his arms, tugged carefully, and he lurched to his feet. Swayed. Steadied. She was young, the girl still clinging to one elbow, attractive, and she had been crying. He blinked and cursed at the tears that still blinded him.

She made a feeble attempt to brush at his chest, then dropped her hand and stood a pace back. "I don't believe it." She leaned toward him, squinting. "I don't believe it! That's not you, Ty, is it? Is it you?"

The years hadn't changed her, he told himself; her face was no different now than it had been when he'd left, when she was nine and part of his charge. He nodded, and Caro fell against his chest, her arms hugging desperately, her face grotesque in the act of violent sobbing.

"They killed Father," she was saying into the fabric of his tunic. "They shot Father and I couldn't get there. I didn't know it was him at first, I didn't! When I heard, I tried to get there and they wouldn't let me. I don't think anyone believed me. I . . . I didn't know what to do! It didn't happen! Ty, what am I going to do? I have to get home and nothing will stop. I have to get home, Ty. I told a Blue who I was and he pushed me away, called me a name. I told him the man was Father, and he said he was dead and I should run home and hide. I want to go home, Ty, but they won't let me. I want to go home. Ty? They won't let me go home, Ty. They won't let me."

The eruptions of pain at his legs and back subsided to a patient throbbing he thought he could easily ignore if he had to. The cacophony of panic had faded; the amplified orders of the remaining Blues fell away into grumblings. There was only the girl he used to know grabbing hold and crying, and her words and his murmurs and the distant thunder of guns.

A Service patrol, learning the lessons of the Blues, deployed itself on a Keyloft roof. When a ratgang contingent crept around the corner below, the Servicemen opened fire to an audience of newseyes.

A lieutenant knelt at the edge of the roof and wondered how in hell he was expected to take prisoners with resistance like that.

The WatchDog settled into the center of the intersection, emptied its Blues and rose. Hovered. Prepared to dart away when a rocket severed its teardrop shape and it fell spinning to the ground. Onto the Blues. Onto the rats that poured from the streets.

They were alone on the street long after time had lost its meaning, its marking of the night. The heat lifted slightly, but they didn't notice. They were alone.

One 'Dog moving slowly from curb to curb. A handful of Blues ducking in and out of shops. Lights, advocs, all the trappings of enticement were dark, were silent, and there was only the sweeping spotlights of the 'Dog, and the Blues.

Caro choked dryly and lifted her head, shook it, pushed at the wet hair that clung darkly to her face.

Yenkin felt for a lingering moment that he had never left his service, was still the servant/uncle with the shoulder to cry on. He slipped, then, his arm around the girl's waist and they walked hurriedly, huddled against each other, along the debris-strewn sidewalk. No speaking. Not daring to think. Nodding gratefully whenever a Blue suggested in a soft voice that they'd better move on.

Old man, get out of here before you get yourself killed.

Passing through the Prime District into the soaring residential blocks of Keylofts whose lights were bright, whose doors held guards waiting for the newshawks while the women and children sat fearful, still dazed, in front of their comunits watching the bulletins and the taped calming message of the aging Premier. Here the brightness came from the colors of the stone, the steel, the small garden plazas that in daylight were wilted by the heat.

Their footsteps echoed. She stumbled; he held her tighter. He remembered a time shortly after she had been born, when the Senator would spend hours during the evening holding her on his lap, one hand carefully resting on the back of her neck, the other at her chest while he tried to get her to smile.

He never should have left. But he had told the old man that he wanted to prod his ambition before it faded, to learn if he was capable of building his own security.

He had failed, and now he was with Caro again as if the years between had been brief scenes in a play that were shifted so rapidly the curtain stayed up.

Servicemen, now, on special assignments in front of the Keylofts whose residents were families and friends of the Government. Every few meters they stopped Yenkin and the girl, demanding a show of identification, suspiciously and nervously satisfied when he managed to recall the tone of the master servant and gave the girl's name. They received no sympathy. Were ordered to move on.

Finally, when Yenkin thought his legs would turn to melting wax, they stood in front of an upward series of sweeping bronzed arches that framed with hidden lighting gold-railing balconies. A captain, masked, whispered into a grille when Yenkin identified himself and his charge. A quick interchange, and the Serviceman bowed and saluted, and slid open the thickglass door.

Caro smiled and nodded toward the building. "Ty, come in, please! They'll be glad to see you after all this time."

He shook his head. "I don't think your mother would like it, Mistress. I remember her well. She—"

"Shag it, Ty, we're going to need you! Please, Ty, if that's what you want." She softened her frown. "Please?"

He hesitated still, not knowing if he wanted to drown himself once again, and knowing he would because the end of the world had underscored his defeat. He looked down at his Host's uniform, unable to keep from grinning when Caro started a quiet laughter. He brushed at his chest, she brushed at his shoulders and they went inside to begin the official mourning.

Delia listened to the first news of the revolution as she showered, the cascading water partially canceling the voice of the announcer from the comunit speaker over the lavroom's circular mirror. At first she thought it a hoax, and a bad one poorly timed, but before she had rinsed the soap from her back she was convinced. And angry. Not wanting to waste time, then, with the dryair nozzles, she toweled herself briskly, fluffed at her hair and snatched a soft robe from a peg on the wall. Slipping into it, she glared at the speaker as she tied the robe closed, then rushed into the living room, shivering slightly as the cool air met her skin.

There was a pounding on the door. Her neighbors, she thought, no doubt hunting for new rumors she would have picked up while she was out with Caro. But did they have to pound so hard?

She dismissed them by not answering, switching on the comunit's wallscreen instead and looking into the face of a newshawk whose somber expression only aggravated her excitement. She was positive beyond hesitation that the so-called revolution was only a ratgang incursion that had been blown out of proportion by people frightened of war shadows. But she cursed loudly and viciously when the report proceeded to link the alleged uprising to one of the EcGroup's minor leaders, Shanlon Raille. She knew the man only slightly and thought little of his Hill abilities, less of his prowess as a sex-performing male. A little man in more ways than one, she'd judged, and hadn't had personal contact with him in well over a year. But that he and the other members of the Group had conspired with some filthy ratnests to overthrow the Noram Government was ludicrous in the extreme. Yet the newshawk seemed to believe it; and so would the citizens listening to his report.

She slapped furiously at the comunit's cutoff and decided to call those whom she knew were on the Group's Central Committee. She had activated the vione and was lifting out her first coded card when she realized that by implication she would also be considered a part of this bogus revolt.

She stared at the blank screen.

Heard the pounding on the door turn to splintering.

Looked over her shoulder in time to see the men charge through the jagged opening their assault had made.

The only time she thought to scream was after they had opened the window. And she fell.

Though he was only semiconscious, Sergeant Caine's training warned him not to groan, not to whimper. Forcing himself to be patient, he waited as he sifted through the noise around him for the state of his situation. It was difficult. His ears were still ringing from the rockets' explosions. But once his head cleared he heard furtive movements, shoes against concrete, scrapping bits of metal, the steady small blast of the still-burning tank. A hand touched his shoulder. Moisture dripped to his forehead, his lips, and they opened involuntarily to take in the cool water. Whispering. Fingers netted behind his head. He choked, swallowed, stretched his neck for more. Then he opened his eyes and saw three women kneeling beside him, silently taking blades to his clothes, sucking in breath when his wounds gleamed redblack in the flame's wavering light. They must have sensed he was still alive, had given him numbing poppers, so he watched with horrified detachment as they used their soiled fingers to pluck out the jutting shards of metal from his wounded flesh. Whispering again. Someone–another woman, he thought–was behind him telling him everything would be all right. He felt nothing. Remembered striking the corner of the building. He decided, then, in a remarkable calm that his back must have been broken, or his neck, or his legs. He grunted, unwilling to trust to words, and his head was lifted gently. He saw the useless mesh, the fiery mating of truck and tank, the huddled silent corpses of charred Blues. There were other bodies, rats from the first wave. He looked a question at a face that moved in front of him and smiled. The woman shook her head. He tried to whisper but his throat began to burn and she slid more water between his pale lips. He tried again, averting his eyes from the workers at his legs, and this time she understood. With one bandaged hand she pointed toward City Prime.

"They kept going," she said. "They didn't stop at any of the shops on the next block. I don't know why, but they just kept going."

James studied the door to the Premier's office for several minutes before the silence threatened to force out a scream. He nodded to himself and strode across the antechamber floor to the sliding glass door that opened out onto the terrace. He hesitated. Looked over his shoulder before stepping out and closing the Hill in behind him.

The heat was still prevalent despite the efforts of a cooling breeze that had apparently lost its way. He tucked his mask into his belt, closed and opened his eyes in time to a deep breath, less of a sigh than an expulsion of curiously tainted air. His arms folded across his chest.

The cloud of light that generally obscured the night sky was gone. The city, as though there had been a power failure, became a darkened pool whose depths flashed blue-and-red at irregular intervals. When the afterimage faded, the city was invisible again. James didn't like the illusion. He thought of the courier run he had made to Colony Luna and the halfway point when he joined the bridgemates to stare out at space. Vertigo wasn't unmanly, he had been told, but nevertheless it took him a while to grasp without panic the idea that there was no solid ground beneath him, above him, around him. He had become irrationally frightened, had stiffened in front of the port, and was grateful none of the regulars had tried to joke him out of his new/old fear. And it was the same now. He knew that if he walked carefully to the chest-high scalloped parapet at the terrace's end he would be able to look down at the streets below. Dark they would be, but he would know they were there. But he couldn't push himself away from the wall. And the city spread itself before him in unaccustomed nightfall.

He was close to exhaustion.

The Premier had required him to stand at his side while the weepers and wailers had wrung through their paces; while the Service Chiefs had outlined their plans and nodded when they were approved; while the ambassadors wept for the safety of the world; while the Team returned with instructions for the Premier's safety, instructions reviewed and refused.

"They won't get this far," Alton had said confidently, nodding toward the comunit scanner messages. "A few might make it to City Prime, but surely not in sufficient numbers to cause us undue worry. They'll retreat. Take my word for it."

James had thought it an impressive, even inspiring performance. Though he was still as confused as the rest of the city, he felt calmer at each instance of reassurance, each comunit view of the Service reinforcing the beleaguered Blues and pushing the ratgangs into captvans or oblivion. In a way that made him feel oddly guilty he pitied the outlanders attempts to overrun; they were so far outclassed that not even a rout would adequately describe the on-going action. It couldn't be a revolution, not by any stretch of any-one's imagination. So he contrived to stand taller, more stately, the Premier's live symbol of the might of the Service specifically de-signed to calm the congressional Reps who begged for informa-tion.

Then the Consuls arrived. Alton had had barely time enough to rise in greeting when the lower banks of screens flared warning red. The Premier had almost tripped over his own chair in the effort to get closer to the system's eyes. The dark-skinned Cenam Consuls flanked the door, apparently unconcerned. Consul Bendal moved to stand by Alton, one hand lightly on his shoulder. While Consul Faux sat on the edge of the desk and placed his feet on the Premier's chair. Smiling. Nodding absently to James, who had moved to stand in front of the wallmap.

Alton glared at the two lower tiers. "Sandy, what the hell's going on there? What have you people—" and he stopped himself when Faux coughed loudly. He bent over, then, to read the leg-ends of white flickering across the bottoms of the screens.

"Sir," Bendal said, "I'm sorry, but I don't know what you mean. There's . . . well, I'm sorry."

James watched them carefully. This wasn't the same. The mood had changed. The emergency the Premier had handled with rela-tive ease for the past five hours had somehow shifted into some-thing altogether different. He frowned slightly, smoothed his face instantly the Canam Consul glanced his way.

"What is this? New York, Denver, I can't make that one out, Chicago . . . damn you, Sandy, you told me on your oath—"

"Sir!" Bendal cautioned, and the Premier straightened, pulled at his shirtwaist and walked slowly back to his desk. Faux didn't move until Alton had stared at him for several seconds, had slapped the Canam's boots from his chair. He sat. Folded his hands over his stomach.

"Captain Thrush," he said without looking around, "there's no need for show now. Please wait outside until I call you. And," he added quickly as James moved to obey, "thanks for your help. The others do tend to get a little nervous."

James had saluted, nearly hesitated to ask a question as yet unformed, then left with a nod to the Cenam Consul who opened the door for him.

He stared blankly at the starred sky. A newseye suddenly popped over the wall, scanning until it spotted him. He donned his mask quickly and one hand reached for the weapon he had strapped to his belt. He hissed. The newseye swooped as if ducking, then spiraled away to the floors below.

A flash of red in the pool of the city, lingering, dying. The distant wail of sirens.

So it wasn't just Washington after all. Perhaps, he thought, the Premier's confidence was ill-founded. He had seen from the corner of his eye the reports of the cities the Premier had named, plus Houston, Los Angeles, three others he didn't quite catch. Something bothered him and he frowned in searching, dismissed it as he felt the relief of conviction that Shanlon wasn't involved, not to the extent that the newshawks were claiming. In the first place, EcG wasn't all that extensive outside the Noram Capital; and in the second, the creds for arming even half the number of reported rebels would fill ten times over the meager EcG treasury.

It was nonsense. He knew it. And wondered then if the ratgangs had been planning this attempted coup for at least a decade, if not more. Secreting weapons sufficient to overcome the Blues, supplies to the sparsely populated hinterlands, organizing slowly, forming vast chains of command and communication and the timing to go with them. Yet the Service supposedly had infiltrators in the largest nests, and as far as he knew (admitting he knew little after the past few hours) no reports of such nearly impossible-to-hide activities had ever been filed. Certainly not through the Team to the Premier, as they should have been.

Puzzled, and still slightly unnerved by the darkened city, he returned inside to feel the cooled air.

The Premier's antechamber was a carefully designed twenty by forty meters. An empty guard's desk was positioned in front of the office door, facing the central lift/drop pillar. A scattering of paired lounges and pedestaled comunit screens filled the remaining space; most of the waiters and petitioners would get no further than this. And now, except for James, the chamber was deserted.

He wandered, touching chairs and screens, glancing every so often at the glass walls, feeling the weight of the dome above him. Finally, knowing he was making himself too nervous, he chose an armchair that faced the lifttube and amused himself by projecting images of too few fine memories on the transparent cylinder. When he had done, he swiveled around to activate the entchannels on the nearest screen, swore when all he could find were newshawks' faces. It wasn't until he heard the first step on the polished bare floor that he realized someone had lifted to the Premier's floor.

General Manquila stood adjusting his uniform.

"General!" James said, rising to quick attention.

"Ease it, Captain," the general said. His black hair, contrary to his own regulations, flowed gleaming to the tips of his high collar, his mustache and beard were trimmed close to his weather-lined face. No taller than James, and the oversized chest and womanly waist made him awkward to look at while he was standing still. James had never been able to shake the uncomplimentary feeling that unless the general kept moving he would topple to his face because his legs couldn't balance him.

"Sir," James said hesitantly when Manquila moved toward the door, "the Premier's in conference with the Consuls right now. I don't think you—"

Manquila waved the words into the air. "He called me just a moment ago, Captain. But keep it up. You're doing just fine."

James acknowledged the insincere compliment with a slight nod, but did not resume his seat until the general had thumbed the door, waited for the admittance chime and had vanished inside. What he saw, when the door slid to, was the Premier seated at his desk, his hands clasped and pressed to his forehead. He was angry, James thought. He rose again and walked to the 'tube, looked down and saw nothing. He shrugged, turned, and the general was again on the threshold.

"Captain Thrush, the Premier wants to see you inside. Don't worry about intruders, if that's what you're doing. There are enough men below to handle whatever might come up."

Of course there are men below, you sobitch idiot, he thought angrily as he strode past the officer. There are always men below. What the hell does he think I am, someone from . . .

Alton was standing now at the side of his desk. He nodded when James looked at him. The Cenams and Faux had their backs to him, watching the reports of the fighting. Bendal was slouched in the Premier's chair, his face waxen, his eyes closed. No one moved.

"Captain," the Premier said, "it seems that our Usam Consul, Mr. Bendal, has been stricken. I understand you're trained to handle such things. Would you please step over here and—"

"Sir, excuse me," James interrupted, "but I'm not really a med, you know. May I suggest, for the Consul's sake, that you call the Hill—"

"I'm sorry, James," Alton said, stepping around the desk, "but we . . . you have no choice."

"The revolution, you understand," Faux said, turning and smiling. "Extraordinary measures for an extraordinary time, Captain. That's the way it has to be for now."

"I'm sorry, sir," James said as Manquila took his arm and prodded him forward. "I'm sorry, but I'm afraid I don't understand."

"The revolution," the Premier said. "It seems there really is one."

The city was framed in the tunnel's mouth. The sky was sparked by rare stars, the only lights he could see since all the windows appeared dark and shuttered. Pressing against the wall he edged up the ramp toward the street, huddling once when a flurry of footfalls raced by without accompanying words. As was the tunnel, the outside was unnaturally silent and he couldn't imagine how the assassination of a Senator, however popular, could drive an entire city into hiding. On hands and knees, then, he reached the open air, squinting and averting his face as a steady breeze kicked dust and paper debris into his eyes. The barrier around the tunnel's entrance and exit had been flattened, cracked, the pieces kicked aside. As far as he could see ahead of him all street lamps had been extinguished save one per block.

He listened. To the silence. Rubbed the heel of one hand over his forehead. Judging by the drabness of the buildings he could see nearby, he had reached the Fringe though he couldn't tell which section of the city's compass he had run to. Looking behind him, he saw a scant dozen blocks distant the faint blue glow of a meshnet and a glare of lights from a huddle in the center of the road. Blues. He ducked without thinking, taking several seconds before realizing they wouldn't be able to spot him.

A spattering of papers blew past his hands and clung briefly to his chest, his legs, vanished into the silent tunnel. He plucked at them and tossed them aside impatiently. And kept one when he noticed its silverblue trim. An edition news. A source. He held it up to catch faint light from the nearest lamp and looked at the Senator's picture and, below it, his own. He didn't need to read the entire story to learn what the accusations against him were, but his eyes traveled quickly to incredible reports of a ratgang uprising supposedly organized and led by EcG and Raille. Pitched battles in the vulnerable Fringes–he looked up at the Blues, scurried below the level of the street and sat against the wall–heavy Blue casualties before the Service began moving in its troops. States of emergency reported from over a dozen of the largest Noram cities. The word *revolution* in glaring red print.

Shanlon Raille.

There are jagged gaps in nightmares through which darker shapes escape, he thought; and he knew then that he had fallen through one of them. An alternate universe. A black grim Hell. Some splitseam tear in the sheet of reality–all he had to do was locate the edges and pull them together and the world would change back to his tricks and his stall and the offices in the Hill.

He sat for nearly an hour, numbed and shaking his head. Moaning once and clamping stiff fingers to his lips. Holding the paper up to watch it flutter in the wind, rip from his grasp and scuttle down the ramp.

There was, finally, anger.

The why of it, however, would have to be temporarily shunted aside. The *why me?* would have to come later–the fact of it was, it had happened and was happening. He stared at his fingers and counted his options.

There was no home to run to. It would have already been thoroughly ransacked by Blues and Servicemen for clues. Probably it had been stripped. Most certainly it was guarded against his unlikely return.

The EcG offices in the Hill were similarly banned. As would be the lofts of the Committeemen (those who had survived their own assassinations, he thought) and whatever EcG members who were known to be more than simple status-seeking temporaries.

He had planned on dropping in to see Morag after his venner stint, but since the hospital where she nursed was directly across from the Hill, she too would have to wait for his truth. Though she would probably be one of the few who could actually believe in his innocence, without his professing it.

To go outland, then, would seem to be the best move for his safety. Run. Hide. Scrounge time to think while the revolution raged on, doomed from the start to a sputteringly ignominious end. Change name and face and try to enter a city somewhere else. Or look for assistance in one of the smaller outowns. Or even flee the country to either Eurepac of the still-splintered SA.

Or he could search for some witnesses from the scene of the murder, witnesses who had known and would know that he had not killed anyone, and definitely wasn't the leader of some abortive ratgang insurrection. But that Consul had been too quick with his pointing and . . . with something else, a flicker of a movement his mind had caught and would not play back. He scowled but could not remember. And whatever anyone had actually seen would be colored, disfigured by the disaster's swift onset and aftermath. He wouldn't be surprised if later accounts had him drenched to the teeth in sophisticated weaponry, spewing death to countless hundreds instead of only one.

The outland.

The anger flared.

No!

Not again.

Not . . . again!

To do it now, at this moment, on this day, would be more than an admission–it would be an abdication. Childhood dreams had already stepped down in favor of adulthood's compromise. When his parents had been killed, he'd floundered in his schooling, in his training, in his subsequent noncareer. Good, but not great.

Good, but not great.

But he knew it now, in shades of lightning, for what it had been and what it was: all of it a hiding of a kind, a running into an outland he had created in his mind.

Tell me something, Shanlon, he said to his palms, aren't you shagging tired of being a venner with tricks?

He was.

And he was mad.

Three

The decision, once made and twice repeated, weakened him. Instead of rising immediately, he slumped. The ramp wall was damp and bled through his robe. He squirmed but didn't attempt to escape the chill that settled along his spine. Shanlon Raille, leader of men, he thought: Shanlon Raille, leader of rats–somehow that was more fitting. He lifted a hand to catch a breath of the wind and dry a sweating palm. His shoulder twitched involuntarily and a flower sprang from his sleeve and fell to the ground before he knew it had been in the air. He stared at it as though it were a face he knew he should recognize and couldn't. When the wind nudged it, then shoved until it began to roll awkwardly down the concrete slope, he reached out and grabbed it. Spun it between his fingers until the stem finally snapped and the drying petals fell into his lap. He sighed. Shrugged. Felt along both arms until he was satisfied there were no more tricks to keep him company. He chewed then on a corner of his lower lip and wondered why his angered determination hadn't transformed him instantly into a formidable machine of vast destruction. Where, he asked the fluttering petals, were the clever plots and countermoves that should have leaped full-blown into the space beside him? Why didn't they grab his arms and yank him out of the tunnel into the streets where his redemption waited, patiently, smiling?

If anything, he was more confused than ever. Having finally decided to do something, he didn't know what to do. Easy to say, impossible to act, as his father often muttered when a customer wanted something special from the shop. What the elder Raille did, thus confronted, was fly through his shelves snatching pieces here and pieces there, his lips muttering incomprehensible incantations while his hands became a blur in the creation of something new. Flying, then, and muttering and blurring until the customer shouted stop and the bargaining began.

One piece at a time.

"All right, then," Shanlon said to the last of the petals lifting from his lap. "All right, one piece at a time."

He straightened, shifted his hands as if to brush himself clean, then changed his mind. He stood and moved slowly down the tunnel, feeling along the walls until he found what he needed. A glance to the ramp and a strain to hear, and he rubbed his hands against the stone, against his face, brushed them twice through his hair and resisted the temptation to smooth it down. There would be no need to add grime to his clothes: he had fallen enough in his flight, crawled enough in his fear to do the necessary damage already. When he felt himself sufficiently filthy, he opened the robe's central seam and reached to his side. From a small sheath clipped to his belt he pulled a small knife encased in ridged ivory, flicked out the blade and made small rents in the fabric of his sleeves, at his knees and hem. He stared at the cutting edge for a moment, thinking it a shame he hadn't met the right woman that night for whom he could fashion an instant god. That girl in the queue, perhaps–he shook his head, annoyed that he was unable to quash her image as he had so many others. The last pleasant sight of a dying man was the most likely answer. Her face would probably be with him as long as he lived–which won't be that long, idiot, he told himself, if you don't move it, and fast. Quickly, then, he tore at the gaps he had made, widening them to jagged tears, then rubbing at their edges to rid them of their artificial look. A snap that tore the robe's low collar, and he moved back up the ramp, wishing he had a mirror, glad that he didn't.

The street was still quite dark, quiet, and behind him the faint luminescence of the Blue's station. It took him a disturbingly long moment to remember there were people dying in other parts of the city.

Rising slowly from the belowground warren, he turned cautiously, seeking direction. There would be no crowds in which he could lose himself, and he suspected that City Prime was infected with Servicemen protecting the government and its myriad kin. Shelter, then. He darted from the street to the sidewalk when a strong gust rose to cover his footfalls. He pressed against the Keyloft walls and moved from shadow to shadow, stopping only at the unornamented entrances to check for unbidden watchers. Inward. Marveling at the silence of the streets, the lofts, shaking off the forbidding sensation that he had risen from the dead only to find that the world had died waiting for him.

A name floated. Hazy. Uninspiring. He crouched at a corner and waited for it to resolve itself.

Delia. A woman of ambiguous loyalty to the principles of EcG, as loyalties went with waning fads. He frowned. He recalled bedding her once. It had been after an office celebration, something to do with a passage of a minor bill that affected scarcely anyone. In her drunkenness she had berated him for not being able to stay with her as dream men should. He'd felt sorry, but not pity. And he hadn't apologized for there was nothing he could have done to satisfy her further. He couldn't remember how the night had ended. Probably he had awakened alone. But she kept returning to the offices to kill the time she had with volunteer work. There'd been no conscious avoidance; he just never ran into her again. And if she, Delia, Delia Something, hadn't constructed for herself an important position within the lobby structure, she might still be free of harassment from the enemies of this incredible revolution; and if she didn't remember clearly his blameless failure, she might be willing to allow him to stay with her while he worked to find a better grasp of the vise that was pinching at his chest.

An address. She wasn't going to come floating down to his aid on a pink-and-gold cloud. He scowled in concentration, realized his efforts would be fruitless and hurried on several blocks, turned several corners, until he spotted a translucent glass door set into a loft wall on the opposite side of the street. Sliding into a shop doorway, he watched the deserted roadway, listening as he fumbled in his sidepurse for the coin he would need. A shout slammed his hand into a fist, and he pressed himself back as a window opened above him and a woman's voice screamed hysterically. Her words were unintelligible, and so was the answering shout of a man Shanlon imagined was struggling with her. She cried out again, and the cry was abruptly stifled, the window slammed shut. Shan flinched at the expectation of falling glass.

Only the scream remained, hefted by the wind and shattered into moaning echoes that sprang lights in several keys across from the shop. But no one poked a head out, and the lights soon went down to their huddling darkness. He waited several minutes before taking a deep breath and dashing across the road, sliding back the door and slipping into the vione booth.

He sat heavily on the short low bench. Pressed his head back against the plastic wall. Perspiration iced down the center of his chest, down the sides of his legs and into his boots. He wanted to close his eyes, but he dared not. He wanted to lick at his lips, but feared the taste of salt. He reached out instead and touched lightly the small gray screen in front of him. It was cold to his finger tips. He withdrew his hand, slowly. And nodded to the reflection of a battered madman that stared darkly after him.

He shivered, then, and realized it was cold in the booth. Twisting slightly on the bench, he pried the door open with his foot, as much to ease the press of the frigid air as to keep an ear tuned to the street outside. He heard only the wind.

Delia. Delia what? He looked dumbly at the simplified console beneath the screen. What the hell was her last name?

Anders. Delia Anders. And if the truth be known, he told himself sourly, she wasn't such a memorable bedmate herself.

He grinned and jabbed his coin into its slot, waited for the tiny red glow of the ready light. When it flashed he lowered the shutter to keep his image from being transmitted and spoke softly into the rectangular grille to the screen's right. "Delia Anders, please. A home connection if it's available. This city. I'm sorry but her address escapes me."

There was a flurry of static across the gray face, so bright he had to turn away momentarily. When it cleared, he groaned silently. A simulcomp woman's face greeted him, smiling efficiently, as bland a creature of mechanical imagination as he himself could conjure in lackluster nightmares. He saw it noting the pull of the caller's shutter, but its expression didn't change. "Delia Anders, home connection," the face said sweetly, its lips barely moving.

"Correct," he said after clearing his throat to make his voice sound more rough.

"I am sorry, sir, but no connection is possible at this time. There is damage to the line. Emergency repair is unfortunately unavailable at this time. May I locate an alternate for you?"

He hesitated, knowing that the continuing lack of visual on his end would be alerting the comsystem's Bluetag as a matter of course. "No," he said, "but you might be able to help me with her address. And while you're at it, tag the number of this booth. It's been damaged rather badly. In the emergency, I gather. I'm afraid I can't see you very well. Static."

The face wavered, informed him the address was in fact available and gave it to him before requesting he repeat the booth's number. Without hesitation he did, changing the last four digits in the sequence, and released the connection. The screen grayed, and he felt the cold again.

One piece, Shan, he told himself and left the booth to hurry to the corner where he checked the inset gleaming locplaque to gear his bearings. That damage to Anders' home system might be a perfectly innocent breakdown, but if not he wasn't going to take a chance on explaining his innocence to a patrol of battle-scarred Blues.

A moment's quick thought and he moved away in the opposite direction of the loft number he had been given.

Caine dreamed.

Rockfaces. Mountains. Snow. Cold.

Patrolling Denver's Fringe that was as clean as Denver's Prime.

Talking, once, with a rat that had fled her nest. She'd told him she had damaged the steramp in her forearm, had gotten herself too early pregnant and too late aborted. A throwback shame that had pushed her into the hills where she waited until her name, she thought, would be forgotten and she could move back to the city and try starting again. Caine had walked her to the nearest city bath, waited until she had cleaned herself, then gave her (not knowing why he gave her) thirty creds in coin and showed her the way to the best hostelry he knew. Employment was easy in Denver back then. He never saw her after she left. And when he told his dying wife, she laughed at him.

Talking.

Patrolling.

Using Bluecred priority to fly to Washington.

And the rats.

The rats.

He moaned in his sleep.

There was something about those rats that he wished he could remember.

Thrush knew Bendal was going to die. Since the death of his colleague some months before (a reported cardiac blockage, but now Thrush wondered) he was the only Usam Consul, and soon there would be none.

He stood in the center of the room. Waiting for instructions from Faux or Manquila. Praying for the first time since his baptism under fire that he would live long enough to think enough to do something about dying.

Praying and, seeing the bleak expression on Alton's long face, not believing.

Shanlon ordered himself to be more cautious. Three-man Service patrols were sweeping through the streets at irregular intervals, and WatchDogs were beginning to streak high overhead. He was in recognizable if not familiar territory now, close to the sectors of official residences. It would be too much to expect that his present condition would continue to go unnoticed as the patrols increased and permanent servgards sprouted from each luxury loft entrance. It was small comfort that he was able to spot solitary pedestrians even at this late hour; they were probably the restless or the drunk or the fearful testing their thresholds of courage, but they would not provide him with sufficient camouflage.

He huddled in a recessed shopface and stared at the now motionless simuls, and the women's clothes they modeled. It was less a conscious process of moving deliberately from one point to another than it was a sudden and desperate instinctive grabbing. He stared at the simuls, grinned and poked his head out to check the street. At the far corner on his right a small cluster of peds, civilians by their nightcloaks, were hurrying though not running from one loft entrance to another; a man and a woman strolled unconcernedly opposite him, their heads close together in silent conversation, and he ducked back to huddle in the dark. He had seen enough, however, to encourage him. There were three shops with their attendant topside offices on this block, the rest of the area filled with Keylofts. None of the shops were of immediate use to him, but he suspected that no more than two or three turns through the neighborhood would give him what he wanted.

Battling against a hope that made him want to laugh, he waited until the street was empty and slipped to the corner on his left. Looked around it. Smiled. A string of shops, four on a side, on the same block. Most of the Keylights were on here, but he could see no one in the windows, no one on the sidewalks. In the distance, the harsh sputtering of a landcar Service patrol. He hurried to the first shop on his side, passed it when he saw the displays of exotic foodstuffs arranged in the window. At the second was a display of Falline clothes. Men's. He stepped into the recess and tried the door. Locked, but he shrugged without moving. Soon enough he knew he would eventually locate the door that had not been locked, the shop owner too panicked at the initial outbreak of revolution news to be cautious; the fear for his wares would come later and if the owner were brave enough, he would return to secure his store, especially if the fighting remained as it had, in the background western districts.

It was the fifth try two blocks distant that gave without the squeal of alarm.

Shan wasted no time for self-congratulations. Working mostly by the diffused glow of the streetlights, he made his way to the rear of the narrow shop and into a small back room that evidently served as office for the business. He brushed a hand over the light switch, dimming it instantly the ceiling became a dull white sun. Models were leaning against the back wall, already dressed, apparently part of a new display for the shopface. It was easy to pick out the one he needed: not quite the shortest, but definitely below what the statistics deemed average. A quick doublecheck of the street again, and he stripped off his robe, the shirt and trousers beneath, the apparatus he wore to aid him with his tricks. There was no other door that could lead to a lavroom, but he discovered behind a tattered satin screen a mirror, basin and tank. Using all of a small jar of soap, he washed face and hands as best he could, soaked his hair several times while wincing at the filth that muddied the basin's water. He rinsed, fumbled for a dryair nozzle before realizing he would have to make do with strips of cloth lying about the office. Once done, he stared in the small mirror affixed to the wall above the basin, preened as well as he could with his fingers and turned to the model.

"Not my style," he muttered as he stripped the simul. Then, after a moment's hesitation, he slipped into his spring harness and slid his knife into the casing where the flowers had been. He practiced only twice, unaccustomed to the unbalanced weight on his forearm, and hoped his fingers would remember to close quickly enough should he have to use the weapon. The clothes—tight shirt and trousers a dark and smooth brown—were uncomfortable but clean, and to hide the telltale bulge on his left arm he yanked a walking cloak off a larger model and fixed the clasp at his neck, set the front seam shut from the inside. The sleeves he folded inward at the wrists, and regretfully ripped the shoulder braid from the warm fabric. He would never be mistaken for a rank of importance, but he hoped he'd display at least a confident status.

He was staring down at his scuffed and dirt-caked boots when he heard the grunt of a motor stall outside.

A glare up at the dim ceiling light, but he didn't take the time to curse his carelessness. Instead, yanking the cloak's hem that brushed at his waist, he pressed against the wall and listened.

Spitting dryly when the door opened and there were footsteps.

"Damned stupid old man," a voice said. "Can't even remember to lock up his own stupid shop. Why the hell we have to do his work for him when he could get off–"

"Barnes, why don't you just shut up for a minute? Take a check around this crap and see if his precious clothes are–"

"Hey, Sarge, there's a light on back there. I don't remember him saying anything about leaving on a light. Did he say anything to you about leaving on a light?"

"Maybe he forgot," a third voice, and younger, said. "A guy like that would forget to take a crap if he didn't have a med on his wrist. You see all the damned poppers he has to down? No wonder the shagging taxes are so shagging–"

"Enough is enough," the sergeant said, though his tone didn't match the manner of his words. "There ain't nothing out here so let's go in the damned back and see what the hell's up."

"You go first, Sarge," Barnes said.

"Not him," the third man said. "He's afraid of rats. You see the way he jumped when we–"

"Enough!"

Shan edged to the lip of the jamb and waited. There was no place to hide–the satin screen was worse than useless–and there was no rear exit he could duck out to safety. He was going to be flushed, and he could either brazen his way to a chance for an escape on the street, or he could fight. And the latter made him uncomfortably cold, while his palms stayed moist no matter how many times he wiped them on his sides.

"Nice clothes," Barnes said, the footsteps coming to a halt less than a meter from the back room door. "Hey, look at this stuff,

Abe, will you? Guy'd look like a balloon wearing something like this."

"You got no sense of fashion, Barnes. All the best Consuls are wearing these things."

"Shows you where their damned brains are. I don't believe it. Look at this! Now who would pay a flat hundred creds for something like this?"

"The Sarge would. That's right, ain't it, Sarge?"

There was a low growling answer and the two men laughed. Shan tensed, glanced once at the ceiling and flexed the fingers of his left hand. His knees dropped him into a slight crouch.

Barnes was the first through the door. Shan didn't notice the man's size or the silvered mask that covered his features: he saw instead the gleaming rod of a stunton hanging loosely from the soldier's utility belt, its handloop wrapped only halfway around the broad black plastic for quick release. Shan grabbed it and thumbed its charge to full even as he swung it left and right. Barnes, startled, was caught in the act of turning around–his face glazed instantly, his arms flung up, and he fell; Abe took the swing full in his stomach–with no time to double up, he staggered backward and collided with the sergeant following directly behind. Shan pushed at the falling man and jabbed the 'ton at the Serviceman entangled behind him, catching his forearm before his handgun could be drawn from its holster. The only sound was the slumping of bodies to the floor.

There was no time to see if the shock had killed or only incapacitated. Shan dropped the weapon onto the floor and sprinted out to the street. The three-man patrol vehicle was still idling at the curb. He ignored it–he had no inkling at all of passwords, patrol routes or the dozen other things that would inevitably kill him for his ignorance. His legs were his best opportunity, and he took it. He angled across the street, trying to recall the directions the bald man had given him earlier, desperately wanting to look back over his shoulder to see if another unit had already been summoned. But he kept his eyes forward, his arms pumping, until he suddenly realized he had been hearing but not listening to the sounds of a nearby battle. He raced around a corner and threw himself against the nearest wall, grabbing at a protruding piece of statuary to stop his flight.

There were Servicemen in the street, 'Dogs in the air, and they were fighting.

Caine awoke. Wrinkled his nose. The odors sharp and lightly burning, the bland pale green of the ceiling, the mumblings human and mechanical, and the occasional escaping moan were identification enough—he was in a hospital ward, and it was crowded.

The utilitarian squat bulk of a diagmed unit shadowed the corner of his eye. Without raising his head he looked down and saw the slithering of the unit's tentacled wires across his chest, the varied coded colors vanishing under the sheet that held him down. He was groggy, and there was no sensation at all below his neck; but once he knew where he was he decided to worry about his ability to walk some other time—right now he had a number of gods to thank for the simple gift of his still being alive. However, before he could begin, the diagmed withdrew and a nurse looked down at him, her smile broad and sparked with relief. She winked from behind a falling fan of short black hair, and Caine winked back.

"You came pretty close, Blue," the nurse said as she pulled at the perforated sheets rippling from the diagmed's side. "Nice to have you back again."

"I suppose I shouldn't ask about the others," Caine said, his voice rasping through a throat dry and raw.

The nurse paused in her readings, looked away and back before nodding. Caine thought of another question, dismissed it and closed his eyes, opened them again and the lights were markedly dimmer, the noise level in the ward reduced to a surf-like whispering. The nurse was slipping an IV into his arm.

"I shouldn't talk so much," he said, and she laughed quietly, nodding. "What time is it? Have I been here very long?"

"It's just about dawn," she said.

"What about the fighting? Is it over? Has anybody won?"

She shrugged and made a show of smoothing the sheets over Caine's chest. "All we get here are the comunit bulletins. They're supposed to be right from the Hill across the way, which doesn't mean much. Alton's still hanging on, he's still in control from the looks of it, but I wouldn't take bets on how long it'll stay that way. Fewer casualties, but that doesn't mean anything either. You can still hear explosions when you get to the roof for some air. It's cooler, though. I think the heat has finally passed."

"Thanks," Caine said. He didn't ask about his back or legs. He could see from the abrupt stiff rise of the sheets that he had been placed in a cast, with only his arms, neck and head free. He felt nothing. Not even hunger.

He watched the nurse reset the unit, waited patiently until his forehead had been wiped with a cool cloth and a glass of lukewarm liquid held to his lips was taken away.

She was not young, not as young as her voice, but lovely with the lines and quiet confidence nothing but age could evoke. Dark hair, dark eyes, dark lips–when she smiled, her slightly flat nose wrinkled and her eyes vanished. Her laugh would be soft, he thought; and told himself he had been given too damned many drugs.

When she patted his hand and moved on to her next patient, he wondered, then, if he were going to die.

Under the cautiously casual eyes of Manquila and Torre, one of the broad-chested Cenam Consuls, Thrush returned to the antechamber and ripped several cushions from the now empty lounges. After making three trips in strained and brittle silence, he fashioned a reasonably sturdy, uncomfortable-looking bed in a corner by the windows. Then he and Alton lifted Bendal and carried him over, lay him gently. Alton hovered a moment before returning to his desk, and Thrush stripped away the Consul's jacket and tore open his shirt at the throat. The man's breathing was halting and shallow, his face more pale, his nose and lips more distinct. James knew that the Consul would be dead before the sun rose.

With no further orders moving him elsewhere, he sat on his heels and clasped his hands over his knees, his back to the wall. To his left the windows, to his right the door to the outside world. He shook his head slowly, allowed his eyes a moment's closing.

Faux, less nervous, waved Alton away from the desk and sat down, turning to face the screens. There were several quiet conversations with the Team's leader, messages that were passed from the general to a succession of colonels. Torre and his colleague, Degaldon, stood silently in front of the world map, both heads cocked to listen to the faint and constant commentary of the networks' newshawks.

It was obvious to James that, however successful now, the movement was still quite a small one, and he was angered in his attempts to find a way to turn that to his advantage. He had been disarmed almost immediately, and the Premier, once removed from his desk, moved about the room as though he were a zombie, not speaking, stumbling over invisible objects on the floor, bumping into the desk whenever Faux demanded a conference. James told himself that the Premier was merely stunned by the incredible turn of events and would soon enough regain his wits, and the thunderous bluster for which he was famous. Soon enough. And James kept wishing he weren't lying to himself.

While on the screens fighting lessened. Once past the Fringe, however, there were no pictures, but he could imagine the relentless driving through the tombs of the suburbs, and the unspeakable numbers of bodies that would rot beneath the trees. He shook his head and concentrated on what he could see, rather than what he could imagine. There were still isolated pockets of resistance, then, and the tolls on the Service/Blue side seemed inordinately heavy. He wondered as he watched what the rats could have been promised that would make them willingly throw themselves into such embattled blatant suicide.

Faux laughed, and the sound was too loud.

Alton stood at the windows, his hands pressed against the glass, his forehead down and touching the pane.

Something had to be done and soon. And he ground his teeth in his failure to spotlight just what.

The lifttube opened onto a small spartan foyer painted a flat white. The streetwall was glass from ceiling to floor, and blocked by a pair of tall potted shrubs with their leaves gleaming from a fresh watering. Directly opposite was a short ebony bench set under a line drawing of Colony Luna as it had been with only a handful of inhabitants. Facing the tube, a dark intrusion on the long wall, was a nut brown door that led into the Key occupying the entire fourth floor. At the front of the loft, the living room—expensively decorated over a period of twenty years; nothing radically altered, Ty thought, except for the carpet, which had once been white and now was a tangled weaving of tan and metallic gold. On the far right a setting of armchairs clustered about a holvid cube, the center of the room with its divan and lounges reserved for guests and seldom used, and the far left still kept clear to provide easy access to the Key's private balcony.

Yenkin stood at the balcony's French doors, his hands clasped loosely behind his back. From the bedroom suite at the rear of the Key he could hear the intermittent sobbing of the Senator's wife, a woman ten years Talle's senior and too dependent upon the dead man's will to survive his assassination unscathed. Caro remained with her, dry-eyed finally and determined to keep the world out, the grief in, with the prodigal Yenkin as her surrogate protector. From the moment they had stepped through the door into the squall of the older woman's hysteria, the vione in the Senator's study had chimed incessantly: newshawks unctuously sorrowful, colleagues stunned, the ordinary curious—all put off with glacier apologies until he had been able to locate the privycode and lock it in. Since then there had been silence, and he was beginning to wonder why none of the Consuls or the Premier had yet called in their condolences. He had convinced himself temporarily, and thereby calmed the women, that the war's intrusion had kept them far too busy for amenities and sorrow; but now that he was alone, waiting for the lighting of the sky to announce another sunrise, he wondered again.

His hands moved from back to front. Found nothing to cling to and fluttered again to his back.

Surely, he thought as he stared unseeing at the lights across the street, there must have been one minute, a single block of unused seconds when Alton could have made a swift connection—after all, it was the Senator's brutal slaying that had supposedly sparked this insane revolution, rallied the Service, united the country, and everything else that the newshawks proclaimed. One minute. It couldn't be too much to ask for a bereavement.

He sighed quietly, reached out and extinguished the living room lights. A low ornate pedestal squatted at his left hand. On it a canted screen framed in helix marble. He switched on the unit without thinking much about it and watched the Capital's prime commentator working feverishly at a map of the Noram Community, pin-pointing the scenes of conflict while casualty estimates flashed in red at the bottom of the screen. It all seemed to be going well, he thought as he followed the Service's progress. The rebel forces, for whatever their initial worth, were falling back to the outlands in great disorganized numbers, the Service following cautiously but without pause. Stock footage inserted to show Premier Alton working hard at his desk in the Hill, flinging out scraps of scribbled-on paper to anxious subordinates gathered around him, his hands a blur while his eyes seemed locked on the elaborate comsystem arrayed before him.

It was dramatic, it was morbidly fascinating the first few times Yenkin had watched it, but now he ignored it. Something about the newsroom's picture bothered him.

Something.

He worried at it, staring at the screen, but the cameras refused to accommodate his bother by constantly darting back and away from the commentator's position. And when finally they settled, he was interrupted by Caro's return. She had changed into simpler clothes, trading her streetsuit for blouse and slacks a carefully shaded green to complement her hair, accent the fine pallor of her complexion. Yenkin smiled sadly, and she nodded without speaking, drifting to his side and turning off the pedestal screen.

"She's sleeping, finally," she said. "But she had to pop four of those big things before I could leave her. I don't know how she does it without any water."

"Is that wise, Mistress?" Yenkin asked. "She never was able to take much medication, even in the best of times. I remember that Eurepac doctor lecturing her about unsetting her tolerance levels. Something like that."

Caro shrugged as if to say, what did it matter now, with her world already smoldering?

A silence, weighted, before Yenkin became disturbed at her closeness and pushed aside the doors to step out onto the balcony. The gold spotlights were off, the room behind him a dark curtain, and he leaned his forearms on the black twist of a railing and looked down into the street. Caro stood beside him, close but not touching, and he could hear her breathing falling like a string of strandless sighs.

The Keyloft was situated in the middle of the block, and it was subdued now as residents, some of them, fell into uneasy slumber. Private security had given way to Service guards who were drifting from their posts at the individual loft entrances to group at the curbs, smoking, talking quietly, shifting to new locations whenever an officer passed with a soft word. At the northern corner was a hovbus ramp, it's barrier taken down and placed in sections along the nearest wall; four men stood across each of the tunnel's two mouths, facing outward, their MLs at the ready.

A faint *click,* and Yenkin jerked his head around. Caro was holding a fan in her hands, spread, and he leaned over to look at the picture etched across it. She smiled at his curiosity and made a silent offer to hand it to him. He almost took it, refused instead.

"My hands are still shaking, Mistress," he said, holding them out to prove his point. "I'm afraid I'd drop such a beautiful thing."

"It is beautiful, isn't it?" she said.

"A gift from an admirer, I expect," he said, smiling, then fading to a puzzled frown when she shook her head. "Oh, I'm sorry. Then it must be from . . . your father. From one of his trips?"

"No, Ty, you couldn't be more wrong. I got it from a venner, in fact."

"But, Mistress—"

She took his arm briefly and shook it, her smile only an arrangement of her lips. "Ty, people stop calling people things like that when people get older." She laughed, then, and mimicked his stance at the railing. "I'm too old for Mistress or Younger or any of those things. As much as it will kill you, please start calling me Caro. Especially now. Most especially now."

"Well," he said, awkward in the face of the death of a formality, "I can't believe, if you'll forgive me, that a common venner gave you that thing there. It's much too fine to come from a stranger. It's probably even valuable."

"It may be," she mused, turning it over in her hands slowly, "but it was given to me anyway. And he wasn't a common venner, either. At least, I don't think so. He was . . . what do you call them, Ty? . . . a trickster, magician. He pulled it out from here," and she brushed at the area behind her ear.

"The restaurant!" he said loudly, surprised, startled into grabbing at her arm. "The one at the restaurant! The one who—"

Caro stiffened, snapped shut the fan and tapped it nervously against her palm. Yenkin turned abruptly back to his scanning of the street. Idiot! He was not three hours back where he had started and he'd already blundered into a tactless remark. He was right; nothing had changed but the carpet. His thoughtless utterances had often driven the Senator to head-shaking despair, and now he was apparently cursed to inflicting the same on his daughter. Haward would have whispered *I told you so;* be perversely thankful, then, he thought, that Haward was in no position to whisper anything to anyone.

A WatchDog wailed past the block's northern intersection.

Only two of the Servicemen bothered to look up.

"Ty," Caro said finally, changing the fan's tapping to a slow sawing motion across the back of one hand, "you were . . . you were *there*. Would you . . . could you tell me what you saw?"

He shook his head at once. "It's not the time, Mistress . . . Caro. So soon after the event . . . no, it's not the time. We have to think about your mother, and we have to think about your health."

"My health," she said, cementing the word in disgust. "There's nothing wrong with my health. Everybody in this house worries about my damned health except the meds. Father worries . . ." She swallowed and looked up at the sky, down the length of the street. "He worried about my moral health, and Mother was always going on about my mental health. As if I wouldn't go into a craze living in a place like this where all my friends, such as they are, are either doomed to be chained in the Hill to their politics or have to pass a thousand thousand million interrogations by the security men before they can even come up to see me. It isn't my *health* we should be worried about, Ty."

"Caro, please!"

"No, Ty, *you* please. I want to know what happened. I was too . . . well, you tell me. Now. Please."

He pushed away from the railing and turned to stare back inside; but without the lights all he could see was his reflection in the glass, a ghost hovering on the brink of extinction. No anchors, no binds. He felt slightly dizzy. She prodded him again, and still he resisted. The dizziness passed and left an acrid trail of nausea. Caro had grown stronger, there was no doubt about that, but it wasn't her persistent demands that stalled him. Sooner or later—and he was surprised that it hadn't happened already—there would be armies of investigators flocking around him with the same questions, the same desperate tenacity, and he wasn't sure he would be able to give any of them the correct answers . . . or even the answers they wanted to hear. It had happened so rapidly, all of it, that he was fast losing control of what was fact and what was only conjecture.

He looked to his reflection, lifted a begging hand, then turned back to the railing and confessed his confusion while his hands waved helplessly over the four-story drop.

"I keep trying to bring it back," he said, almost whining, "even when I don't want to think about it, but it's never the same."

"Ty."

"Sometimes the Senator isn't dead at all, and it–the riots–are all for nothing because there's nothing to fight about. Sometimes it's me on the ground and I'm lying there and the Senator is laughing and then, suddenly, he's dead. Sometimes there's–"

Caro took his arms and wrenched him around to face her. She was crying, soundlessly, but concern rather than grief broke the lines in her thin face. Yenkin listened to himself babbling and shook his head violently to shut himself up. Then, his tongue stilled, he sagged in her grip and leaned back against the railing. Turns and tables, he thought when his mind ceased its racing–the comforted becomes the comforter, a role nobody wants. He glanced over his shoulder and down, and saw several of the Service guards staring up at them, but none of them moved toward the loft entrance. They must think it odd to see a Host standing on a balcony in a place like this, he thought; and an unbidden image of the scene he was in made him smile, reluctantly, and Caro released him, smoothing his tunic and touching, once and lightly, the point of his chin.

He sniffed. Raised his eyebrows to loosen the skin of his forehead. "I don't know," he said. "I honestly do not know what it was that I think I saw. My back was at the restaurant door, holding it open for the Consuls and your father, see, and one of them was trying to get the others to hurry it up. A crowd had started to gather, I guess because he was recognized, and–"

"Faux," Caro said. "The man's name is Faux."

Yenkin tapped a knuckle to his lips. "Oh . . . yes, yes, you're right, that's who it was! Anyway, he was calling to them, and then your father came out and the other one–it must have been Bendal, now that I think of it, because whatshisname, Devereaux, is dead–God, I should keep up more with current affairs, shouldn't I? I mean, I don't even know who the Consuls are any more. How can a man survive if he doesn't know who his–"

"Ty, calm down!"

He reached back and grabbed at the railing, squeezing until its ridges cut into his palms. "Anyway, he was standing there between them, your father was, and suddenly there was this shot and the Senator went down like he'd been clubbed and Faux was pointing and screaming at that venner outside there. I remember the venner because he had recommended the place to a customer earlier in the evening and Haward thought it was odd and wanted him taken care of before he caused trouble." He laughed, shortly, made a fist and tapped it to his chin. "He wanted to get some ratgang members to teach him a lesson. Poor stupid Haward–the venner's stall got him when it went through the window."

Caro gestured toward him with the fan. "That venner," she said, and turned the gesture over her shoulder. "They said he was someone called Raille. A lobbyist or something. They said he's the leader of this fighting going on!"

Ty shrugged. "I wouldn't know about that, Caro, but–"

"But what?"

An impulse, then, to drive off her questions by leaping from the balcony into the arms of the gutter. He wanted something to throw.

"But what, Ty?"

"But I don't know, damnit! I don't know, but I don't think that venner, whoever or whatever he was, shot your father. I was looking right at him. All he had in his hand was a bunch of fake flowers he was waving in front of some woman. Of course, there might have been something hidden inside the flowers, I guess. I just don't know."

And as he said it, he knew that he was right. There had been the crowd and the Consuls and the Senator and the shot; Faux suddenly shouting, the crowd scattering, and the venner just standing there, emptyhanded, white shock drawn across his face before he turned and fled from the Consul's accusing finger. Yenkin felt weak. Caro must have sensed it because she hurried inside and returned a moment later with a low benchseat she placed at his feet. Avoiding her eyes, he sat gratefully and held onto the railing, staring at the buildings across the street through the black spiraled bars.

"I didn't know it was my father," Caro said, quietly, to no one in particular. "This Serviceman took the hov from us, and I was so mad I couldn't see straight. Literally couldn't see! I didn't know it was him right away, not until someone ran by screaming his name. And he wasn't tall, you know, not at all. He . . ."

Her litany/confession faded into a faint distant buzzing. Ty let go of the railing and stared at his palms dumbly, then clamped them over his ears. Caro rambled on; he looked up at her, wondered why she didn't hear the noise. Suddenly she stopped, snatched at his wrist and forced him to stand.

"Down there, Ty!" she said, pointing with the fan. Then she clutched it to her with both hands, hiding it, protecting it.

The guards below had gathered uneasily in the middle of the street. One was speaking into a micbut on his uniform's lapel. They had all slipped on their masks, slipped their weapons off their shoulders. Several peeled away from the group to race to Keyloft doors where they spoke urgently into the entrance comgrilles. Ty listened but heard nothing in the Key behind him but he understood why when those lights still burning began to wink out. He ducked unthinkingly when a guard pointed an ordering finger at them, pulled Caro down beside him. Before the man could repeat his instructions, the buzzing became a shouting.

Caro hissed and pushed him to look toward the hovramp's twin mouths.

The men who had been stationed there were facing downward now, their rifles aimed, the silent red of their laser discharge forming a webbing that vanished into the darkness. Two others joined them, and two more after that. The webbing blended into a sheet of red, and they followed it down and out of sight, and the shouting faltered, rallied suddenly, and a white-red sunburst forced Yenkin to look away and rub at his eyes.

The thundering followed, and the hot lifeless wind, and within moments of the explosion's passing the street was filled as a ratgang poured from the tunnel, fanned out along the sidewalks and quickly engulfed the remaining Servicemen before they had cut down more than a dozen. It seemed, then, to Yenkin that men by the thousands had joined in the street, grappling now hand-to-hand. A woman on a facing balcony began to scream, but the uproar below rose in a steady tide to drown her terror; several men on various other balconies had run out from their Keys with civilian-type weapons and began firing indiscriminately into the melee. It didn't take long for their stand to be attacked, and Yenkin saw one take a shell through his neck, drop his weapon and try to stem the flow of his blood while he stumbled backward, bounced hard off the wall and careened over the edge of his railing. Less than a minute later, several rats had stationed themselves in doorways and set up a cross fire to prevent further sniping.

Yenkin dropped to his stomach.

A half-dozen Service patrols shrieked around the corner, plowing their vehicles into the mob, stalling and emptying before they could be trapped inside. A rocket blew a crater into the street. Caro shouted a warning to no one, about nothing, pressed her forearms to her ears and clasped the back of her head.

Curiously, then, the invaders stopped their forward movement at the middle of the block, and Yenkin watched as at least a dozen rats ran for the entrance of the Senator's loft. Grabbing Caro, he shoved her back inside, knocking over the comsystem pedestal in his haste. "Get to your mother," he said when she protested. "You've got to get her out the back before anything happens!"

"But why are they coming here? Haven't they done enough?"

He shoved her again, twice more before she moved where he wanted. "How the hell should I know, Caro? Just go before it's too late!"

He watched as she stumbled across the darkened room, didn't move until he was sure she wouldn't turn around to argue with him again. Then he ran into the foyer and saw that the lifttube was already lit for use, a soft glowing blue that seemed to pulse into darker shades of the same warning color. Dropping to the floor, he crawled to the 'tube's edge and chanced a look down against the faint pull upward. He could see heads, rising, vanishing when they reached each of the floors below. There was muffled pounding, an explosion, a scream sliced into silence, and heads once again. Scrambling to his feet, then, he pried loose the utility panel in the wall next to the 'tube and stared at it. Too many wires and no key to their functions. He lifted a hand toward them, dropped it and rubbed it anxiously against his side. Another explosion, and the floor seemed to lift beneath his feet. He looked around wildly, spotted the bench and ran to it, lifted it and jammed one end into the panel. There was a static-filled explosion, sparks and a flare of fire that instantly darkened the edge of the opening. He dropped the bench only when he heard the falling screams of men plummeting down the 'tube into the basement below.

There was no way up, now, but neither was there a way down except at the back; and he hadn't a doubt that the rats had already found the escape route and were using it now that their primary access had been forced from them. Weapons, then, to protect the women; and he ran into the Senator's study just as Caro ran back from her mother's room.

"Rats," he said to her unasked question.

"I know," she said. "I could hear them climbing the well from downstairs. I locked the door. It's thick. They won't be able to break it in."

He nodded absently, not bothering to tell her about the explosions he had heard. It didn't make much sense, this concentrated attack. It would have been better for them had they used their manpower and tactics in an assault against the Hill where the power was, not on the luxuries of the people who wielded it. He attacked the Senator's desk, yanking out drawers to the floor in search of the firearms he was praying he would find.

"What are you doing, Ty?" she said when she saw the debris he had created.

"Everything's been changed. I know he had a handgun in here, and I think it was in the safe, but I can't remember where the damned thing is!"

She gaped at him, then ran to the desk and pushed it aside as though it were made of paper. "Here," she said, stamping her foot on the floor. A panel of carpeting slid aside and there was a dialock gleaming in the dim light.

Ty shook his head and moved to kneel beside it. "Can you open it?"

"It's keyed to him, Ty," and she slumped wearily against the wall.

"Forget it," he said, "I'll think of something else. Wait a minute! What did you do with that—"

The explosion blew in the door, threw Caro on top of him, and they were instantly coated with still-warm debris.

"Mother!" Caro screamed as she tried to scramble free of Yenkin's terrified grasp.

But he only held her tighter. There was a man standing in what was left of the doorway, dust swirling about his face. He was too sore to move, and the man was grinning.

"Delan? Delan? Hey, Sergeant Caine, are you awake?"

He opened his eyes slowly, blinking against the ceiling's light. Clouds drifted, resolved to faces: two on the right, one on the left. As he stared, the shadows passed and he recognized the smile that was his nurse; the others were Service officers–one might have been a colonel, but the other's insignia couldn't possibly mean the man was a general. It was another drug dream, he thought wearily. He closed his eyes.

A hand to his shoulder, shaking gently. "Sergeant Caine, please. Try to stay awake for a few minutes. These men want to talk with you."

Caine tried to shake his head, but it was gripped tightly behind his neck. A brace? More of the drugs that kept him from feeling? He opened his eyes.

"Sergeant Caine," the man who might have been a general said, softly, smiling his sympathy, "we know you are in a lot of pain from your injuries, but we need to know something that is vitally important. Something we believe you can tell us. The only one who can tell us, right now." He paused, glanced at the nurse, who nodded. "Sergeant, yours was the first Fringe sector that came under attack."

The first? Attack? Why didn't the man speak more clearly? Why didn't the nurse make them all go away? He was tired, and he wanted to sleep.

"Sergeant, did you notice anything unusual about the attack? Or perhaps you were able to spot something out of the ordinary about the rats who came through your defenses. Did you see anything at all like that?"

Caine closed his eyes, drifted until they were prodded open again. He licked at his lips and groaned in an effort to think, to answer the questions repeated endlessly until they spiraled into sparks behind his lids. He could have said no and driven them away, but that wouldn't have been enough, nor would it have been the literal truth. Though he didn't know precisely what the truth was.

"I was out of the attack almost from the first," he whispered after the nurse had slipped some cooling liquid between his lips. "It all happened too fast."

"So you were unable to see anything at all," the colonel said.

Caine lifted his eyebrows in a shrug. "Faces. A car. A rocket hit our tank. It–"

"What about the faces, Sergeant?" the perhaps-general asked. "Could you see them clearly? Were they anything like mine?"

Dark, lined, framed in gleaming black hair. High cheeks and staring black eyes. Had it been only the filth that coated the rats? He tried to shrug his shoulders, and failed. "I don't know, they could have been. You don't understand any of this. They were too far away. One rocket, see, and then there must have been another. I was blown back, I remember that. I hit a wall. I was out when they came through."

"They came through? Sergeant, are you sure of that? Are you sure they came through?"

"Oh yes. One of the lofters who worked on me until the hospital people came said they kept right on going. What's happening, sir?"

"If you'll excuse me, sirs," the nurse said, "I think that should be enough. The man's . . . tired."

"Sergeant Caine, are you sure you couldn't tell?"

"I don't know!" He was angry now, wanting desperately to sleep and return to Denver. The dark-faced men were no longer smiling, and he didn't need their frowns to stir shadows in his dreams. "Yes, they did. No, they didn't. I don't know! Why don't you just leave me alone?"

"I think they did," the colonel said to the might-have-been general.

"Good."

"We should have tagged them from the beginning."

"They would have been found."

The nurse muttered something Caine could not hear, and the officers nodded. One of them, the general, patted Caine's shoulder heavily.

"You've done a fine job, Sergeant. You'll receive a medal for what you've done, you know. And I'll be sure that the Premier gives it to you personally. He'll be glad to do it. Nurse, do you have an office we can go to? I'd like to talk to you for a moment. Take care of yourself, Sergeant."

Fine, fine, Caine thought, wishing he could rub at the shoulder the man had touched. The faces drifted away. He kept his eyes open in case they should return with their questions, but the ward grew silent when their footsteps faded and he wished he could rub at the cramp that was drifting across his chest. The cast was too tight. He raised an arm to summon the nurse, but it fell, leadened. Denver. His vision blurred at the edges. His eyelids flickered. Denver. He had had too many drugs. He knew he should be feeling pain, as the officers thought he was, but there was nothing at all. Soporific. Denver. Darkness, then, though he didn't remember closing his eyes. Thinking: dark-faced rats and dark-faced Service, and one more day and I'll get the hell out of here.

Sleeping.

Waking when the pain was too great for the drugs.

And he was glad he could scream just before his heart shut down.

James sat with his back against the wall, his legs straight out in front of him. He watched the three Consuls huddling in front of the comsystem's screens, whispering, nodding, once in a while breaking into a laugh that was curiously mirthless. Alton had left the window for the wall map, his right hand tracing the Eurepac boundaries as high as he was able to reach. A colonel stood stiffly on guard by the door. Manquila was gone, had been gone for nearly an hour after a message had been brought to him by a red-faced, puffing civilian.

And as the sky lightened, sucking its stars into oblivion, James daydreamed of the heroics he would accomplish in singlehandedly overthrowing the revolution's apparent success. A sudden surge of speed and strength would overwhelm the colonel, wrest away his weapon and fell the Consuls before they could be stirred into action. Adrenalin desperation would permit him to lift the massive desk and heave it into the screens, which would cause a power shortage; and in the resulting darkness he and Alton would race from the room, drop the 'tube and alert the forces below that all was well . . . and not well. He grew progressively more superhuman as his hope diminished, and once he wished he had one of Shanlon's varied tricks to aid him in his escape. But one man against four was literal death, and he'd be no use to the Premier lying lifeless on the floor.

What puzzled him now was the Consuls' delay in announcing the coup. No move that he could determine had been made to contact the newses, or the rest of the army, or any of the politicians and diplomats who had been denied entry by reason of the crisis. He guessed, from single words dropped in too-loud discussions, that Faux was hoping to stall things long enough, stretch the silence out until Meditcom and Eurepac had been alerted to the situation and left to decide whether or not war would come in spite of it. He doubted the war's outbreak, from the Consul's reasonings, and estimated there would be at least another day, perhaps two, before Noram's breakup was announced. That, he decided, had to be the point of it all. Neither Faux nor Manquila nor either of the Cenams seemed to be grappling for a lone hand on the helm, and he doubted further there was anyone waiting silent in the wings for matters to fall firmly in hand.

He wondered what Faux would do if war came anyway.

And he wanted to ask questions, but something more than fear kept him silent. To be too wise now would be just as deadly as trying for an escape.

The sky grew lighter. Manquila returned, grinning, and Faux spun around to face him, his eyebrows raised. The general glanced at Alton and James before nodding, once, sharply.

"The last of them," he said. "Now we should know in an hour or so. It depends on how long it takes them."

"Who?" James asked, and instantly regretted it.

Manquila strode across the floor and looked down. "Why, the rats," he said, his smile still broad. "Or haven't you heard what's going on out there, Captain?"

"I've heard," James said.

"Fine. Then hear only, and please do not speak again. I would say that your life depends upon it, Captain, but that would be too melodramatic."

"You've just said it."

Manquila shrugged elaborately. "Ah, my failing, then. I do not listen to myself very often." He laughed, loudly and long, and James wanted to lash out at the groin positioned only a breath from the tips of his boots. His lips thinned and he shifted, but the moment passed as the general turned on his heels and walked back to the desk, leaned against it and carefully scanned the screens.

"Soon enough," Faux said. "They'll be moving outland soon enough. They'll get us when they're ready."

"Nice," Torre said, picking at his teeth with a thumbnail.

"Very nice," the general agreed.

"Yes," the Consul said, rubbing at his arms as if he were cold. "Isn't it."

The street was filled with combatants for at least two intersections that Shanlon could see. Servicemen grappling with rats, sniper fire from balconies on nearby Keylofts, smoke hovering like yellow-gray mist. There was an explosion that made him wince, his teeth ache, his eyes water. He rose from his crouch and turned to run, froze as WatchDogs streaked by overhead, helpless to do anything but spotlight the battle. Patrols were converging at the corners, and he had to throw himself into a gutter to keep from being struck. But the men inside the vehicles ignored him. They were masked and armed, and their first objective was the chaos that had begun to split into isolated pockets of threes and fours. As he scrambled to his knees, gasping, a blast from another explosion lifted him, drove him against a shopface and he lay stunned, unable to do more than listen to the screams, the anger, the high shrieking wails of fear and injury that counterpointed the voices of the 'Dogs wheeling in frustration.

In pain. Weeping. Until his arms moved, his legs twitched and he rolled onto his stomach, pushed and rocked back onto his buttocks. He shook his head in an effort to clear it, then cried out and retched dryly while he grabbed at his stomach. Rose to his knees. Spit and hauled himself to his feet and leaned against the wall, using it like a ladder to pull himself painfully around the corner.

Lights red and white and gold and agonizing blue surged and dimmed as he spotted the twin mouths of a hovtunnel station. He glanced back at the fighting, then launched himself away from the building and into the street. A score of rats broke from the battle as he staggered toward the tunnels. Firing followed them, and chips of stone and tarmac drove into Shan's face and back, his hands and neck. He stumbled once as the ratgang swept by him, was knocked to his knees before huge hands snatched roughly at his shoulders and heaved him up.

Carried.

His left arm was still numb, but his right thrashed wildly until something struck the back of his skull and he was stunned again, aware that he was being transferred to someone's shoulder, aware of the shouting that pursued him and a perhaps-flare of a nearby explosion that drove all color from his vision. His cheek thumped against someone's back. He turned his head. And as he finally yielded to the cover of unconsciousness, he saw a thin face and red hair and knew he was dying.

Four

The suburbs had been strangled. Like fish on a barbed multitude of hooks, thrashing about mindlessly until flesh began to tear and blood flowed unfeeling. From a thrashing to a quivering, to spasms of undirected energy that ripped the barbs loose here, set others there to biting far deeper. From quivering to trembling, and trembling to a stillness that was glassy-eyed and staring.

But dreams of land, no matter how small or sterile the patch of earth, died hard and not without wailing shrieks of lingering pain. There were, from time to time, spates of flashy turbines, stolid lectrics and, for the more affluent of the dreamers, the windrush of hovercats. Men's castles became men's fortresses became men's dungeons, until they looked wildly about for another Key and found it nestling boldly in their palms. The companies that had moved out of the cities quickly moved back to escape the ghosts of the taxes they had been fleeing. Subsidies federal and local, massive renewals, intricate breaks on rents and purchases and personal incomes. A blending, then, of foresight and desperation. The outer perimeters began to fall back, slowly, tentatively and apprehensively, until a momentum was achieved and the transystems blossomed, and the landcars and hovercats and tiny lectrics were superfluous now, except for show. Suburban names became names of city districts became names in memories scratched on the backs of yellowing photographs.

And when the city stopped its building, the houses beyond were burned to the ground. And beyond that, far beyond that, they rotted, and burned, and became crumbling masonry cairns in a new/old wilderness.

Shanlon watched it pass by him. Macadam gouged and upheaved by a ruthless succession of winters. A few stubborn foundations still discernible through the trees. Here and there a collapsed trench, a thicket grown around a sagging fence, a field of weeded rubble where a neighborhood once had been. His vision was still blurred and generally unreliable, and a persistent sharp headache kept his eyes closed for much of the time. The ratgang, having snared him, had vanished almost immediately into a well-guarded transtunnel. And suddenly there were torchlights, and he knew there also had to be maps since the movement of the 'gang was rapid and seemingly unerring.

He passed out twice. From his wounds, and the distortion of the drugs they needled into his arms.

Awakening the second time, he found himself in a vehicle, turbine by the whine, then transferred to a battered hovercat when the roads ran out. If there was pursuit, he did not hear it; and if the rats had planned on killing him, he was glad for the postponement. But when his vision did finally clear, tearing at the glare of the sun, he was blindfolded almost instantly.

But not before he was able to catch a disheartening glimpse at his companion captors.

They were dressed as rats and spoke the muddled language of rats, but something in their manner, the methods of their attack and ultimate escape, bothered him, as well as the looks of them. Only a glimpse, but it was sufficient enough to convince him that their wearing of the tattered robes, the soiled cloaks, were more costume than custom. Only a glimpse, only a sensation, it was more sense than logic; and when the 'cat stopped and he was picked up and carried off–relief at the feeling of cool/warm air filling his lungs and clearing his head still more–the 'gang jargon was dropped in favor of a dialect English he was sure came from Cenam. Whispers only. A phrase, a word, nothing more. He strained to listen, and understood nothing. He tried to create a map of his location, and failed. All he knew was that he was outside the city, and until he could get a look at the sun, he could only guess that it was a fraction past noon.

Carried, then, sacklike over someone's shoulder, descending into a darker cool; a waiting, a mumbling, a door opening, and he was thrust to the ground . . . and the door slammed.

He hesitated, still listening, turning his head in startled jerks until his hands found the courage to rip off the blindfold. Blinking rapidly, then, and wiping at his eyes, instantly aware of the blunted pains in his back and head, knees and elbows. He allowed himself a long moment's luxury of free-flowing curses: at himself for the role he had failed before he had even begun; and at the rats-not-rats who treated him with less care than they should for their mythical leader.

Then he looked around the room he was in. Slightly less than three meters square, windowless, rough walls dug inexpertly from earth, tangles of roots and angles of stone protruding darkly into a faint light from a basin lamp, wick floating on oil, set on a single wooden table. There were no chairs, no pictures, and against the far wall a narrow, uncomfortable-looking cot covered with dried grass. He was sitting in the center of the dirt floor, huddled close to himself in sudden reaction to the realized weight of the ground above him, around him, pressing against the thick wooden door that was the room's only exit. It was the transtunnel again, but this time there were no ramps to run to, no human sounds of passage. He shuddered and, once begun, was unable to control it.

He stared at the single small flame and watched it blur into a minor conflagration, his eyes refusing to focus until finally he closed them until the trembling ceased and he was able to extend his arms and legs without cramping.

He stood, staggered to the cot, and wincing at the easily imagined colonies of insects flourishing within, brushed the grass to the floor, poised to stamp out any of the more repulsive hordes. The bed was smooth slats, and he sat with his back to the wall, knees drawn to his chest, arms clasped round with hands gripping elbows.

So much for the grand design of heroic confrontation, he thought; so much for the fireworks.

And then he realized he was letting it happen again. Flowing instead of rowing, drifting instead of swimming. True, he told himself; but what good was that realization when he was trapped without hope of escape? Wrong! There *was* hope, but to sit and wait was the sensible thing now; and this time floating merely the conservation of energies yet to be.

Besides, he was getting hungry, and the hunger was contributing to the headache he had been nourishing since his flight (however assisted) from the city. He rose after a time and walked cautiously to the door. There was no judas window there, no inside knob. He considered an indignant pounding, but after several seconds with his ear pressed to the wood, he could hear nothing at all on the other side; and he decided he was quite alone and would only bruise his hands for nothing.

He turned to stare at the lamp, the cot, the walls of his cell. He wondered if he wouldn't be more relaxed screaming instead of standing.

The footsteps decided for him.

The first dawn. And there was fighting still in several sectors of the Fringe.

A man and three women were cut down by a tank because they refused to drop their ration of food, their bundles of clothes, given to them by the Blues just the morning before.

They looked like rats. No one apologized.

Morag Borsen watched as the bed was wheeled into a sealed-off section of the ward. Walls of clear glass, diagmed elaborate and already reaching for the arms, the legs, the throat of Delan Caine. She wanted to say something, anything, that would let him know she had not given up hope. The heart had been the easiest; it started at her first pounding. But the rest . . . she turned and headed for the next wave of victims.

A score of rats broke into a warehouse previously planned to be subdivided into Fringe Keylofts. They scattered quickly to the hundreds of windows on the dozens of floors, sniping at the 'Dogs yowling through the air, dropping oddly sophisticated handbombs onto the Blues who were massing in the street. Once the strength of the 'gang was known, however, and the blueprints of the warehouse distributed in triplicate, the Blues decided not to call for the Service. They lounged instead against the neighboring buildings while four 'Dogs blasted cannister bombs through the hundreds of windows, and the gas that leaked through the gaps was soon followed by bodies seeking the air.

There was no longer any fighting in City Prime itself. But the screams of the dying lingered, the sweet smell of blood.

No one counted bodies.

Only the bright blue flares of the ashers.

Shanlon hurried across the room and sat on the edge of the cot, hunched his shoulders and lowered his head. The only positive sign he had received in the past few hours indicated that his captors were not, at least, gleefully sadistic. The more vulnerable he appeared, then, the better his chances of keeping his neck in one piece while he fumbled for escape.

The door opened, its hinges quiet. A young woman, and a man trying not to be old, were shoved in from behind. The man nearly lost his balance. The woman only took the necessary step inside and stood motionless, her face taut. Shanlon unfolded as the door closed, pushed with his heels until he felt the wall at his back. The man stared at him, blinking; the woman only noticed that she and her companion were not alone. She moved out of the direct light of the lamp.

Shanlon nodded his greeting. "You," he said to the woman, "I'm sure I know. I hope you liked the fan. You," he said to the man, "I think I remember, but I don't think we've been introduced."

"I don't believe it," Yenkin said.

"What? That we haven't been introduced?"

"You're the man on the street, the venner," Caro said, her uncertainty clear in the hesitant step forward, the anxious step back. "You're the one they said killed my father."

Shanlon plucked at his still seamed and ragged cloak. "I didn't, Mistress," he said. Quietly.

"He doesn't think so, either," she said, her voice calm but not trusting. "He used to be my father's man, you know. That was years ago, of course, but he's come back. Haven't you, Ty?"

Shanlon grabbed for the old man's wrist and tugged until Yenkin yielded and sat beside him on the cot. There was deep shock on the man's lean face, a numbness that seemed to have spread to his limbs, his mind. Other than a few scratches and bruises, some grimy streaks of dirt, however, there was no evidence of injury, and Shanlon puzzled at the reasons for the man's partial withdrawal. The lips were moving, but there was no sound; the eyes were open but they were no longer truly seeing. "You don't think I killed Talle?" Shan asked in surprise and hope, but what response there was came several moments later, and then only a barely perceptible movement of the old man's head. He glanced at the girl edging nearer. "Is he all right? Was he hurt?"

Caro shrugged, helplessly, and knelt in front of them, taking Yenkin's hands and covering them with her own. Her face aged suddenly as though a life-prolonging elixir had been withheld on the brink of the drinking. "They came for us," she said in monotonic recital. "They killed my mother, too. She would have died anyway, sometime soon, but they killed her blowing their way into our Key. They grabbed us, I didn't even have a chance to say good-by, and one of them stuck a hype into my neck and I passed out." She looked to Shan, who nodded and pointed to the fading bruise on his arm. "I guess I'm supposed to be a hostage or something for the revolution. Except I'm not important any more, so I don't know. No one's left to care any more except Ty. Ty, he went away, you see, and then suddenly he was back. It might have been the same, you know, except for the fighting and all that blood. And there was a 'Dog that somebody hit with a rocket or something when it was right over us, and we were nearly crushed. All dead we would have been then, all of us dead and nobody left. Ty always took care of things in his own way. Now, he just keeps looking like that, sometimes saying something, but most of the time just looking just like that."

She took a shuddering deep breath and continued to talk, disjointed, dredging for grief, fighting for tears, and Shanlon listened quietly as he slid off the cot and forced the old man to lie down. He took off his cloak, then, and spread it gently as a blanket, but Yenkin only moved his lips soundlessly while a bubble of saliva formed and broke, trickling down his chin, his neck, to vanish untouched under the high collar of the ludicrously bright Host's uniform he was still wearing. There was nothing Shanlon could use for a pillow.

He looked, then sat on the floor, his back to the cot. He interrupted the girl with a slow wave of his hand. It was important that she listen to him. She would be the first, and the most important. "I didn't do it, you know," he said again, though the scene of its happening was blocked out of his memory.

She glanced at him once before returning her anxious gaze to Yenkin's pallor. "He said you didn't. He said you might not have, that is." Her hair trembled as she tried to shake her head. "I wish I knew. A part of me says I should be screaming and yelling and tearing your throat out. But I haven't the energy. I haven't . . . anything."

"You have him," he said, tilting his head back.

"Yes. No, not really," she said. "When I first saw him, after I knew who . . . Father had been killed, I thought he was some kind of an angel who would protect me and Mother. But not now. He's a memory, that's all. Lying right here in front of me, he's only a memory. As dead as my parents. As dead as . . ." She wiped a hand under her nose, her eyes, with a sleeve, and dropped Yenkin's hands gently, folded them over his stomach and turned around until she faced the door with Shanlon. "This is stupid, you know. It's going on what, twenty-four hours since everything fell apart, and I should be yelling and trying to slash my wrists and throttle you and . . . I had a friend, too, Delia–"

"Delia Anders?"

She started, and stared. "You knew her?"

"Vaguely. I was on my way to her Key when I got mixed up with the wrong crowd. Sorry. A lousy time for a lousy joke."

"It's a good thing you didn't get there. She's dead. Her neighbors heard the early broadcasts and thought she was part of your revolution. They threw her out her window."

He tried to imagine Delia's face, her body, the long ago touch of her hands; and when he could not, his immediate surge of weak grief faded. Delia. A statistic, nothing more.

"I wish I knew what was happening."

"You and me both, Mistress," he said, fighting not to sound morose, succeeding only in getting her to look at him again. "It's supposed to be my revolution, like you said, but those dills out there don't know who I am. And even if they did, I doubt that it would do me any good. Ensure my frying, most likely."

"They can't win."

"Thank you for the 'they,' Mistress."

She shrugged. As if it were a small thing, that there were no big things to concern her any more. But he was grateful just the same.

"But you're right. They can't win. And I'd like to know why they even tried. Or why we were picked on. The EcG, I mean. We aren't big enough for a convention in a joyhall."

"Coincidence," she said. "Coincidence."

"It's only coincidence because I don't know what the hell's going on."

But she was right, he thought. It was all totally and unredemptively stupid, and it was senseless. A simple day ago and he was a venner, a runner, a mediocre lobbyist protesting mildly and without much conviction. One simple day, and now he was a fugitive and an accused murderer, and he hadn't the slightest idea why it had to be that way. It would have been a burlesque of living if it hadn't been for the people he had seen dying, the blood on the streets, the destruction by the rockets. He had wanted, then, a chance to think, a refuge of sorts to plan some kind of defense—he had it now, and he smiled with a sardonic twist of his lips. Some refuge. One that required his escaping before he could do what had to be done. Now, if he only knew what it was that had to be done.

They sat by the side of the cot, listening to Yenkin's slow breathing, thinking of the things they could say to each other and not knowing which of those things could or should be said aloud. Finally, when he grew tired of trying to count the seconds to mark their captivity, Shanlon pulled his legs to him and gripped his shins. "I wish I had a trick for you," he said, in nearly a whisper.

Caro, whose hands had drifted up to cover her face, lifted her head and stared at him.

"What I mean is, Mistress, I wish my magic could open that damned door for you so you could get home again."

"What home? The loft our Key was in was burning to the ground when we left."

"Then I wish I could put it out for you."

She twisted around on her buttocks to face him, one arm resting on the cot, the other in her lap. "What are you trying to do, turn me into an instant friend?"

"No magic for that," he said, biting back the sorrow.

"No kidding."

"But . . . you said you believed! Ty—is that his name, Ty?—you said you believed him when he told you I didn't do it. I don't know why I got nailed, but I did not do it."

"Then who did?"

He scowled and tugged angrily at his jaw. "I don't know. I was there and I don't know. I try to play things back, but I keep missing things. All I see is that Consul pointing at me and yelling. But you said—"

"I didn't say I believed him," she said. "I don't know what to believe. If you didn't, and I knew why everyone said that you did, it would be easier. Wouldn't it?"

"If I were the leader of this mess, Mistress, why the hell am I stuck in this blesséd cell?" he demanded, suddenly tired of the alternating sympathy and prosecution in her eyes. He pushed himself awkwardly to his feet and paced the width of the room, turned and stalked back to the door where he glared at the spot where the knob should have been. "They'll have to bring us food soon. Maybe they'll answer some questions."

"Don't bet on it."

He faced her. "Did you like the fan?"

She blinked her confusion, then reached to her waist. But her hand came away empty. "I left it at the Key," she said apologetically. "It was pretty. I thought you were trying to set for me."

"Maybe I was," he said, grinning, "but I don't think so. Pretty fan and pretty girl, things move in pairs, you see."

Her scoffing laugh was forced. Shanlon waited, leaning against the door. When she had done, she pushed self-consciously at her hair. He thought the color more like gentle embers than angry fire. "Did you make it?" she asked.

"Not the fan itself, no. Only the picture."

"It must have taken you a long time."

"A couple of days here and there. Between speeches, so to speak."

"Does it mean anything? The picture, I mean. Is it symbolic or something?"

"Only to me I think," he said. He scratched at his chin, wondering if she would understand, wondering how unresolved her hatred of him really was. "When I finished school, I deferred a workcall for several months. My parents . . . died, see, and I didn't want to run my father's shop. I sold it, after a little bit of trouble with the taxers, and used the receipts to make a little trip around places. No place special. Just around. Before I came back to Washington, I stopped at an outland town in the Midwest. A farming place where you can go into the fields and not have to worry about ratgangs. Rats don't like it much out there anyway. Nothing to steal, no Fringes where they can find abandoned buildings to sleep in when winter comes. It's pretty nice out there, actually, if you can stand all that open space and all that sky just going until you can't see it any more.

"Anyway, I found a fairly friendly family to live with for a while–a couple of days, actually–and I was sitting outside once, after I had gotten used to it, just before I left, and I saw these birds tearing around just before sunset. The moon was already up, and I was daydreaming about heading for the Colony one of these days. Heading for the Colony is always one of my daydreams. And one of these days is always when I'm going to go. It was an odd picture, though, those birds and the moon. It was like they could fly up there anytime they wanted to. The old man of the family told me later the birds were ravens, a fairly intelligent beast, or so he said.

"Anyhow, from where I was sitting, when they finally left it looked as if they were heading straight for the moon. They kept on flying, getting smaller and smaller, not going to one side or the other, and pretty soon I couldn't see them any more. It was strange. Very unsettling. They just kept on going and disappeared as if they had really gone there. I was mad. Jealous. And when I feel like telling myself truth, I was damned sorry for myself."

"So you made a vow that somehow, some time, you were going to get there if those stupid birds could, right?"

Shanlon laughed quietly and shook his head. "No, Mistress. I just keep on feeling sorry for myself. And those blessèd birds just keep right on flying into the moon."

By early afternoon, it was apparent to almost everyone but those living on the Fringe that the ratgang incursions had been stalled. A number of WatchDogs had been shunted away from the direct fighting and into positions of guidance for the Service patrols prowling the boulevards, or to combating the hundreds of fires that had gutted an equal number of buildings old and new throughout the City.

The heat slowed movement to a crawl.

The shadows that had added nightmare to the fighting were gone, hiding in tunnels and doorways and beneath multicolored awnings shredded and flapping like banners searching for a parade.

Blood was red, instead of black.

Corpses were bold, instead of mysterious.

An explosion in a transtunnel gutted a street, sent great chunks of pavement and pipes, small pieces of men and equipment, spouting into the bright sunlight in a geyser of cloud-high flames and cloud-wide smoke. Windows shattered, walls buckled, and the Service patrol that had set the charge heard an hour later that the rats it had been after had fled ten minutes before. The captain in charge shook his head and moved his men out. The Blues would be around to take care of the wounded; the asher would follow to take care of the dead.

A teener, racing away from the rubble of his Fringe home, found himself trapped between two approaching ratgangs pouring from the tunnels. He threw himself onto a pile of half a dozen bodies unclaimed from the night before, held his breath, closed his eyes, and listened as the two 'gangs met, muttered and moved away. He waited. Counted several hundred seconds before lifting his head and staring into the sockets where a woman's eyes should have been. If the rats heard him screaming, they did not turn around.

The heat.

The sun.

Four Blues lay in a hospital ward trading stories, speculations, intimations of their promotions. All had lost at least one limb, and all were looking forward to retirement on full pay.

Another Blue sat at a precinct console monitoring the movement of a ten-Blue guardforce moving through City Prime under the eye of a 'Dog. Unlike the others, he was glad to be out of the fighting and away from the dying. The statistics that came in, when anyone found the time to compile them, he placed in a pigeonhole over his head, pushed a green button and sent it away to those who liked numbers. All he had to do was listen to the guardforce commander. Wait for a HelpCall, or wait for a clear. He did no vicarious killing. Only waited. Until he could go home.

Caro kept her silence like a blanket to warm her. She watched as Raille wandered about the small room, stopping every few paces to tug at a protruding root and follow to the floor the dirt he had dislodged. The lamp's flame had weakened, but neither of them moved to straighten the wick. A permanent golden twilight, then, that forced her to strain to see clearly; and finally she tilted her head back to rest against Yenkin's thigh while she stared at the low ceiling and waited for something to happen.

As Shanlon continued to walk, softly, with measured steps and face averted, she felt as though a great piece of flesh had been torn from her side, reducing her to a creature somewhat less than the original, yet just as capable of survival as soon as it found the means to overcome the loss. With hysteria spent, she postponed her grieving for a more peaceful time when the grief would be a comfort and a purge rather than a way to escape as Ty had done. It had saddened her to call him a memory that had achieved corporeality; but it was true, painfully so–he was a past with a future now, and she . . .

She was searching for a way to put substance to her anger. She was, too, convinced that Raille was all that he claimed to be, such as it was. If nothing else, that story of the fan–however true–was, somehow, sufficient proof. She had thought at first it would turn out to be a simplistic parable of their situation, a lesson he was trying to convey to bring her hope. But it turned out to be exactly what he said it would be–a story, and nothing more. And it told her more about him than she thought he realized.

And, in an odd way she was immediately unable to clarify, she was pleased that he did not fill the room with grandiose plans of escape, magnificent deceptions that would bring their captors to their knees in supplication and send her and Ty and the curiously strong venner back to the city in sunset triumph. Hope, whatever its definition turned out to be, would have to come in a different form, from a different source.

A smile, then, and a short silent laugh. Delia. Thinking Caro vitally interested in nothing more than a shag with a good-looking stranger. No, she corrected; Delia would call it a shag and think Caro would prefer a more romantic euphemism like "making love" or "being together in tremulous anticipation of heaven's reward." Poor Delia. The pretense of being committed to a cause had killed her for a cause no one understood, least of all the man supposedly leading it.

She squirmed, turned and knelt to see if Yenkin was still awake. He wasn't. His eyes were closed, his breathing steady. She made a ceremony of adjusting Raille's cloak and gently pushed the man's legs closer to the wall so she could perch on the cot's edge.

Shanlon Raille, she thought, why do I think you're going to save us all?

And: "Company," she said a few minutes later. Raille stopped his pacing and moved beside her, his head cocked toward the door.

It sounded to her like a struggle outside, several men grunting and cursing over the shrill protests of one or two others. Raille made a movement to locate something he could use as a weapon, but she only folded her hands in her lap and waited. As the door swung to and a man was tossed bodily onto the floor. Packets of powdered food followed, and Raille snatched them to place on the table beside the lamp.

The man was dressed in a ragged jerkin and torn trousers caked with pale red clay. His hair, possibly brown, was long, twined with bits of leaves and grass, and merged with a beard that just touched at his scrawny chest. He lay still for a long moment, his head covered and protected by bare arms laced with old scratches. There was no covering for his feet, and she could see with a wince the scars that had hardened his soles.

"We're not going to hurt you, if that's what you're afraid of," she said finally, dispassionately.

Raille glanced at her, then knelt beside him and touched at his arm. The man jerked away, scrabbling to the nearest corner. With his face uncovered, Caro saw that he was young, certainly no more than two or three years older than she. If not, she thought, younger.

"This your nest?" Raille asked, still on his knees.

The man/boy spat dryly.

"Do you have a name?" Caro said.

The man/boy pushed himself deeper into the corner, lifted his thumb and flicked it against his teeth.

"Interesting," Raille said. "You must have had a fight with the nestOne, right? So good old nestOne decided he would throw you in with the cityfolk so they could have you for dinner. Or lunch. What did you do, try to shag his wife or something?"

Again, the spitting.

Raille looked back over his shoulder and Caro shrugged, frowned, and beckoned him closer. Without standing, he moved and she bent down to whisper. "I don't think this is his nest," she said, her eyes on the rat while her lips brushed at Shan's ear. "Look at him. He's blond, for one thing, and under all that dirt he's white. I saw—"

"I know," Shanlon interrupted. "I think maybe the boys upstairs have made mistake number one. Ten more like it and we'll be able to walk out of here in one piece."

She tried to answer his grin, but knew she looked more confused than amused. Covering herself, then, by rising, she moved to the table and picked up one of the plastic packets. They were undated but still sealed. She tore at the corner with her teeth and let some of the yellowish grainy powder fall into her hands. Licked at them. Grimaced, but emptied her palm before spilling out more. Raille joined her and they ate silently, making sure the rat in the corner could see their every move. There were a dozen packets in all and they finished six, set three aside for Yenkin, and Raille picked up the remainder.

"Hungry?" he asked carelessly, dropping the meals at the rat's feet, though just out of his reach. "Maybe you'd like to see a trick first. A trick, maybe, to whet your appetite."

"Shan!" she said angrily.

"Relax," he told her without taking his eyes from the rat. "I didn't bring my flowers." He knelt in front of the rat and lifted his arms to chest level. The rat squeezed back, and Shanlon smiled broadly. "Just watch my hands, sir," he said in the flamboyant manner Caro remembered from the night on the boulevard. "Just watch my hands and see that they have nothing in them, nothing at all. Just the air passing through and the funny strange things you can pluck out of the dust."

Caro shifted to stand by the door, watching as Raille cast patterns in front of the young rat's face, blinking suddenly when there was without warning a small gray casing between the venner's fingers, holding back a gasp when a blade flicked blue-black into the dim light.

"Magic," Raille said when the rat hissed and crossed his thin arms over his chest. "Does it every time. Now, suppose you move over here and join us for a breaking of our fast. Be nice, however, because the Mistress doesn't like you very much. You're not very polite, spitting on her floor."

Shanlon backed away slowly, his blade a funereal metronome that made Caro turn away from her staring and return to the cot. Yenkin stirred when she sat, but did not awaken. She pressed a hand to his brow and shook her head at the cool dry skin; it would have been better had he been ill, she thought; then she might have been able to recapture some of the feeling she had had when she first saw him on the street. When her father had died. Had been murdered.

Finally, the rat moved out of his corner, cautiously, his eyes narrowed, his tongue flicking at his lips. He snatched at the packet Raille offered to him, but his subsequent move to retreat was stalled abruptly when the venner warned him with a wave of the knife. He glared, then spat into his palm and poured enough of the powder onto the saliva to make a thick paste. Caro shuddered and had to stiffen to keep from hugging herself. But she ordered herself to watch without expression until the packet was empty and the rat held out his long-nailed hands for the others.

"You must have a name," she said, surprising herself by sounding as disinterested as Shanlon. "Your cityname, if you have one. Or your nester. I don't care. But I don't want to have to call you rat."

The back of her neck tightened when he looked at her, scanning her figure slowly, almost impudently, from breast to ankle. Then, when Raille waved the blade again he seemed inside his tattered clothes to sigh resignation. "Cityname is Viller," he said, the sound of his voice confirming his youth. Not born in a nest then, Caro thought, but probably one of the restless romantics who found out too late what it was like to live in the outlands in a ratgang. And her appraisal was verified—and she allowed herself a small grin—when, at Shanlon's quiet prodding, Viller told them he had left a Houston school when he had fallen into trouble trying to comp answers to a final examination. Rather than renew his term under disgrace the following year, he left the city and almost immediately fell into a nomadic nest.

"Houston?" Shanlon said, his head cocked in doubt. "Then what in the blesséd priest are you doing up here?"

"Key and eat, hom, Key and eat," Viller said, still eying the packets in Raille's free hand. "Houston kisses your past once you cut the Fringe. If you're not spacer, then they don't ken your life."

"It's a rotten way to have to live," Caro said. "And you picked a rotten time to get in it, didn't you."

Viller grinned and ducked his head. "My life, yes? Lick a meal and a wash from some Fringe and hit the market when you can before the cold blows. Badly, badly, my luck though. What I get is nailed. This morning—yes?—I found this nest and I see no rats so I nudge around braining I be a nestOne myself if I can find a shag. Then, from no call at all, this dill swings to split my skull. I keep yelling I'm rats too, but he just thunks me and tosses me. Can I have more of that eat, hom?"

Shanlon stared at him thoughtfully, made no move when Caro took one of the packets from his hand and tossed it into the rat's lap. The judgment of his sincerity she would have to leave to

Raille for the time being: a venner, she thought, would surely know more about rats than she would. All she had ever heard were the complaints from her father every time November rolled around and those formerly beguiled, now disenchanted rats became soured with the so-called natural life and crept back into the cities. Their numbers, never huge, never overwhelming, seldom caused any strain on the employment pool. But once in a while the not-so-petty criminal also made a bid to return, and that was the trouble spot Talle had wanted calmed. And never could.

And now never would.

The door opened suddenly, and before any of them could react, a hand pushed a small pitcher of water along the floor and pulled back, and slammed the door. Viller dismissed it as he pasted more of the meal and chewed it as though he enjoyed it. Caro waited for a signal from Raille. Receiving none, however, she fetched the pitcher and carried it to the table. There were no plates, no cups, and after a moment's indecision, she finally poured a little of the food into her palm, sprinkled it with the cool water and sat near Yenkin's head. The paste was faintly repulsive and her fingers could barely touch at it, but the old man took it eagerly, without opening his eyes. She wanted him to talk, then, to let her know he was over the multiple shock of his world's disintegration, to at least provide her with a semblance if not the fact of a functioning protector. But he ate only, his eyelids fluttering but not opening. And sleeping again deeply when the first of his packets was depleted.

She made another useless adjustment of his blanket cloak and turned, arms resting on her thighs, to face Shanlon and the rat. She wanted to ask the younger man what it had been like living such a sparse life, being part of a subculture continuation. Besides the cities and the outowns, she knew there were also isolated clusters of homes scattered between the Appalachians and the Rockies, the news-labeled Pioneer Breeds, who seldom extended their numbers, were mostly descendents of earlier small farmers who had reverted to the handplow and child labor. She wondered why the rats insisted on drifting instead of settling like that.

To her own surprise and Shanlon's startled look, she asked him.

"Creds and Blues, hom, creds and Blues," he said with a twisted grin. "Not enough one, too many the other. Sides, who wants staying where the eat is worked? You can live for a while. Not bad. Fair. Dull, though. See, the flying is easing, no problem.

Landings another thing. Wash has big Fringe, and about her be big nests and the cityfolk jump a lot. Other places, the Fringes not so bad, you can get in no problem. Not much. But it's best flying. Walk out. Find a nest. It's the okay thing and you can shag and eat and go with the light." He shook his head, then, and made a self-conscious attempt to push the hair back from his face. "Winter's bad. Bad. You have a nest, see, maybe was a house, a store, something like that. Small hole sometimes, and you're side to side, butt butt, for months. Nice for sometime. Not me. I get over my mad and I want to land again." He grinned, and Caro and Shanlon grinned back. Then he sobered and pointed to the ceiling. "Ain't rats, homs, ain't rats from nowhere. Not them. You get bads, course, once in a while, 'cause the Blues set the 'Dogs to them. They settle sometimes. Not always. But these," and he pointed again, shaking his head and scowling. "They not be rats. Like you. You not rats, that's okay. They not rats too. And this ain't nesting. Sides, they talk funny."

It was difficult to keep herself from smiling, but Caro managed it by turning to check on Yenkin again. And again, wondering why she bothered, and why the little man with the magic tricks didn't stop staring at the rat and do something! It wasn't necessary to dig a tunnel to the outside, or even overpower a guard the next time the door opened. A speech would have done it. A signal for hope. But he did nothing but sit on his haunches and watch the rat, his head tilted like a stalking bird.

She knew she was contradicting herself, then. She didn't expect anything. Especially not from Raille.

But a vagrant slip of whimsey disrupted her. Why, even while the rat was talking, did Raille turn and smile at her the way he did?

If anyone noticed the unnatural stiffness of the Consuls arranged carefully around the wall, if they spotted the forced and enforced cheerfulness in the Premier's demeanor, nothing was said. Diplomats and Reps, lobbymen and Sens passed through the office chamber in groups of no less than six, no more than ten. Alton received them all, by name and by rank, as though they were brothers. He assured them in his best fatherly and commanding voice that the city would be soon cleared of all ratgang pockets remaining from the initial assaults, but the Service troops were now, on his order, committed to a continuing pursuit action which would leave metropolitan safety largely to the Blues. No, he was not worried; Raille had not yet been captured, but a recent message assured him such an event would be forthcoming before the sun set again. And yes, of course he understood the implications of giving the Service such an order pushing them into the outlands, but wasn't it about time those same outlands were cleansed of infection?

Muttering and nods.

A rep from the network pool prided himself, preening, on an elicited comment that the spacefacs would reopen the suburbs within the decade, if all went well and prognostications were closely, if not precisely, achieved.

The Commander of the Blues placed on his desk a sheath of commendations for his men wounded in action, another sheath not quite as thick for those who would receive their awards, with sorrow, posthumously. Alton spoke quietly to him, his hand shaking the Blue's constantly, strongly, until James thought the policeman would explode inside his uniform.

They came. They went. Business as usual in the midst of a revolution.

Several minutes past noon, then, the office was ordered cleared. Alton slumped into his chair. Thrush moved quickly to sit by Bendal, whose makeshift bed had been cut from the room by a screen brought up from a Star Court chamber. While Faux and his men huddled, relief as blatant as the grins they wore, James placed a hand against Bendal's neck, pressed lightly, and froze. He searched for a wrist and pressed. He leaned down, his ear close to the heavy man's lips. Then, gently and resigned, he unfastened the man's shirt and lay a hand against his chest.

The eyes were still open. He blew lightly, and the lids did not blink.

He sniffed, rubbed at his chin and his brow, then rocked to his feet and stepped around the screen. He ignored the angry stares of the others as he moved to stand in front of the Premier's desk. "Sir?" Alton took a long minute before looking up. "Sir, the Consul has died. Mr. Bendal is dead, sir."

Alton blinked, his lips working for a phrase, and saying nothing.

Faux made a noise of uncharitable sympathy and snapped his fingers at Manquila, who, without waiting for a verbal order, whispered something to one of the colonels in the antechamber. A minute later, a detail of officers rushed in, threw a wrinkled and soiled white cloak over the body and carried it out. In silence. Without respect, or a gesture for the office. James followed them to the door and, in front of Manquila's disgusted glare, saluted the departing corpse.

"Gentlemen," Faux said, striding quickly to stand behind Alton's chair, "we have a situation now that will tax the purpose of our meeting." He smiled and rubbed a knuckle against his lips. "This afternoon, our Premier must speak at length with our dear friends from Continental Europe. He will, of course, tell them that he cannot possibly reinforce anyone's armies or ship further supplies beyond our own borders until and unless the crisis at home is resolved to his complete satisfaction, in terms of the safety of Noram's citizenry. He will, and we'll remember that he planned it all this way so we are assured that he will not fail us here, he will urge them into immediate negotiations. He will give them all the hope he can muster for the 'facs, though euphorically more than is strictly accurate, and will use all his well-known persuasive powers to at least let the respective communites walk out of it without slitting their throats. What he will also do is plant, very carefully and carefully couched, seeds of speculation as to the future of Noram."

"I will not," Alton said, so quietly that James barely heard him.

"You will," Faux said, not so quietly. "And you will not try any sabotage because you are suddenly feeling the strain of current events. The consultation, or whatever you wish to call it, will be held over vione links between here and my chambers, where the reps from those idiots will be waiting for you. It is," he said, suddenly louder as Alton made to rise in protest, "already arranged!"

"I will not play an unwilling Brutus," Alton insisted.

"Willing or not, you will play him well," Faux said.

"He'll kill us," Torre said, Degaldon nodding.

"Not if I can help it," Faux answered. "By the time he gets an opportunity . . ." And he shrugged.

Food was brought in. The Consuls and Manquila ate as though they were attending a feast, without speaking but interrupting themselves at intervals with great explosions of laughter. Alton only folded his hands on his desk and stared at the tray a colonel set in front of him.

James ate little, unable to override his distress. And though he tried to camouflage it, Manquila, then Faux, noticed.

"If we dig him now," the general said, "there'll only be the old man."

James stiffened and pressed his back to the windowwall, as if hoping that somehow the glass would shatter and set him free.

"A waste, for the moment," Faux said. "And too many, unfortunately, have seen him playing the right-hand symbol to our Premier's stability. He'll stay. At least until after the meeting. After that, he'll have to prove himself."

James relaxed, but only partially; and he was, hours later, tension rigid again when the Premier carried through with the vione meeting without once, to his knowledge, betraying the position he was in.

Helpless. As bound as if wire had been woven into and around his limbs. He wondered about the fighting, about those isolated pockets he could see in the screens' eyes where the rats eventually dropped back to be replaced by Service, to be replaced by Blues. Soon, if all went well and he saw no reason why it would not, the city would be cleared and safe again. Then, once the ultimate plot became general knowledge, what would be the reaction? He suspected, sadly, that there would be a few lonely uprisings, but nothing more than that. The Confederation had been a convenience that had become accepted through habit rather than far-reaching loyalties to some dawn-of-man inspired goals. One nation or three made little difference as long as services continued uninterrupted and the tax creds made a gallant show of being used. Only a few would really understand what the collapse meant; and he was just beginning to. The move to an essential, perhaps even vitally embryonic form of world government would be set back, too far back to beat the nukes and their missiles.

Nationalism, a dormant poison, would be activated again, and all the 'facs in the universe would not be able to stop the onslaught of destruction.

But Alton, knowing all this as James knew he did, acted as he was bidden. And when the meeting ended, he and James were taken to a smaller room behind the main office. Two meters by three, a lounge, the hiding place Alton used when he felt his burdens too heavy to throw off with a shrug.

For a time, then, they were silent. Alton slumped, almost slumbering, in a chair placed in front of a comunit screen. James stared at a boxlike projection to the left of the screen, ceiling high and covered with what looked to him like a jungle scene mural. Closer, and there were locks and hinges at top and bottom. He guessed it to be a decorative type of wall safe, turned and stood by the single wide window, stared out at the terrace and beyond to the city he would never be able to alert. Barriers beyond his vision protected this sanctum from newseye probing, and neither 'Dogs nor military aircraft nor anything else that flew were permitted to come near the Hill under any pretext whatsoever. He might, he thought, be able to smash the window. But it would be too noisy, and there were still those guards in the antechamber. And those below.

And below.

He grabbed at the sill and his knuckles whitened. He stared across the way to a pyramid building layered in whites and blues and softly reassuring grays. A hospital. The Hospital. Connected with New Hill by an underground tunnel through which the Reps and the Sens, when stricken, could be rushed. But not Bendal. The tunnel had not been used for him.

He stared and his vision blurred until he shook his head sharply.

Shan, he thought suddenly, and as though telepathy were a reality rather than a dream; please, don't be the same damned man. And for all your little gods' sake, don't get caught.

Five

The room was quiet, almost preternaturally so, when Ty opened his eyes and thought that he had been allowed to die. There was absolute darkness unrelieved by the sounds of movement, and he grasped quickly at the sides of the cot as the sensation of falling billowed strong and undeniable. And in his grasping, he felt the smooth course of Caro's hair. Dead? He bit at his lips sharply and slowly, gently, moved his fingers until he was able to imagine her slumped on the floor, her head resting against his leg. He wanted to awaken her and comfort her, but he was afraid.

Afraid of the darkness less warming than smothering.

Afraid of the men who had drugged and abducted him.

Afraid of the man who claimed not to have killed Talle, and who refused to leave the side of the rat.

And more than all of this, fearing that the upheaval which had brought him unmistakably home would snatch it away again before he knew what it was like.

His fear made him angry, but he felt helpless to respond to it. He was old. Weak. What could he do that the man Raille could not, and better? It was a contribution, then, that he searched for, lying rigid and quiet while the others slept. A groan from somewhere beyond his feet. A nightmare, he thought, and knew what it was like.

Suddenly white replaced black and he was blinded by a small sharp glow that settled and became a wick in the lamp beyond the cot. The man called Raille was standing over it, staring at the single faint gold flame, rubbing at his jaw as if he had just received a blow he had not expected. Caro was as he had thought—awkwardly sleeping by his leg, and the rat was crouched asleep in the farthest corner of the room.

"Raille?"

The venner turned slowly, a smile at his lips waiting to be born, and was, as Yenkin rose on his elbows and carefully swung himself from the cot, lowering Caro until she was stretched face down on the floor, her arms twisted into a pillow for her head.

"What time is it?"

Raille shrugged. His hand hovered over the flame as though it needed warming. But the flame sputtered, and he pulled the hand away.

"What are we . . . what are you going to do now?"

Raille sniffed and sat on the floor in front of him, legs crossed, hands idle in his lap. "Escape," he said simply. Then, as Ty felt his face contort into wide-eyed shock, the venner broke into a laugh with a palm over his mouth. "I'm sorry," he said when control returned and he rocked on his buttocks, "but I couldn't resist it. I'm supposed to be the revolutionary leader, you know, and I've been thinking about how insane this is that I'm captured by my own loyal troops. And would you believe they don't even know who I am? Picked up by mistake I was. Damn!"

Ty felt his lips quivering into a smile, felt a large bubble in his chest expand until he could contain it no longer. He laughed, clamping both his hands over his face as the venner had done, glancing guiltily down at the sleeping girl but laughing harder, so hard that finally, as he gasped for a breath, he began to hiccough. He slid off the cot onto the floor, his knees brushing Raille's, and the two of them laughed silently until their faces flared red and tears flowed, cheeks ached, chests threatened to explode.

Rocking on the floor like children with a secret between them.

And when it was done, and he was giddy at the relief, he asked again: "What are we going to do?"

Raille sobered, shook his head violently and stared over at the rat still sleeping, his stringy hair clustered darkly in front of his face. Then he looked at the girl, and at the locked door behind him.

"Escape," he said again. "I mean it this time. It's a long story, Ty, and if you ever get to know me better, maybe you'll understand. But I'm not staying here. A fluke brought me, but I'm not waiting for chance to get me out. Opportunity, yes. There's a difference. But there are things I have to know first before I can do anything."

Yenkin listened to him, the voice droning in a half-whisper as he asked the same questions he had posed to himself during that nightmare time when he had withdrawn into hiding. If this was truly a revolution, who was really doing the attacking? Not the rats, if Viller was to be believed. And what about Mordan Alton? Dead, alive, captured . . . what? And why should Raille (assuming his innocence, Ty cautioned himself suddenly) be singled out among millions for the role of the man who fomented the fighting? Too many questions, and not a single satisfactory answer. He blew out a short breath and hoisted himself to his feet, moved to the table and looked down. The packets of food were gone. His stomach growled. He glanced up to stare at the wall, and turned abruptly as Caro groaned suddenly and rolled onto her back, her small breasts flattening against her chest and giving her a boylike figure belied only by the eyes, the mouth, the soft curl of her hands.

He had no time to move before she blinked, groaned again, and pushed herself to sitting. She stared around the room until her face told him she remembered where she was.

"What time is it?" she asked, sleep still heavy in her voice.

Raille laughed, and she frowned.

Yenkin reached out a trembling hand, intending to assist her to her feet, clenched his fingers suddenly, and doubled Raille's laughter.

Morag sat in front of the terminal screen, the lightpen held tightly in her left hand. She stared at the Progress of Patient form with its interminably long choices and finely worded instructions, and considered waiting for the doctor to come on for the ten o'clock morning shift. Under the heading marked Regression she could have ticked off any number of points, but still she hesitated, chewing at her lower lip.

Caine was doing better, thanks to her reflexes and the work of the diagmed.

But he should have been doing well. Very well.

Mangled he had been from the explosion at his sector, but those lofter women who had treated him on the scene had known enough what not to touch and where to press and how crude bandages and splints should be applied. That the Blue had been alive when he reached the hospital was an enormous advantage; that he had lasted through the night on a steadily upward curve of recovery should have been an obviously favorable omen. Augury? She shook her head. He had, in fact, been coupled to a diagmed unit almost from the second he had arrived on the roof.

Damnit, she thought, he shouldn't have gone under like that!

But he had.

His heart had stopped.

Shock to the system, added to which she could not forget that intolerable visit by those pompous birds in Service uniform.

And the older one, taking her into an unused office and questioning her for nearly ten minutes on what Caine had said since he'd arrived in the ward. She had lost her temper then and ordered him out, reminding him that the screaming from the other beds would not stop while she was wasting time.

She had wanted to make the tests exhaustive, but there had been no time. Too many dead, too many wounded, and too much blood for her to worry about cleaning.

Maybe now, she thought then, while it was relatively quiet.

She set the lightpen into its holder at the side of the screen and pushed wearily away from the terminal. Not so young anyway, girl, she told herself, and wondered then why she'd insisted on primping whenever Delan had looked at her, had asked for some help. With the pain. With . . . she rose and walked heavily to the window in the small room, leaned against the narrow sill and pressed her forehead to the cooling glass. Dawn was already giving edges to the city, and she could see curls of black smoke drifting like clouds from several points on the horizon. Below her was a block-wide plaza of scattered trees and benches, dry fountains and small stands where refreshments were sold on holidays, snacks and newses on ordinary mornings. On the other side of the plaza, New Hill looming. She often thought that through sheer dint of straining she could telescope her vision and see into the Premier's office.

But all she could see was a black-faced wall, blind thick glass and the sparkling of the dome as the new sun was entrapped.

She wondered about the fighting. The casualties had dwindled to less than half a dozen an hour, and all of them Service and Blues. So she was told. And she hoped then that the rats had been driven unmercilessly back into their jungle.

She wondered about which tests she could safely run on Delan without getting anyone mad, without using too much of what should be saved for the less seriously injured.

She wondered if the Premier would actually come over and give him a medal.

And she wondered, a little angrily, just what she would do if he did, and she were there.

A lieutenant paced worriedly across the mouth of the street. The meshnet had crumpled, useless, and crackled metallically under the crush of his boots. His men were strung out in a ragged line from building to building, staring wearily at the tangle of foliage that grew slowly lighter from the sun and resolved itself into trees and wild shrubs at the far side of a cleared barrier nearly two hundred meters wide. None of the men spoke to the officer. They were too exhausted to think about more than staying on their feet. And they did not want to put any ideas into his young head. During the previous night's fighting he had been as a madman railing at his cell, urging them on, driving the small ratgang slowly back under writhing, unmerciful fire.

Now he was waiting. Impatiently. Worried that they would not come back. His men were ready, he knew, to repulse another, even larger assault. He scratched at his mask, then yanked it off with a snarled curse and jammed it into his waistband. Glared. Turned almost arrogantly and watched as a massive wide-bellied tracked vehicle thundered around a corner and stopped in the center of the street. The lieutenant counted to one hundred before the driver approached him, waving gold-edged papers and holding up his other hand to prove he was not armed.

He was dressed in black. With a small red cap.

"How many you make it?" the driver asked, looking around at the bodies still dark, still red.

"Thirty-two. Six mine, twenty-six theirs," the lieutenant said. Then he pointed with his rifle to a bulging sack propped against one of the buildings. "I've got the effects."

"All right, good," the man said, gave the lieutenant a half-hearted salute and ran back to his vehicle, shouting. Almost instantly, four others dressed the same sprang from the passenger cab and began dragging the corpses toward a rectangular opening over the rear bumper. They tossed the dead in uncaring, stepped back but not quickly enough to avoid having their faces illuminated briefly by a flare of red and gold.

Soundless.

But the lieutenant imagined he heard the fire's roaring.

He hated ashers. They made his skin grow cold.

He turned away and faced out of the Fringe.

Damnit, he thought with an angry grin, when the hell are they coming back?

A fat man crouched naked beside his bedroom window. He was shivering. He was crying. Below, in the street, a half-dozen women scuttled like hooded spiders over the corpses of twice their number Blues. They bent, poked, picked, and shoved small items into the deep bulging pockets of their knee-long aprons.

The fat man had retired from the Service more than ten years before. He had missed the current fighting and, he knew, would miss the coming war. Now, all he could do was watch helplessly as crone scavengers clawed at the bodies of his brother Blues.

Ten minutes earlier he had tried to contact the local precinct, to tell them, to warn them, but all vione calls had been pre-empted for the duration of the emergency.

On the comunit screen in the next room he could hear a newshawk's voice droning the latest on the attempted revolution.

The fat man wept. Because he was too old. And because he had seen the weariness and the rage in the face of the Premier the last time he had appeared on the comunit screen.

Suddenly, with tears drenching his jowls, he rose, belted a Service dress kilt about his waist and snatched at a chair beside his bed. He smashed it time and again against the wall until he held two stout legs in either hand.

I'm not dead yet, he told himself repeatedly; if those Blues out there can't take care of their own, then I will, and be glad.

Caro wriggled until she was seated crosslegged on the cot, her back pressed loosely against the damp dirt wall. She had waited patiently until both men had stopped their insane laughing, and was not at all amused or understanding when they tried to explain what had brought the fit on. They were finally cracking, she thought–half in sorrow, half in frustrated anger–big strong men who couldn't save me if they tried. She watched as they wiped their eyes, gasped, every few seconds exploding into giggles, chuckles, then back into constrained silence. She watched and was disgusted and looked to the rat, who had awakened during the commotion and had stayed in his corner, puzzled but grinning.

"Better laugh than cry," the rat said to her gaze. She stiffened, and wondered why she had thought he would be more sensitive.

"Yes, exactly," Raille said from the floor, "so why don't we just relax and see what we've gotten into here. Maybe then we can do something to change it."

Caro remembered her earlier dream of a speech of hope from the venner; but this, she thought sourly, wasn't exactly what she was looking for.

"Our rat here–"

"Cityname Viller, please."

Raille nodded in his direction. "All right. Viller says we're not in a nest. He should know. I wouldn't." He glanced suddenly at Yenkin, who shook his head, to Caro, who only glared at him. She knew he must think her a snob, City Prime popper who never soiled her hands beyond reaching for food. He shrugged and continued to address himself to the ceiling. "Not a nest, then, but filled with rats. No," he corrected himself immediately as Viller made to interrupt. "Not rats, but fakes. Like," he said with a wry grin, "my little gods. And if they're fakes, what for? And why us? Not us, actually. That much I've figured out. You," he said, and pointed to Caro so abruptly she jumped.

"Why me?" she demanded.

"Come on, Mistress," he said, suddenly reverting to the formal. "You're Helman Talle's daughter. Talle is . . ."

"Dead," she supplied, and was shocked at the coldness in her voice, the refusal of grief to stir itself, however briefly, within her.

"Dead," he repeated flatly. "Yes, and you're alive. It was no accident that they hit your block out of all the others in Prime. They wanted you, they got you, and don't ask me what they're going to do with you because I haven't any idea."

He stopped. Caro waited. Then: "Is that all? You said you were going to see what we had here. Is that all you can come up with?"

"No," he said. "Yes. Yes, that's all. One piece at a time, as my dear old father used to say."

"That's all we seem to have."

He grinned and she turned from him, staring at the door until she realized she had been listening to footsteps approaching their cell. She tensed, felt the others move from the center of the room back to the walls. She wondered if, failing the actions of the others, she could spark something, lunge for whoever came through first, throw him off balance and let Raille and the rat do something. Anything. Slowly, then, as the idea took hold, she uncrossed her legs and edged away from the wall, one foot braced against the cot, the other on the floor. Her hands were loose at her sides.

She heard Raille's quiet laughter and ignored it.

The door opened cautiously, and a handgun, hand, arm, shoulder poked into the room. Before Caro could act, however, a man sidled in, his back to the wall. He was dressed in rats' rags, but she could see now Viller's point. This man belonged to no ratnest, no 'gang. He was, for one thing, too well fed. And so was his companion, who moved in beside him.

"Talle," the first man said, pointing vaguely at her with his weapon. "You will come with me, please."

She looked to Ty, her gaze demanding action, or a promise, but the old man was trembling visibly, and his eyes would not meet hers. Raille did nothing but whistle tunelessly between his teeth; and the rat, being a rat, cowered.

"Why?" she asked, her braced foot lowering in defeat to the floor.

"We'll talk," he said, smiling brightly. "Talk, maybe have a drink. I want to keep you happy. That's what they said."

"Who?"

The man grinned at his companion. "Who. Good. She thinks well."

Caro felt like screaming, like lifting her fingers to claws. Instead, she slumped and all her resignation showed in her shrug.

"Good," the man said. "Him, too," and he jabbed a thumb toward Yenkin.

Not alone, then, she thought, not alone. That, at least, was something in her favor. Alone, and they might . . .

"Could you use a magician at your party?" Raille said.

The man ignored him, moving to one side and waving the gun until Caro linked arms with Ty and headed for the door. She wanted to look back–hating herself for the wanting–to send something . . . comfort, scorn, a plea . . . to Raille, but her other arm was grasped too tightly and she was hustled out before anything could be done.

The corridor's boarded ceiling was low and sagging, barely clearing the two men's heads. The walls were, as was the cell, roughly dug and supported by irregularly placed, half-rotted beams. Crude brackets of blackened metal provided holding cups for small torches, most of which were extinguished. The air was foul, stale, and Caro swallowed hard to keep from coughing as the second man pushed Yenkin away from him and pulled the door to. And as he did, and before Caro could say anything, Ty suddenly collapsed, pulling her and her guard down with a combination of yells.

There was a tangle, then, a scuffling interwoven with angry threats, and Ty was yanked roughly to his feet, cuffed once alongside his head before she could right herself and protest.

"That wasn't necessary, he's old," she said when they began moving, quickly, Yenkin stumbling as though he had popped one too many.

"He's not old enough," the first man said, laughing over his shoulder at the other, who joined him.

Caro bit down hard on her tongue, gnawed at the inside of her cheeks and took a deep breath to calm herself before she could yield to the urge to bring a knee into the man's groin.

And when they had reached, less than five minutes later, a short flight of stone stairs, she almost sighed at the wash of cool air that breathed down from the open door on the landing.

Morag watched as the two men stripped and sponged Caine. They were brisk, efficient, decidedly cold. She stared at the harsh tapes across his chest, the medcast stiff and creamy white from his hips to his ankles. She tapped at her chin thoughtfully while through the clear wall she noted each gash, each contusion, and . . . an odd bruise just at his shoulder. Alone. Not even a scratch for a companion.

She moved along the wall, pressing as closely as she could, and stared at it, wondering, then deciding that she didn't much care what any of the doctors thought. She would run the tests. Scratch an itch. Nothing, and she could go to her quarters. A shift-and-a-half was plenty without sleep.

But . . . something . . .

She tapped on the wall and waved the men out.

James rubbed the sleep from his eyes with the heels of his hands. He had slept on the floor in front of the door, a gallant act of protection for his Premier, who was hiding somewhere in the still small reaches of his slowly breaking mind.

The comunit screen was activated, showing through the vione channel the room adjacent. As he stumbled about in a large circle to bring circulation back to his limbs, he watched the dumb show of Consuls standing around Alton's desk, arguing about something apparently, and gesturing vaguely toward the bank of screens still monitoring the fighting. He watched for several minutes, ignoring the lightening sky beyond the windows behind him.

"The classic falling out?" Alton said.

James turned so abruptly his neck cramped, and he rubbed at it hard, trying not to wince, trying not to match the Premier's grin. The old man seemed, but only seemed, to have regained something lost during the long night before. The slouch remained, the sag at his face, but his eyes were intent on the scene flickering over the screen.

"Are they fighting?" he wanted to know.

"I don't think so, sir. But it's hard to tell. They're probably as tired as we are."

Alton punched at the volume controls futilely, then slammed a fist against the utility wall. "You realize, of course, Captain, that I should have known this was going to happen to us . . . to me. Sooner or later it was going to happen. But like an idiot, I put the world ahead of my country."

"If you'll excuse me, sir," James said, the apology nothing more than formality, "but I think you were right."

Alton shrugged, but not with unconcern. "Maybe. Perhaps not. At any rate, the question seems to be: what are we going to do about it, James? We need a bit of luck."

The door opened then and Faux stood on the threshold. His face was haggard, his eyes blunted by lack of sleep. Alton drew himself up, and James moved immediately to stand to one side, but slightly in front of him. The Consul watched them position themselves, glanced at the mute performance on the comunit screen and managed a smile James was ready to rip from his lips.

"We're waiting for word from Meditcom," he said, his voice flat and soured. "You may call it a reprieve, if you wish. It seems as if we will have to keep the world out for a little while longer."

James managed to bite back a grin, realizing as the man spoke that they could do absolutely nothing about announcing the coup until they were positive it would not bring the jackals of the world howling down around their heads. Pride in ancestry was one thing to preach about; survival of that ancestry was something else again.

The Consuls were as trapped as he and the Premier, then, dependent upon the talks that must now be speeding back and forth between the capitals of the world's tinderbox.

And from the other room he heard Degaldon: ". . . then we have to find him again. We need his body, in case you don't understand that. Can't any of your men see it? We need his body before he talks to someone Service."

Alton took a step forward but James put out his arm to restrain him and, when the Premier looked at him, James shook his head, once. Faux, who had turned to quiet the others, missed the gesture but saw Thrush standing with his arm protectively rigid.

"Nice, but unnecessary," the Consul said. "I'll send in some food in a while. And, if you like, I'll free the comunit for your pleasure." He bowed, a mocking smile breaking the folds of his gray face. And closed the door silently behind him.

"Damn the man," Alton said, spinning about to stand at the window and glare out at the city.

"But bless the war," James said. "As long as they keep on talking and speculating, we still have a chance."

"To do what?" Alton retorted in a burst of welcome anger. "Fly off the parapets like some misbegotten, superpowerful bird? Thrush, you're . . ." He stopped, closed one eye and considered what he had just said. "Thrush," he repeated slowly, then shook his head and laughed, his voice soft and somewhat relieved.

James waited, watched, frowned as he pulled a chair to him and sat, propping his boots up against the wall. From his position he could see only the sky, and the profile of the Premier outlined against it.

Rain, he thought as clouds took vague shape and scudded ponderously over the city. Well, why not?

"You know," Alton said after he had quieted and had stared at the clouds for several minutes, "if we only had something to write with, and to write on, we could plaster a message on the window and maybe someone in the hospital over there could see it. Maybe one of the newseyes could pick it up."

"And what would anyone do, sir?"

Alton shrugged. "Fly back over here. I don't know. But a fist is better than nothing, Captain."

There was silence.

"It was a good idea, sir," James said, with a shrug in his voice.

"Of course it was, James, don't you think I know that? It was a brilliant idea, perfect for a comunit entertape. We can't do it, that's all." He sighed heavily and touched a palm to the window. "We'll just have to be brilliant in another way."

"How, sir?"

Alton turned and looked at him, a somewhat amused and disappointed smile on his face. "James," he said, "for a man with your reputation, you're not exactly overwhelming me. Why do you think I kept you with me? For your good looks?"

"Sir," he said, "I've been accused of being brash, in action and to my superiors, but I'm not reckless. I know the difference between stalemate and defeat. We're–"

"Defeated."

"No, sir, not at all. Stalemated. As long as Faux has to wait on Meditcom, we still have–"

"Hope?"

"Opportunity. We just have to watch a little, that's all. I haven't given up, if that's what you think."

A familiar voice bothered his ear then, and he twisted in his chair until he could see the comunit, saw they were running the tape of Alton's let's-be-calm-citizens speech from the beginning of the crisis.

"Sooner or later, someone is going to notice that I haven't changed my clothes," the Premier said wryly.

"Great. Then they'll think you're a rat or something."

"They already do, James."

"That's not what I meant."

Alton stared at him, shook his head and looked back out the window. "I know that, James. And I wish you had more of a sense of humor. We're not going to get anywhere at all if you insist on deliberately ruining my puns."

"I'll try to do better, sir."

"Don't try. Do it."

James watched the face on the screen for a few moments longer, sniffed and turned back in time to see a pair of small dark birds swoop close to the dome, separate and dart away just as lightning flared on the horizon.

"Rain," the Premier muttered.

"Isn't that what you do anyway?" James said with as much innocence as he could muster.

Alton turned slowly, one eye at a time. "That," he said, "was awful."

"I'm trying, sir. I'm trying."

"You certainly are."

Shanlon watched as the door slammed shut, prepared to wince when the latch turned over on the outside. Instead, he heard a scuffling in the corridor, rapid footsteps, mumbling, and then . . . nothing. He stood with his back against the rear wall, staring in disbelief, refusing to look at the rat kneeling expectantly in the corner. Suddenly, for no reason at all, he realized he was still wearing the cloak he'd stolen from the City Prime store. Without taking his eye from the door, he fumbled inside it until the seam gaped, and he let the soft cloth drop from his shoulders into a shimmering black puddle on the earthen floor. He hugged himself as if he were cold. Rubbed his arms vigorously. Traced the line of his cheek with a forefinger knuckle. He was waiting, not very patiently, for the door to swing open and a laughing face poke in for approval of a cruel and apt joke.

The door had not locked.

He was sure of it. But he did not want to take the step to test it. For the moment he was satisfied that the possibility existed. He would act on that as soon as he understood more of what he was going to do.

Back in the hovbus tunnel he had told himself, finally, that he was tired of running. Tired of gliding like those damned birds of his, on the fan, and in his mind. This, then, was the first opportunity he would have to work at it. And he didn't know what to do.

"No rats they," Viller said, his voice cracking.

"I know," he said, "but do you know how many of them are up there?"

Viller held up his hands, toyed with his fingers. "Five, six, no more. I peek, I don't see. Maybe other dills in the trees outside, but no rats they. No rats here anywhere. This a nest long time, but long time since rats nest here."

"If," Raille said, sliding down the wall to squat on his heels, "we get out of here in one reasonably working piece, what are you going to do?"

"I look for eat and wash in Wash. I try again. Why not?"

Shanlon snorted his exasperation. "Haven't you been listening to us talking, you blessèd idiot? Don't you know there's a revolution going on out there? Supposedly rats." His laugh was bitter, and short. "You stick one small toe into a Fringe and they'll burn you to an ash not even the wind can pick up."

Viller twined his fingers into his filthy hair, plucked a blade of brown grass from behind his ear and chewed on it until he grimaced and spat it out. He rubbed a knuckle under his nose. Stuck a finger into his mouth and poked at a molar. Then he took the finger out, chewed on the nail and spat.

"Have to wash in Wash, then, hom. Cut a hair, maybe two."

"You wouldn't recognize yourself."

Viller grinned, his teeth yellowed where they weren't black.

Shanlon returned the grin, touched at his forearm to check the position of his knife and rose, groaning silently at the crack of his kneecaps. Timidly he approached the door, searching over its surface as though traps of explosives or poison waited for his touch. He sniffed once, then felt along the frame until his fingers found gaps between door and jamb. They hooked, tightened, but his arms would not pull.

"Do it, venner," the rat said.

His arms tensed, tugged, and he drew the door to him as slowly as he could without screaming his impatience. He felt suddenly lightheaded, but the door moved unencumbered. Finally, he was able to peer into the corridor, squinting at the draft that brushed coolly into his eyes. He heard the rat scuttle to stand behind him, fetid breath warm on his back, a black-nailed finger jabbing him excitedly in his side. He shook his head and the rat grunted, shoved him aside and darted over the threshold, crouching to spring back at the first flicker of a menacing shadow. Shanlon followed him when there was no cry of discovery, closing the door carefully, then grinning as he twisted the lock over. Viller immediately snatched at his arm and began tugging him to the right, but Shanlon balked. Not daring to speak, he indicated with head and hands that the rats-not-rats had taken Caro and Ty in the opposite direction. But Viller would have none of it.

Go on, then, you shagging ass, Shanlon mouthed at him, and hurried away, not caring if the rat followed, but more than slightly relieved when, after a few paces, he heard Viller racing to catch up with him.

The corridor twisted only gently, giving him no place to hide, no corners to sidle up to; and when he reached the flight of stone stairs he hesitated, one hand resting nervously on his thigh. The door above was closed, a thin bar of light blurred beneath it. He could hear no voices on the other side, but nevertheless took the steps cautiously as if they were wooden and ready to creak. Thinking all the while that these men, whoever they were, had to be inordinately confident of his cowardice not to have posted guards every inch of the way.

At the door then, his breathing labored, he pressed his ear to the wood. Nothing. Only a faint coolness that promised ease to his lungs.

He glanced down at Viller, whose face had paled beneath the patina of dirt, and whose lips were drawn back from his teeth as he panted his apprehension.

Shanlon shrugged, took the dulled knob firmly in his hand and flung in the door, stepping quickly aside as he did so, his arm tensed to loose his lethal magic.

The room here was sparsely furnished, but by hundreds of degrees more comfortable than the cell below. The walls were painted a soft gray and obviously recently cleaned; a divan, two armchairs, a bookcase and tapeslot built into the far wall. A single window placed high toward the ceiling was uncurtained and glowed with the day's first soft light. To its right, a door.

Shanlon blinked until his eyes adjusted, trying not to sag as he realized he would not be attacked. Then he saw a dark form slumped in a far corner. He ran to it, rolled it over and looked anxiously into the pinched and pained face of Caro's old friend.

"Ty," he said in a harsh whisper. He slapped at the man's face, softly, then hard, pressed a palm against his chest and waited until he could thank his little gods that he could feel the strong presence of a heartbeat. An ugly black-and-yellow lump on the man's left temple solved him one riddle as he glanced around the room for water, for something he could use to bring Yenkin around. The rat, meanwhile, had posted himself at the exit door, waiting, listening, then pointing to an alcove Shanlon had missed. There was a basin built within, and Shanlon hurried to it, filled his palm by drops and rubbed the cool water into Ty's cheeks and forehead. Twice more, and he had to slap a hand over the man's mouth to stifle a groan.

"You're all right," Shan said, leaning close for his lips to brush against an ear. "Relax. We'll talk in a minute."

The minute dragged, became five, became ten, and finally Yenkin was propped up into the corner.

"The door wasn't locked?" Ty said.

"Magic, I guess," Shanlon said.

Yenkin grinned and gingerly placed a finger to his injured temple, winced and sighed.

"There were five," he said, gulping at the air. "They took Caro, I don't know where, and I tried to get away. One of them hit me with something."

"How many?" the rat hissed from the door, one finger jabbing at his wrist.

"An hour. Less. I don't know."

"Don't worry about it," Shanlon said. "Someone will be back, no question. We just don't want to be here when they do."

"But Caro!" Yenkin insisted, trying to get to his feet before Shanlon put a hand to his chest and carefully shoved him back.

"She's gone for now," he said. "We can't just go chasing after her, now can we?" His hand waved about the room, trying to shatter the walls so he could embrace the outside. "They think I'm the cause of all this. I'm not. I didn't kill anyone, and I didn't raise the rats to rebellion. The only way I can convince anyone of that is by staying alive until I can find another piece."

Yenkin frowned, puzzled.

"Don't worry about that, either," he said. "It's between me and a man I once knew."

Viller, trying to listen to the outside and the conversation simultaneously, gave up in disgust and scurried to the comunit wall. The screen was canted and small, obviously a makeshift addition with a screen barely large enough to cup in his hands. He turned it on anyway and grunted when a tiny face filled the screen.

"Our Premier," Shanlon said. "Still telling us everything's just fine."

Yenkin ignored him. He watched the screen and Shanlon, readying himself to climb the nearest chair so he could look out the window, saw him suddenly scowl.

"What's the matter, Ty?"

"Last night," the old man said. "Or is it two nights ago, now? Two nights? Anyway, I was watching the first reports of the fighting at the Senator's Key. There was something about the newsroom I couldn't . . . I still don't know. The map there, the one behind Alton. It looks to be the same."

"So? You can buy one from any venner on the street."

"Yes," Yenkin said, pushing as though there were something jammed in his throat. "But it had lights. The lights . . ."

"Pretty," the rat said, waving to hush them.

"No!" Yenkin said, so loudly that Shanlon hunched his shoulders, expecting an army to come crashing through the door. "Now I know," he continued. "But I don't know what it means."

"Well, what is it, damnit?"

"The lights! You know . . . here's fighting, there's fighting. But now that I think of it, there were no lights in Cenam or Canam. They were all in the center. The rest of the map was dark."

Shanlon was about to dismiss it and leap for the sill again when, suddenly, the scene he had retained only in fragments came back in a rush, as though it were happening again. And this time he saw everything.

The restaurant, the stall, the Consuls leaving through the door. Yenkin—and he glanced at the old man with a puzzled grin—holding the door back deferentially. Talle apparently arguing; an older, more weary-looking Consul leaning toward him and whispering something, something short, something that made Talle snap his head up with a look that could only be a mixture of fury and fear. The other, the imperious one . . . standing by Yenkin and muttering something, a bulge in his cloak and the glint . . . damnit, the glint of a handgun, firing, vanishing, and that damnable finger outstretched and pointing . . . and the mob set on him.

"Blesséd, blesséd priest," he said, and sat hard on the floor as though he had been struck. "You aren't going to believe this, but I've found another piece. And I don't think there are any more."

Six

It could have been a holiday, the second full day after the world imploded. A holiday. Noram Unity. Canadian Remembrance. The Mexican Festival of the Holy Light. The celebration of the birthday of Henré Laker, the first Premier, founder, father. Lincolnday. Juarezday.

It could have been a holiday.

The streets were deserted long after the hour when offices should have been opened, lit, chattering, settling. Not quite deserted—empty. A few racing peds ducking in and out of doorways as though they expected rockets to land at their feet from the clouding sky and extinct them. Hovbuses lifting out of their tunnels on no particular schedule, poised, waiting, diving again and leaving behind them a swirl of dust and paper and a few shredded clothes. Joyhalls with oddly silent voices, blind fronts; restaurants with aromas stifled; Keylofts with heavy ironwork grilles caged across the entrances to their lobbies.

Blues walked in quartets down the center of the street, one looking back, one to either side, the first with eyes front, as WatchDogs, curiously subdued, drifted overhead as if yearning for a summons.

Service had roadblocks still at prime intersections, but the manpower had been steadily reduced to a smoking, muttering, sneaking-drinks-from-a-flask few. They were primarily young, and eager to slip the leash and race into the suburbs, but they'd been chosen to protect rather than pursue. They all wore their masks.

And in that silvered anonymity, the clouds were reflected.

Towering fluffed white that scraped at a harsh blue, shading down to a thin layer of uncertain gray, shading finally to a black that no midnight could contain. Islands of clouds, continents of clouds, all massing at the horizon and ponderously, inevitably, closing in on the city.

Lightning stalked, forked, knifed, flickered at the edges of vision like the swift clawed jab of an angry cat.

Assault.

On nerves as well as concrete.

"The details," Faux said to the Premier, "are what you are still alive for. I can't be expected to do everything. Not even my colleagues believe I'm divine."

Manquila was gone; the others were alone in the main office. Food had been brought in by a colonel whose nerves were obviously frayed, obviously breaking. James kept himself posted at the door to the back room, where he had spent the night and had seen the dawn. Shortly after a meager breakfast, the Canam Consul had ushered them out, seated the Premier at his desk and stood back to allow the new flow of reports to be rushed in by hands that still did not know what had taken place. The strain on the old man, James noted, was telling. His face had once again taken on that somnolent glaze, and though he managed to rouse himself to a performance each time a Cabinet or Justice official bustled in, he sank further back when it was done.

It won't last long, he thought, his eyes trying not to stare at the comunit screen tiers. Sooner or later, someone is going to ask him what's the matter, and he won't be strong enough to deny anything.

"About six, our time," Faux continued, "there'll be what we hope will be a final meeting of the Meditcom and Eurepac ministers. They'll expect you to have a statement for them."

"They can expect all they want," Alton muttered.

Faux bridled and took a single step toward the desk. James saw his hand clutch into a trembling fist and he tensed, ready to spring at the pompous toad's throat should he dare lose control and strike. But Faux, blowing out a breath, snapped his head back as though yanking on reins with his teeth, and turned the step into a slow, methodical pacing that quartered the room.

"They will expect the statement, Mordan, and you'll give it to them. In this respect, nothing has changed and we are still allies. You will tell them what you've been telling them—no troops, sorry—and they will scream and, I've no doubt, foam and rattle their childish silos. Then—as you yourself had planned it, may I remind you—they will most likely thunder away the night in their respective rooms, come to terms tomorrow and announce the new peace before sunset." He glanced at the ordered row of timepieces over the world map. "That gives us, I make it, something less than thirty-six hours before we can breathe freely again."

It was a mangled kind of madness that James knew he was witnessing. A coup that no one knew of, and yet the old Premier and the new were talking as if nothing at all had happened. There had been no incursion into the city of ratgangs bent on the city's destruction, no retaliation that swept bodies of rats and Blues and Service alike before it as brigades poured into the dead suburbs toward the known and suspected nests encamped in the surrounding hills. And from all other beseiged cities, the same. The rats were on the run. To be exterminated despite the Premier's cautionary orders. And still, in the relative quiet of Noram's heart, the country was falling apart. Manquila, he guessed, would return to Cenam as its leader, Torre and Degaldon notwithstanding, and Faux would undoubtedly want Canam for himself. Had Bendal been promised the center? And if so, who would take it now?

And that, he thought as he watched Faux come to a halt in front of the desk, is a stupid question.

"It's a foul choice you've given me," Alton said.

Faux grinned and bowed, as though accepting a compliment.

"War will save the country, but not the world; peace will save the world, but not the country. You should be congratulated, Faux, and damned. And damned most of all."

The Consul shrugged without actually moving his shoulders. "We can fence our philosophies later on, if you wish. Right now, you have a statement to prepare for our friends across the water. And you, Thrush!"

James came rigidly to attention, hating himself for it but unable to defeat the conditioning. He relaxed, then, and tried not to smile into Faux's glare.

"I want you in the antechamber again. There'll be more visitors. Newshawks, friends, the usual clutch of garbage. I want you to look very official, Captain. And be very quiet."

James nodded once without looking to Alton, then fairly marched to the door where Degaldon leaned over and opened it for him, a feral grin on his dark face. "I will join you later," he said. "You'll appreciate the company, I'm sure."

And suddenly, James was alone, facing the huge open room and disgusted with himself that he had no dramatic plan to throw into action. He could go, as he'd once considered, to the terrace and try to get a message to one of those omnipresent newseyes–but he had no doubt Degaldon would be with him before a move could be made, had perhaps even planned to present him with this opportunity. And it would be a tragic thing for the Premier's personal Liaison Service Team member to take a tumble to the plaza below, just when it seemed to the city that things were getting back to normal.

A peripheral casualty, they would call him.

He strode to the lifttube and heard, in the waiting area below, the murmur of voices, the handful of officers who had been moving in since the fighting began. They would no doubt be screening all visitors quite carefully, and unobtrusively. A rise in the level and he heard Manquila's rasping laugh.

So few, he thought in frustration. So blessèd damned few.

Degaldon came out as he turned from the 'tube. The office door hissed loudly shut behind.

The Cenam Consul, in a dark tunic and black trousers, wore a handgun clipped to an elaborate broad belt. Ostensibly for show. He took James's mocking salute with a grin, then reached into a side pocket and offered him a nic.

"No, it's insane," Morag said, slapping away the newsheet her shiftmate had been pressing at her. "I know the man, Arley, and he is physically, emotionally, constitutionally incapable of it."

Arley, short and stout and lined with weariness, seemed ready to argue, then only shrugged and dropped the sheet into the waste. Morag watched it vanish into bluefire, sniffed and stalked out of her office with white tunic flapping. She strode angrily through the wards, around the beds stuffed and jammed into the aisles, alcoves, corners, anyplace where a diagmed wasn't urgently needed, or wouldn't be before the day was out. She was tired, but a second wind had temporarily driven away the stinging behind her eyes and the pull at her legs that urged her to sit, to sleep, to wake again only when the sun was down and the war over.

First Delan, now Shanlon. None of it fit. None of it made sense.

Especially Delan, who had almost died because the bruise on his shoulder concealed a puncture.

She hadn't yet made up her mind to bring it to the attention of the doctor on duty. She was unfamiliar with him, working as she was into a shift she normally slept through. And even if she did, how would she say it?

Doctor, I think there's been an attempt to murder one of the patients.

She decided to talk to Delan.

And she walked through the wards.

A child moaned beneath a tent of clear plastic, her legs amputated at the knee, her left arm encased in smooth white.

Another child–boy or girl she couldn't remember and couldn't tell–was bandaged from eyes to toes. The bandages leaked blood. She pressed the "call" on the side of the bed and moved on.

A civilian woman thrust into a cylindrical glastic casing. Her lungs had been seared, her eyes lost and she was fighting the antibiotics that attempted to graft her a new way to breathe. But not to see.

Attendants mechanical and fleshly ran mops and sponges over the bloodstained floors, the hot water steaming from conduits in the walls, disinfectant lifting like a faint green fog to burn her nostrils and make her gag.

Shanlon?

The shifts were changing.

There was, in spite of Shanlon, the evidence: the dead, the dying, the muttering through the ceiling of copters bringing more in from the Fringes and immediate outlands where ratgangs still lurked, from the hovbus tunnels from which they'd been flushed with scalding water, bursts of acid, sweeps of lasers. The rats were detained in the armed ward on the top floors, where only those with pink passes clipped to their collars could enter. She did not have one, did not want one, preferring instead to deal with those she knew were civilized.

Those she had once thought were civilized.

But . . . Shanlon Raille?

She rounded a corner, pushed past a groaning, moaning, quietly sobbing bedridden clutch of wounded, and made her way to the rear of the room, where Delan, released from the cubicle, was resting quietly. She had ordered, quite without authority, a complete flush of his system, and as she stood by the side of the bed, she noted with modest pleasure the color slowly drawing back into his face. How old, she wondered, refusing to look at the tape spindled on the headboard; in his forties like me, she decided.

His eyelids quivered, fluttered, and he stared at her for a full minute before smiling.

"Hello, Morag," he said. And coughed until she slipped a thin tube into the side of his mouth and watched as the clear nutrient was sucked into his throat. When he'd done, he raised one arm weakly to wipe at his lips.

"No taste," he said.

"Be glad," she smiled.

"What happened?"

She frowned only slightly before leaning over and telling him. And when it was over, and when he did not panic or bluster as she'd expected him to, she knew her face had paled when she realized there was something in the air besides the lightning.

Caro said nothing though her first impulse was to scream; not out of fear, because she felt herself curiously beyond that now, but simply for the relief she knew it would bring. The two men, who called themselves Harrow and Gaito, had taken her into a small room where they met with three others. There was nothing to drink or eat, and they immediately moved with her toward the door. It was then that Ty did something, she couldn't see what, and one of them struck him into a corner where he lay, doll-broken and silent. She hadn't cried, nor had she pummeled Harrow, who gripped her arms in anticipation of a reaction. She only watched as a man named Vererro knelt by the old man, checked his pulse and the side of his head and grunted.

Then they had taken her outside. That was when she wanted to scream.

Trees, shrubs, the fractured tinted light of the sun through thickly green foliage. A cloud lumbering darkly, and a cacophony of birdsong. Her muscles strained, her legs ached, to run, to sprint; and Harrow sensed it and tightened his grip. But she only grinned stupidly and let herself be taken down a narrow, twisting path to what remained of a macadam road. A landcar, its gulldoors extended, waited in dusty silence. As silently as the men who escorted her to its side.

Then, with watchful glances up and down the road, four of them began tearing at their rats' clothes, grunting, two of them laughing once until the rags had been discarded behind a nearby bush. Beneath the clothes were uniforms, Service, and though she did not recognize any of the battalion ensignia, she noticed that on Harrow's left shoulder was a small patch resembling a leaf, and on Gaito's another resembling a stylized Aztec calendar.

Vererro stood back, saying nothing, his lank nervous frame swaying like a tethered animal.

Caro was glad he appeared to be staying behind. She did not like him, or the small black eyes that roamed her red hair. She was about to comment, then, on the change of dress, when Harrow signaled to the others and they slipped into the landcar, two in front, she in back, in the middle. The turbine instantly whined over and the vehicle shuddered for the brake to be released. Vererro leaned against the right-hand side of the car and whispered something to Gaito, who nodded with a jerk of his thumb in the air.

They pulled away suddenly, and she craned her neck to watch through the narrow rear window as Vererro walked slowly back up the low hill toward the house she could no longer see between the trees.

They weren't going to kill her. Shanlon was right.

And finally, after ten minutes of avoiding the breaks in the road and the trees snapping down to block them, she said, "Where are you taking me?"

There was no answer.

"Please." Exhilaration had faded, was pre-empted by a silence that seeded fear. The two men on either side of her had pressed themselves back against the walls of the car, as though she had been plagued and touch was the carrier. "I can't run away. Four against one? Please, where are you taking me now?"

Gaito looked to Harrow, who was doing the driving. Harrow nodded, once.

"New Hill," Gaito said with a barely suppressed grin. "You're going to meet the Premier. Or see him again, if you've already met."

She gaped and knew she looked stupid. "No," she said.

"You asked," he said, and turned back to watch the road.

It was nonsense, of course, and she began to create vivid scenarios of her fate, from the melodramatic to the heroic, all of them incredible and none of them comforting. Each time she came to the precipice of decision, and fell, plummeted, joined her parents in their unnatural, abrupt deaths. In the distance, above the quiet whine of the engine, she could hear faint thumps, grumbling thunder, and though she could see no more than a few towering clouds, she wondered. Then recognized, and wondered again: who was fighting? Service against the rats? Service against . . . ?

She looked at the men more closely, puzzling over their uniforms. It could have been, she thought, that their disguises were simply methods of infiltrating a ratnest organization, to expose their war plans before it was too late.

It could have been, but the smile that flashed briefly was more melancholy than satisfied.

Had it been, then she would not still be a prisoner, nor would she ever have been. And despite their careful treatment of her—a fragile package not to be bruised more than necessary in the delivery—she harbored no illusions any more that she was anything more than what she appeared to be.

And if they weren't Service spies . . .

She shook her head vigorously, startling the man on her right into grabbing at her wrist.

"Let go," she said coldly.

He gazed at her, turned stare into glare and slowly released her.

"You're not from around here, are you?" she asked suddenly, and out of the corner of her eye, she saw the one on the left shake his head before he could stop himself. Gaito looked over his shoulder and scowled.

"Well," she said without flinching, "I'm not going to sit here all day and keep my mouth shut." She lifted her head, then, as she had seen her father do to a Rep who presumed too much. "The least you can do is tell me something."

"What?" he said, lifting a broad arm to rest it on the back of his seat. Harrow grunted as they thudded slowly over wooden debris, rotted branches and thick splinters of shattered boles. "Relax," Gaito said to him. "Ease it awhile. You heard what the man told us: be nice."

"What man?" Caro asked.

Gaito only grinned.

"All right, then, what's going to happen to my . . . to my friends back there?"

"Vererro will take good care of them. He'll see that they're all right."

She snorted and looked out the window. "You'll kill them."

"Maybe."

She watched the tree pass, only slightly faster than a steady run, gasped when Harrow suddenly swerved the landcar off the main road and onto a dirt lane barely wide enough for the vehicle that lurched violently and brought to the back of the driver's neck a bulging of tensed muscles. She gnawed on her lower lip, imagining that this was the same route they had used to bring her out of the city after the attack on the Keyloft. And as she watched, she sent back to the venner a silent apology for all her doubts. He was as he had said. No leader. And certainly not of these men. And Ty, poor Ty, so soon home and so soon gone. For the rat, Viller, she felt nothing. He was nothing. Only a rat.

The thundering grew louder. Storm or battle she could not tell.

"We'll have to walk it the rest of the way if it gets much worse," Gaito said angrily. "We can't–"

"I know, I know!" Harrow said, shifting in his seat suddenly. "That sobitch will kill us yet, you know. Manquila's an idiot. He should have known."

"Who's Manquila?" Caro asked.

"A friend," Harrow said, leaning close to the windshield.

"Except he gets to live, doesn't he?" she said. "My friends have to die."

"I never said they would die, Mistress Talle," Gaito said, with a smile.

Caro said nothing. Remembered instead the moment Shanlon had eased the fan from behind her ear. She had reached out for it, and he had touched it lightly on her palm, a small caressing cross before her fingers took it. He had pulled it away, gently, then opened it so she could see the tree, and the man, and the birds soaring toward the moon. Opened it, tapped her once on the wrist with a smile that made her start, then lay it carefully, like a feather, in her waiting hand.

And he was going to die.

"Now I know Shan's not your boss," she said. "He wouldn't kill anyone. He's got that much at least."

"Shan? Wait a blessèd minute," Harrow said then, his voice raised nearly in a shout of disbelief. "Shan? Mistress, are you talking about Shanlon Raille?"

Gaito's eyes widened.

She could see Harrow staring at her dumbly in the rearview mirror suspended from the roof.

She could do nothing but nod, and as Harrow wrenched the landcar around in an awkward turn that scraped against trees and plowed through bushes, it struck her then that she might have finally done something right.

If only Shan were not still cowering in the cell.

A stunted, middle-aged man walked into his shop with fearful glances over his shoulder, and back rigid as if expecting a lance to pierce his heart. He stumbled over the threshold though there was nothing underfoot, and stared openmouthed at three Servicemen lying in a huddle at the entrance to the back room.

The first thing he did was put in a call for the Blues, and while he waited he worried about what this would do to his insurance, his family, the extent of his trade. He fumbled in his pockets, found no coin, and wondered how he might be able to bribe the Blues into keeping this silent.

"Right up there," the concierge was saying, slightly uneasy at having to talk to the hovering newseye at his left shoulder. He pointed upward, toward a shattered balcony railing whose twisted struts clawed at the air above the street. "They came right up the 'tubes and the back stairwell. Nearly every Key on the way was smashed. Who knows how many bodies? They're still digging them out. I don't keep track, either. I don't know who was in there. Like I said, I don't keep track. They come and go, they come and go. I don't interfere with these Government people, you know. That's not what I'm here for. Blew the hell out of the 'tubes, though. The people what come back, though, will have to walk. Blesséd, it's a pain when you have to walk."

"You were not in your position?" a tinny voice said.

"Is that a joke? I can't tell if you're joking. Couldn't you send someone . . . real out here? No, of course I wasn't down here in the lobby. Service came right in when the fighting started, told me, told all of us on this block to find a hole and pull it in after us. I did, too. You think I want to be burned when this damned Raille guy comes in here to steal my coin and rape my wife? Hey, tell me something, have they got him yet? Are they going to hang him? I hope it's in the plaza. First time I remember that happening I was six. Hardly remember it now, of course."

"Raille was here?"

"Who else could it have been, huh?"

"No, I can't do it. There are too many others who need me now. You can see that for yourself, can't you?"

"You've got to, Morag."

"I'd have to steal a pass."

"I told you what I was trying to remember. And I sure can't tell it to that general, now can I?"

"The guards will ask questions."

"You don't have to go in there. Just look. See what you can. See if I was right."

"Delan, I don't know. I don't know if I can."

"You . . . can. I'm thirsty. You can. Wait until the shift changes again. Or when you break for midmeal."

"You've got to rest. And I've got other patients."

"Morag . . . please."

"Rest, Delan! I'll . . . I'll see what I can do."

They dug into a packet Viller uncovered beneath the divan. There wasn't much food, but enough to sustain the illusion that they had been well fed. They ate rapidly, without talking, not bothering to add water to the powder, swallowing hard, nearly gagging, but racing against the time when they knew someone would return.

Shanlon tried desperately not to think as he chewed on the paste forming in his mouth, believing that he must have tripped himself at last over the end into madness. It was the terror of being accused, the flight, the explosions, the sudden awakening in a cell with no one knowing who he was except the people who had thought he had killed part of their lives. And to tell Yenkin and the rat would be madness indeed. A false revolution? They would demand–Yenkin would demand because the rat didn't seem to care–they would demand proof, and he had none. Only a glimmering that stuck to his reason like burrs to trousers. Pluck, and they resist while pricking; ignore and they multiply. Yet it stuck, and he worried at it, stroking it, pounding it, thinking it . . . mad.

A game with the world.

They had come so close over more than a century. Eurepac, Meditcom, Russchin, Noram . . . little by little the old ways vanished into new ways into newer. Absorption, stall, reach out and absorb once again. A matter of time, he had been taught and had believed, before it all became one as lessons were learned and nightmares diminished. The spacefacs waiting, keys he trusted to the opening of a door. What lay beyond no one knew. But perhaps, as he had hoped, and as he and James had argued, and as he and Morag Borsen had dreamed, it would be the door to the outside.

The Outside.

Where there were no limits.

Now . . . it was a game.

He stared down at his palms, the lines and scratches encrusted with dirt and blood.

No one had asked him to play, no one had dealt him the chips before the first die was thrown. It was a joyhall blindfold, a variation on a theme in which he had become the hare.

It did not take much speculation to understand that they had expected him to die immediately, not to escape the claws of the mob that had howled for his blood while howling for the Senator. They had not counted on his fear being more prickly than his courage, his legs more swift than those around him. And surely they had not counted on their minions being blind to their prize—he shivered suddenly when he realized how soon dead he could have been had any one of his captors recognized his face, the face streaked and altered and no longer his.

Ty and Viller finished their skimpy meal and looked at him steadily. He angered, and calmed, and thought: what can I expect? I got them this far, and now they'll not let me go.

"We'll take what food we can," he said, tossing the remains of the packet to the rat, who blinked before stuffing it into one of the dozens of small pockets that sprouted from his rags. "And then . . . and then we'll run."

"Where?" Yenkin demanded. "Back to the city?"

Shanlon shook his head with the contempt he thought the question deserved. Stopped suddenly and grinned as Yenkin held up his hands in unbelieving protest.

"Well, sure, why not?" he said. "If all the fighting's going on out here—and I don't see those rats holding on for long inside, do you?—then where else could we be safer?"

"But what are you going to do?"

"Is that all you ever did, ask your customers what they were going to do after a meal?" He pushed himself to his feet, tugged at his shirtsleeves and walked toward the door. "I have a friend," he said, "a nurse who works in Hospital Prime. She's the only one left I can think of, other than a certain uncle who's probably hunting for my scalp. If I can contact her, maybe then we can find out what's going on. Really going on. Then, maybe, I can get someone who counts to listen to me."

"What if she doesn't believe you?"

Shanlon grinned. "That's why you're going with me."

Yenkin sputtered into a brief silence. Then: "All right, then what if those people, the other people, the ones who count . . . what if they do believe you?" He stayed on the floor, refusing to move. "What if they do? Then what?"

"Joke, joke," the rat said, his hands flying nervously over his chest, into his beard and hair and out again. "He say nest, not city. South maybe, away from dills and bashes and like that. Like the birds . . . he . . . say we . . ." He stopped, and swallowed.

"I said city," Shanlon said, "and I meant city. If someone listens, I'm off the hook!"

"Is that all?" Yenkin demanded.

"No," Shanlon said, "but if I told you the rest, you wouldn't believe me."

"Try me," the old man said.

"Try," the rat repeated, grinning darkly, in yellow.

Shanlon took a deep breath, his finger tips suddenly tingling as though they were readying for something the rest of him still did not know about. He turned away from them, turned back. Pressed his ear against the door and heard the steady crunch of boots on the ground outside. Instantly, he waved frantic directions, and the rat and the Host ducked back through the doorway into the underground corridor. Then, with a silent curse to his uncle for not knowing more than he did, Shanlon positioned himself beside the small comunit and leaned back against the wall. He folded his arms with hands gripped biceps lightly, and crossed one ankle over the other.

Never do anything less than give them a show, his father had said when customers came in to rummage for magic. *Give them a show and they'll never know until it's too late how much coin they've put in your purse.*

Father, Shanlon said suddenly and silently to his memories, why the hell don't you shut up?

He wondered how much longer he would be drugged into lethargy. Not that he could move were the drugs taken away, not with the cast and the tapes and those insistent colored wires. But his mind felt caged, the bars widening and thinning and he never quite in position to take advantage.

The murmur of the ward.

Footsteps of the doctor, the nurses, no one stopping to see how he was. He was, however, better, and he knew it. Physically, at least, he would recover from the explosion, with only a few scars on his back and legs that he would not have removed because, angrily, he wanted to remember.

The pat on the shoulder.

He remembered that, too, and the sudden sharp pain that had at the time blended into everything else that ached and burned.

Midmeal had come and gone, and gone, and the hours of the afternoon had become the hours of night as great black clouds loomed and spat in electric fire.

Though he could not lift his head, his eyes strained down the aisle as far as he could see, blurring, clearing, until Morag–and he trembled, with anticipation, for more than her news–came into view.

The look on her face. Not quite masked.

Caine closed his eyes.

Less than five hours ago Morag had moved his bed from the ward into which he had been brought when first he was a casualty. Her officiousness had overcome all the objections of the attendants who didn't understand what she was doing. He knew. He was being hidden, among the dead and the dying, and the barely alive.

When she touched his shoulder, he would not look up. He didn't want to see Morag's soft smile, soft eyes, soft curves of her whites. Caine was afraid, and it was safe in the dark.

The door opened briskly, and Shanlon tried not to jump when the rat-not-a-rat stepped over the threshold. The rags were gone.

The uniform oddly fitting. The Serviceman/rat froze when he finally became aware of Shanlon's falsely bright smile.

"I like this room better," Shanlon said.

Vererro took in the room with a single practiced sweep.

"If you're looking for the others, they've been long gone down one of the tunnels. I came up to see what I could get to eat, and to find out about the girl." He dropped his arms, then, and spread them to prove he was unarmed. "You can shoot me now or later. It makes no difference to me. I'm not hungry any more."

"Harrow was an idiot for bringing you back here," the deceptively thin man said, edging along the wall, slowly, one small step at a time.

"Then why did he?"

"You were there. You saw the fighting and the running, all the confusion. He grabbed you when you ran up, like a simple reflex. He should have dumped you when we got out of the city. He had some idea, who knows what it was. He was an idiot."

"Agreed," Shanlon said, turning on his heels to follow Vererro's none-too-subtle progress toward the tunnel door.

Suddenly, the man lunged for the knob and Shanlon darted to intercept him, stumbling when Vererro abruptly changed direction and leaped for one of the armchairs. By the time Shanlon had regained his balance, the chair was in the air and he dropped hard to the floor as it spun overhead and bounced off the wall behind him and into his back. He grunted and rolled over as a second chair followed the first, was onto his feet and leaping before the man could duck away. His shoulder struck breastbone painfully and they slammed back into the wall, rebounded and tangled, rolling, grunting, until Shanlon was able to break free and stumble backward onto his feet. His left arm was extended, palm out, and he shook his head.

Vererro was furious, his face almost gray with anger, and Shanlon knew he was only toying and could have easily broken his neck, arms, legs twice over. The man was enjoying it, Shanlon thought; the sobitch was actually having himself some fun.

"The lady," he said suddenly, as the other twisted into a rapid crouch. "You didn't kill her?"

"Are you kidding?" Vererro grinned, dropping back to stand in the corner, hands loose at his sides, his chest barely moving. "You must know who she was, don't you? Senator Talle's daughter. She's not going to die. But I guess you'll have to, won't you?"

"You can't kill me," Shanlon said, backing away. "I'm your leader."

Vererro laughed, once and shortly. "Sure," he said, "and I'm going to be the next Premier."

"Come on," he said. "Haven't you ever heard of Shanlon Raille?"

The man stopped his slow advance, his eyes momentarily glazed in puzzlement, and it was enough for Shanlon to flex once and shoot the knife into his palm. He brandished it once before throwing, and Vererro had no time to twist away, to do more than gape in astonishment as the blade sliced into his throat. Then he gasped, reached up for the hilt and drew it out, dropped it, opened his mouth and the blood bubbled over his lips. Shanlon called for Yenkin and the rat, then stumbled to the door and lurched outside, holding onto the jamb while his stomach roiled and acid fountained, and he was on his knees, retching, rocking, unashamedly sobbing.

A wind blew cool across his face, and with it the unmistakable smell of rain.

Run, he told himself, and could not move.

Run! he ordered, but when he stood, his legs were uncontrollable and he staggered until he came up against the low building, his shoulder striking the doorframe. He held on, spitting, wiping at his eyes, until he was able to stand erect, swaying slightly, and move back into the room. He half-expected Vererro to be standing there, grinning. Grinning he was, but the gleaming red slash wasn't his mouth; and his chest, and the floor, was a spreading pool of crimson. Avoiding the body, he snatched up the knife and wiped it hurriedly against one of the chair's cushions. Then he ducked through the doorway into the tunnel, hoping that Yenkin and the rat would still be waiting for him.

And when they weren't, he wasn't surprised.

Or disappointed.

The noise of the fight had most likely been sufficient to send them scurrying, as the aftermath of his killing had sent him panicked. They would have taken to the tunnel, then, and he moved on, passing the cell where he had been kept—kicking feebly at the door and slapping at the latch—grabbing one of the small torches down from its brace when he noticed the darkness closing in ahead of him.

He considered calling out, considered the possible results, and bit at his lips.

Suddenly the tunnel opened onto a large room walled with cinderblock crumbling with dampness. Its ceiling, pocked and darkened with a layer of mold, bulged downward under the weight of something pressing from above. Or, he thought as he headed for the exit, from sheer time-weariness at having to sustain an illusion.

Viller was right, it had been a nest, he decided. A 'gang had laboriously connected the cellars of a number of fallen houses. And from time to time he spotted at the limits of his torchlight rusted wide pipes jammed up into the earthen ceilings, air ducts crude but effective, and keeping any 'Dogs from spotting the nest. He shrugged in slight admiration for the rats' ingenuity, but could not understand how they could have chosen, freely chosen, to live this way. The city, for all its pretense and sterility, was, for the moment, a progression more comfortable, and easier on the stomach.

The torch sputtered, and sparks began drifting to die in the air.

He began searching for doorways that had not been blocked up, boarded, jammed shut with huge boulders dug out of the walls.

There was a reason, he told himself, why he needed Yenkin back, and possibly the rat, but as the flame finally sputtered once, spat and vanished, he could not for the life of him think of the answer.

Yenkin watched, detached, as Viller tugged impatiently at what seemed to be a mass of tangled roots dangling from one wall. He was sweating, he was tired, and his legs were trembling a threat to collapse beneath him. His head ached where it had been struck, and he would not have been surprised if he had learned he had been mildly concussed. Not that he cared any longer. He had done his heroic measure for the outland symphony, had made sure that Raille would be able to escape from that room.

But now Raille was gone, and that man was dead in his bubbling blood.

They had watched through aged cracks in the door, and when it was done and Raille staggered out of view, Viller had grabbed his arm and dragged him halfway through the tunnel before he could find the use of his own feet and trail after him as best he could. He had no other choice but to follow. To stay with the corpse, or to make a try through the woods outside would have been inevitably fatal–he had no sense of direction, could never have returned to the city unaided. To rely, then, on the rat, was his only recourse.

Viller struggled with the matted roots.

"Nice place this," he muttered without turning around. "Many heads, lots of shags. Must have been chased is all. Too big for all to stop flying all the same time."

"What are you talking about?" Ty asked, his head beginning a rhythmic throbbing.

The rat spread his arms to encompass the small room, whose walls still held sagging strips of unidentifiable paneling. "Nest, hom, nest. Big, many rats, took a long time doing the roads here, a long time. This," and he tugged hard at the roots, dirt from the ceiling trailing down onto his head, "the way we get out. No ends either side, see, no ends but where the hom is dead. This way to the outside road."

Ty brightened somewhat. "Listen, you are taking me back to the city, aren't you?"

Viller shook his head sorrowfully. "The venner he could have got me in, soaped, cut, nice. Not you, hom, not you. Me for the hillands and another nest. Maybe next year I hit Wash or York. Not now. Too many guns out there, not enough talk."

Ty felt the ground above him, the ground below him, rise and fall to vise him. The air was suddenly noxiously stale, and the light from the rat's torch jammed into the floor was a sickly pale white.

Suddenly the rootmaze pulled loose and fell toward the rat, who leaped out of the way before he was buried. Beyond was a small hole, barely large enough for a child to walk upright, and the rat dropped immediately to his hands and knees and grinned back over his shoulder.

"Hom, stay or not, your choice. I like sun."

He vanished, the hardened soles of his feet the last thing Ty saw before the sudden realization that he was finally alone goaded him into following. Freezing once as his head tucked into the hole, thinking he heard faint rustlings of pursuit coming from the direction he'd just left. He listened, strained, turning his head like a prowling bird, and decided it was more wishful thinking than someone's boots. He kicked over the torch and crawled.

Feeling small clots and clumps of dirt fall to his head, neck, down his collar, onto his back, work damply below his waistband. Beneath his hands the earth was dry and hard, poked through with dulled stones. There was no light ahead that he could see, but the tunnel sloped downward in steplike starts. Once he went down to his elbows and could smell the stench of his fear. Again he stumbled and went to his shoulders, nearly shrieking when something small, something alive, scuttled across his cheek, past his ear and into his hair.

He could hear the rat breathing heavily in front of him.

He used the sound as a light.

And when it stopped, he stopped. A handsbreadth at a time, finally, moving forward until he reached a sharp bend in the tunnel where it doubled back, doubled again, twice, three times more. Zigzagging, and suddenly permitting a light. Oval light, cracked with dark streaks.

He nearly rose to his feet in his hurry to run, and when he had plunged into the open air, he was grabbed by two strong hands that threw him to one side behind a thick wall of laurel.

"No tongues," Viller said, his eyes narrow, his teeth chattering.

Ty said nothing, only lifted his head and saw through a break in the branches a landcar lurching along a battered road. It stopped less than thirty meters from where they were lying. The gulldoors flexed and he saw Gaito slide out. Viller hissed, pressed at Ty's shoulder and slipped away. Ty struggled to raise himself to his knees and glanced around the forest floor for something he could use as a weapon. As long as Gaito and the others in the vehicle didn't see him, he was safe enough, he supposed; but a flash of red hair in the back seat made him forget his safety.

And as he was reaching for a length of dead branch that might have some use as a club, Shanlon burst out of the tunnel behind him, cursing loudly.

Gaito looked up.

James took the tobac cylinder offered by Degaldon and thumbed it lit, drew on it and watched the first gray flare of smoke waft into the Consul's eyes.

Degaldon did nothing. He only waited. An increase in the murmur of voices from below indicated the arrival of the day's first visitors.

"Tell me something, Consul," James said, deference markedly absent from the tone of his voice, "is Consul Torre or General Manquila going to get control of Usam's new government?"

"You have no right to know, Captain," the Consul said, striding toward the lifttube as he brushed at his clothes.

"Then," James said after him, "will it be Faux? Canam and Usam both?"

Degaldon stopped, but did not turn around.

James crimped the nic between his lips to keep them from smiling. "What are you hoping for, Consul?" he said when he had the nerve. "War, or peace?"

Seven

Shanlon blinked rapidly in the bright light, was stunned into silence by the frustrated dark rage he saw in Yenkin's face. The old man was crouched on hands and knees behind a screen of brush, and looking from him to something on the other side, and down. He listened to the sound of his own voice echoing into the trees and silence, then dropped and scrambled forward until he was at Yenkin's side. Through a gap in the thickly leaved branches he saw a man in uniform hurriedly directing two others to either side of him, all three apparently from a landcar stalled at the bottom of the slope. Two of the men had handguns, the third a long blade casing. On the roadside of the vehicle was a fourth man with light hair, leaning on the low roof and talking with someone he could not see inside.

Yenkin grabbed at Shanlon's shoulder and pulled him close. "Caro," he whispered harshly, and pointed. Then he pushed Shanlon away and retrieved the thick branch he apparently was using as a club.

Shanlon looked back over his shoulder. The hillside he had stumbled out on was steep and heavily forested, yet he could still make out remains of the foundation under which the exit tunnel had been dug. He was unable to locate the place where his own uniform had died, and he imagined from the time it took that it was probably on the hill's other side.

Yenkin grunted then as the incautious thrashing of the three men indicated they were fanning out in pincers, and Shanlon, after a quick thanking slap on the old man's back, darted back toward the tunnel's mouth, veered suddenly to his right and plunged into the brush that pushed against the flaking concrete foundation. He worked his way uphill as rapidly as he could with a minimum of noise and, at the far end of the knee-high wall, ducked around the corner and lay as best he could on his stomach. He could not see through the leaves and branches except for brief glimpses, but he listened to the progress of his pursuit and the arrogantly loud shouts of direction and taunts. A name came clear, and he spat dryly. They knew who he was, then, and though Caro had obviously been marked for saving, there was nothing he himself could tell them that would keep him alive.

Listening.

Noting with a ghost of a grin their eagerness. They would be too busy, he thought, to work on one at a time. It would be either him or Yenkin, then, who would be free to maneuver. He grinned. Not him. It would have to be the old man.

But hopefully not so old that he couldn't swing that club.

The light began to fade as the clouds moved in.

Yenkin suddenly called out, was cut off abruptly, and there was someone racing toward him, over the packed dirt that had filled in the walls. He rolled onto his back, a lick at his lips, and as soon as he saw the shadow of a leg he reached up and yanked, pulled the uniform over his head and into a bush, was on his chest with a forearm across his throat and his free hand grabbing at the black hair. He slammed the head back once, twice, and the uniform slumped still. Immediately, Shanlon snatched the man's handgun from his fist and scrabbled away on hands and knees, up the hill again and angling to his right, the handgun stretched in front of him while he slapped away branches and fought the burning in his lungs and the dizziness that made him blink.

Across a narrow cleared space, and he grabbed onto the trunk of a winterbent birch, spun himself to a halt, squinting, crouching, then freezing when he heard an angry hiss of discovery. Looking left, right, as the air shaded from gray to twilight. He opened his mouth to breathe in forced pants.

"Raille!" a voice called. "Raille, the old man's dead."

He shook his head to clear it of the roaring.

Listening, waiting. If the man in the center had been the one he had stunned, the hunter on his right would be trying to circle to close. He looked over his shoulder, straining.

"Raille, listen, we only want to take you back to the Hill."

Uniformed rats. Rats. Where, he wondered, was Viller?

He glanced back to the foundation and saw a man standing, one hand on his hip, the other idly holding a handgun. Shanlon looked at the weapon in his own hand and smiled. Two, he thought. Then the man was waiting for him to answer, to expose himself. He dropped lower and turned slowly on his heels until he was facing uphill.

"Raille, look, we're not going to hurt you or the girl. There's no sense in making it hard for yourself. You've a shagging poor chance, you know. The old man's dead."

A flash, only a flash, but it was dark blue and moving. Shanlon brought the handgun close to his face, its grip thick and awkward. He had no idea what charge it had left, but there was no time for testing. He stretched out his arm and sighted, following the flicker of uniform as it made its way past a screen of oak and brush. He led it to a clear space beyond, and waited.

"Raille, you're all—"

Waited.

"Shanlon, I'm all right!"

He turned instinctively and saw Yenkin standing, brandishing his ridiculous club as he stumbled toward the foundation. There was a glint of bright red on his face, and the man who had been calling whirled around. Shanlon moved without thinking, dropping forward and firing, the nearly inaudible hiss of his weapon extending like a snake's tongue. It struck the man high on his chest, dropped him with arms flailing and his own shot burning harmlessly into the air. And before he reached the ground, Shanlon was standing again.

The uniform he'd been tracking was standing in the open and staring.

Shanlon grinned and aimed.

"Wait a minute, wait a minute," the man said, and his arms went up, the left too far back however and Shanlon saw the blade catch the last of the light before the wind began howling as though it had been straining, had been loosed. Leaves flew and branches whipped, and the left arm came down as Shanlon pushed himself off his right foot, firing, watching the blade chip at the tree that had been behind him, watching the uniform double up, drop, roll once and stare blind.

"Shan!"

He made his way quickly back down the slope, stopping at the man he had killed and taking his gun, then clambering over the foundation to crouch beside Ty.

"You're an idiot," he said.

"I just wanted you to know."

"Sure," he said, and they looked to the road where Harrow was standing, on the nearside of the landcar now with Caro in front of him. She was pale but calm, the wind pushing her hair into her face, tugging at her blouse and trousers as she squinted up toward them.

"Raille," Harrow called, "I know you can see me."

"Stand up," Shanlon whispered to Ty, who stared at him stupidly until he was shoved with a fist. "Stand up, you idiot!"

Yenkin rose slowly and moved to one side, away from the bush so he was fully exposed. His club at his side, loose and swinging.

Harrow watched but did nothing. The trees overhead whipped and lashed, and Shanlon saw the instinctive pull of his head. Then he began moving, a pace to the right, one to the left, bringing Caro's head in front of his face, away, and back again. His eyes scanned the hillside nervously. Yenkin took one step down, another, and a third before Harrow screamed at him to halt.

"Stop!" Shanlon whispered, the force of the wind preventing his voice from carrying. "His gun's in her back."

"Raille! I'll give you the girl, but you have to let me go."

Shanlon stared at his own weapon, knowing it was useless for all the practice he had as long as Harrow kept moving. He would never have the opportunity for that perfect shot he would need; anything else, any other try would be Caro's . . . he turned away and punched at the ground, heard a confusion of shouting and looked up, stood up, and saw Caro lying on the ground, Yenkin racing down the slope and Harrow . . . Harrow bent backward over the hood of the landcar with a flailing Viller wrapped around him. Before Shanlon could reach him, Yenkin had dropped to the road, had lifted his club and lowered it. Viller jumped away, and Harrow was still.

"Nice, hom," the rat said.

Shanlon reached out a hand and pulled the girl to her feet. The wind was stronger, but she ignored it as she looked into his face, then to the rat and Ty, who were standing quietly over the uniform. And despite the sudden trembling in his legs and the difficulty in swallowing, Shanlon grinned and tried a nonchalant shrug.

"If you say magic," Caro said, "I'll have your eyes."

Amazing, James thought, how normal it all is. There had been no reports of city fighting for the past three hours, and the newses had picked up on the Meditcom/Eurepac conference instead, with one or two items on the spacefacs thrown in. He walked to the windowwall once, stared down at the deserted plaza, then across at the hospital that seemed to shimmer in the darkening air.

"Captain," Degaldon said, "I've been thinking."

I'll bet you have, he thought, stifling a smile before he turned around. His reply, however, was forestalled when a Court Star Justice rose and stepped from the antechamber's lifttube. His head was covered with a silver-embossed skullcap, the rest of him cloaked in red-trimmed black robes. He nodded almost absently at the two men, and Degaldon hurried to the office door to announce his arrival.

The horizon flared a brief bluewhite.

The Consul then moved to a pedestaled comunit by the lifttube and spoke into it softly.

James watched him. Since Faux had ordered him to stand ceremony outside the office, he had been working at a way to get out of the chamber. But he had discarded already the notion of grabbing someone within the Hill itself; to tackle a Justice, or a Senator, or even a Rep with a story of a coup and war would only have him burned before he had finished. Failing that, he would be brought back to the underdome office where his witnesses would find Alton and the Consuls working diligently to stave off a war on another continent. To be believed he wanted absolute proof, and the only way he would get that was if one of the Consuls broke, or Manquila threw too much weight around too fast.

"Quite a bit of company down there," he said, returning slowly to the center of the vast room.

"Only a handful," Degaldon muttered, preoccupied with whatever he was seeing on the screen. "A few fat colonels who think they have ambitions."

James kept silent. If the colonels below were the only ones connected with Faux, then the half-dozen Servicemen he had also seen were aware only of the emergency at hand: the rats. His chest suddenly felt light, and lightly chilled. He tried swallowing, tried a steady pacing that brought him to the windowwall and back to the center of the room again. His hands went numb, then feeling returned with a prickling that made him clench them into fists, open them, clench and spike his nails into his palms.

He stared at the lounges from which he had taken the cushions for Bendal's deathbed.

He stared at the blind eyes of the screens on their stands.

"Time moves slowly, Captain."

He nodded and blinked as lightning brightened the room's dim illumination. His reflection in the glass and, to his left, Degaldon standing by the 'tube, waiting for the Justice to take his leave. Ghosts in ice, he thought.

Lightning, and the hospital.

It was impulse rather than planned reaction that moved him to the Consul's side, quietly, accepting the offer of another nic and, while thumbing it, snatching the handgun from the man's belt. He stepped back, though only a pace, and waited for him to try something stupid. Instead, the Consul smiled and shook his head.

"It isn't charged," Degaldon said. "The general doesn't actually trust us."

"Shall I try it?"

His free hand lifted his mask into place, set it and tapped it lightly. He was unreadable now, and knew that Degaldon would be at the disadvantage without direct eye contact. He also knew that the lightning flares would reflect off the silver and give him a headless look.

The Consul, recovering, bowed mockingly with his head, his hands loose at his sides. "Well. Now that you have me, Captain, what do you intend to do? Storm into the office and save the Premier? I think it unnecessary to assure you that even with that weapon, three against one in such close quarters is not the best of odds."

"Four," James said. "You're still alive."

Degaldon paled and his eyes flicked over James's shoulder, wavered when their gaze returned to his mask before lowering to the floor. James grinned and turned briskly when the door behind him slid open and the Justice walked out, his robes barely clearing the threshold before the door closed again. He was preoccupied with a sheath of papers in his hands, and it was time enough for James to put hand to hip, covering the handgun as though it were still on his belt. Then he moved to Degaldon's side with a low warning hiss. When the Justice looked up, finding his way barred to the 'tube, James nodded sharply. "We'll accompany you part of the way, sir, if you don't mind." The Court Star official only shrugged, moved to the 'tube and stepped in. James took Degaldon's arm and held it tightly, pushed him to the lip and paused only a moment before letting him go. "I can come down burning," he said harshly, "and you can't run fast enough."

At the anticipated shudder, he pushed lightly, stepped out on the reception floor only moments after the Consul. The Justice, having accepted his escort, was waiting, and the three made their way toward the next, primary drop.

James was pleased, though he could not help the tension that locked his joints and fluttered in his stomach. The building-wide room was, as Degaldon had said, sparsely occupied. To one side and close to the 'tube that led to the office were several cots, and on three were colonels playing cards desultorily; two others were speaking softly by one of the pillars near the outside wall and a sixth was arguing with a Service noncom. A handful of other Servicemen were gathered around a comunit pedestal, and only one glanced in their direction as the trio of officials moved across the floor.

The thunder was loud in the dim open room, and James wanted to run, to push Consul and Justice into the 'tube before one of the colonels saw the panic in Degaldon's face.

A few seconds, he thought; just a few seconds . . .

"Consul? Excuse me, Consul, is anything wrong?"

Faux held his hands clasped tightly in front of his mouth as he stared at the storm that had begun with the wind. Alton pushed at papers on his desk, then swiveled around to watch the tiered screens since his alternative was the wolf-hungry look in Torre's dark eyes. And the sneer at Manquila's lips as he whispered to himself. There were 'Dogs covering the action now, and their progress over the fighting in the hills was a series of quick jerky snaps as they dodged the fire from below.

"Tell me something," Alton said, tugging thoughtfully at one ear lobe and turning his head. "How did you get the rats to fight?"

He hoped for an answer, and prayed for a long one. When that fool Justice had left with his disposition for prisoners and Torre had shoved the door closed almost on his heels, he had had only a glimpse of the antechamber, but sufficient to see that Thrush had set on his mask and was standing rather close to the Consul Degaldon. It wasn't until a few moments later that he realized the captain's hand was resting on his handgun. And James did not have one, not even for show.

"It wasn't all that difficult," Faux finally said, leaning his palms on the sill and staring down at the plaza. "Most of them, of course, are my . . . our own men, just enough to get the pack into the cities. The others . . . true rats, from hardnests. It took a while, but bribes and promises of heavens of their own can do wonders to a rat who's facing execution if he ever shows up again in the hands of . . . well, of a Blue."

"Work long?"

"Long enough to weed out the rats who were only larking."

"I see," Alton said. "Then, once the Service moved out of the city, your bogus rats become fighters on our side."

Faux nodded, his face still hidden.

"And all the other cities?"

"The same. It doesn't take much, Mordan, it doesn't take much. Your own army is used against you, in a way no one could fault. They'll be too busy fighting anything but rats for the next several months. And those rats, you see, once the word gets around, aren't going to just throw away what they've been wanting for years. Decades. Practically centuries. The Service will be busy, doing exactly what you want."

Torre looked to the map, the timepieces, and leaned against the door. "Soon," he said. "A couple of hours. They'll start talking soon. We might even know by midnight, here."

Faux snorted and shook his head.

Alton knew, then, how nervous he was, how close to the end of his endurance he had come. He wished there was a way he could throw a safe snag into that conference, but he was too tired and would have to depend on Thrush for the burden. He turned to the deskcom with a look to the general, and asked quietly if anyone else was waiting down below. When no one answered, he grew cold, colder when Faux heard him repeat the question and turned to wait for a reply. When there was none, he scowled.

And in the silence, the voice of the storm.

"General," Faux said, "you'd better go down."

"General," the Premier said, sharply enough to turn the Service around. "Go down, but you'd better be . . . careful."

The markings were clear where the landcar had passed before once it had left the main road, but immediately the spot where Harrow had turned around had been reached, Caro could do nothing to show Shanlon the way. She only knew, she told him twice, that they had said they were bringing her to New Hill. For what purpose she was not told, except that she would meet a friend, a man named Manquila or something close to that. None of the three men knew who he was and, after a useless bout of speculation, they fell silent. Listening, to the scrape of prying branches as the road became a trail became a path that threatened to vanish as the wind dropped twigs and leaves and, finally, rain. The temperature dropped. The headlights shattered into flashes of white.

She was seated in front, Yenkin and the rat behind her, and she kept her arms pressed to her sides, away from the cold metal of the door and the condensation that ran with the rain down the window. And in the silence, and in the thunder, she felt for the first time the dirt that had clung to her, streaked, darkened her hands and face where they'd been scratched when Viller's feet kicked her away as he dropped from the tree onto Harrow. She scrubbed her hands dryly, pushed them impatiently through her hair, and gave up, sighing, wondering instead how Shanlon was planning to storm a city already under seige. She heard at various times explosions she knew weren't thunder, and concluded that the Service had driven most of the rebels out of the Fringes and into the wild. But as much as the thought might have comforted her, she still did not know how they would manage to get back in. Certainly not together, she guessed, and for the moment had no desire to leave Raille behind.

Or Ty, who was working and failing to stifle his groans. He'd been struck on the same side of the head as before, this time a gash opening and bleeding freely. Shan had torn the sleeves from his shirt and bound them about the old man's head, holding the blood back long enough for it to clot. She glanced over her shoulder and back, and he was waxen, his lines deepened by dried red and dirt, the already tattered cloth marked with a dark stain she watched for signs of spreading. The rat was holding his hand, muttering, stroking, and Yenkin responded with a slight brave grin that made her turn away, to Shanlon and the rain.

"What are you going to do?" she asked, wiping a hand over her lips, her chin, resting it on her thigh.

Yenkin laughed suddenly and said, "Escape," and Shan grinned, looked to her quickly and, this time, she returned it.

"There is a way into the city," he said when she asked him again. "And once I'm in there, I'm going to forget about making public speeches on my innocence, at least for a while. There's a woman I know, a nurse in Hospital Prime. For one thing, she can do something about Ty's head, so he doesn't look so barbaric."

"Like a rat," Yenkin said, and laughed weakly.

"Hey," Viller said, and Ty slapped at his leg.

"Have you known this . . . nurse long?"

"Long enough to know that she won't believe I've done any of this. We can use her to get information, like where I stand, and maybe she'll help us get you to see the right people. If there are any of them left."

She didn't respond. He had told her, with apologies and retrenching, what he had surmised with the clue Ty had given him. She could not believe it, refused to acknowledge that all this had happened from the murder of her father. He speculated that perhaps the Senator had known and opposed the idea from the beginning, or had been used, whether he knew or not, as the sacrificial lamb to be thrown to the masses for their fury it would bring. For their confusion, just enough to keep things and the world off balance sufficiently long for whoever was in charge to do what he wanted. This Manquila, perhaps, or the Consuls seen coming out of Ty's restaurant.

Caro thought it was too much and Shan was grasping. It was understandable, she told him, all his raging desire to find out the truth, but it failed miserably on several points of logic.

But logic, he'd said with a grin nearly wry, had nothing to do with politics and people.

"You said there was a way to get into the city. How?"

"I don't know," he answered, "but our rat back there does."

He braked suddenly, then, and the rain slashed through the foliage, blotting out the light, running down windshield and windows in sheets that cast on Ty's face a shimmering shadow that fell in darkedged waves. Caro turned in her seat as Shanlon did in his, and they looked through the gap to Viller, who had released Yenkin's hand and had pressed into the corner. His hair had fallen back over his face in clinging dark strands, and he poked a hand into the maze, pulled it out and spat.

"He tells us," Shanlon said, though he did not look at her, "that he fell into the nest on his way to the city. Out of all the nests in the hills around here he fell into ours, renovated for the comfort of rats not his brothers. Now maybe that part is true. I kind of think it is. But I haven't liked him since the beginning, and he knows something we don't that we have to know. Tell me something, cityname Viller, how had you planned on getting into Wash?"

"Fringe, hom, like all the others do."

"Sure," Shanlon said. "Just walk in."

"There *are* rats fighting," Caro said suddenly. "There *has* to be. An army big enough to cover all the places you said were being attacked . . . . it couldn't be hidden for that long."

"That's right, Mistress," Shanlon said. "So. We have . . . some rats, at least. And rats know what rats do, don't they, cityname Viller?"

"Hom, you talk."

"No," Shanlon said, "you talk. And talk right. If you're as young as you look and say you are, if you're telling us the truth about that much, then you haven't been in any nest so long that you've lost control of the mother tongue."

"Shag!" Viller said, starting to lunge, but Ty suddenly lifted a leg and caught him across his chest, dropping him back, gasping.

Thunder, but Caro ignored it. She only saw in Viller a part, a real part this time, of what had moved to destroy her life. Before anyone could stop her, then, she reached between the front seats and took a handful of the rat's hair, yanked at it viciously while he yowled and bent double, yanked harder and brought his head between the seats. Shanlon replaced her hand with a grip on his neck, and he passed his other hand slowly in front of the rat's eyes.

"Remember the magic blade," he said. "You should know I haven't lost it."

"Hom–"

Caro slapped him, put a palm to his forehead and shoved until he fell back and was sitting in his corner, jumping when a nearby tree split loudly and whitely into flames quickly doused by the rain.

"All right," he said.

The whine was gone, the pitch lowered, and Caro stared at him, wanting to weep.

Someone was standing beside him. Patiently. Waiting. But it was safe in the dark and he didn't want to open his eyes, content instead with the scent of her skin, her uniform, the odors of the hospital she carried with her and were buried beneath something that kept them at bay. He felt the touch on his shoulder, the slight shaking, and sighed as his eyes flickered open, focused, and smiled. She fussed meaninglessly, then, with the diagmed beside his bed until a doctor, pacing the aisles of the still-crowded ward, moved through the double door into the next, trailed by two nurses blank-faced and cold.

"All right," he said, the smile moving to his lips.

"They're rats," she told him simply, her face defeated now and tired.

"No," he said, whispering so low she had to bend over his chest and pull at his sheet.

"But they were, Delan, I saw them. Plain rats, nothing more."

"Can't be."

"Delan, you're impossible. I almost got stopped a dozen times, but I know what I saw. Rats. Just rats."

He grinned, using his eyes to trace the line of her jaw, the disturbing dark pouches already bulging under her tired dark eyes, and the gentle, too gentle curve of her hair as it scooped over her ear in a single black wave.

"But . . . well, there is something else."

He nodded, then abruptly groaned when she poked him as a nurse paused in her rounds at the foot of the bed. Morag shrugged with a passing hand over Delan's face and moved one of the probes from his neck to his chest. The nurse moved away, but Delan saw her frown.

"What," he prompted.

"The ashers," she said. "They've been all over the place yesterday and today."

"So?"

"One of the drivers—they work out of here, you see—he said they were ordered to flare anyone a Service officer declares is dead."

"Anyone?"

She nodded. "And that's where they go, those ones you think you saw. At least here in the city they're not leaving anyone behind."

"But who the hell is *they?*" he said, lips tight and teeth clenched. "What's going on?"

"But I showed you the news."

He shook his head. "I'm sorry, but it doesn't smell right."

"What?"

He grinned again. "One of these days, Morag, I'll tell you all about it. In someplace . . . quiet. But take my word for it now–it doesn't smell right."

His left hand became a fist and he pounded it lightly on the edge of his cast, thankful they'd cut it back from his neck but still frustrated and angry that it left him immobile.

"I have half a mind," she said, sensing his exasperation, "to run right over there and knock on some doors."

"In this rain?"

"Through the tunnel, idiot, for the big men who get sick."

"And who would you talk to? Who could you trust? Maybe I'm just imagining it, you see, and maybe you were wrong about–"

"No," she said, shaking her head. "I wasn't wrong about that."

"But still, you can't go over there, can you?"

She shrugged, and laid a palm to his cheek. "Relax," she said. "I'll think of something."

Less than a meter, less than his shadow.

A gray-haired colonel rose from the card game and laid a hand on the shoulder of an officer beside him. Then he slowly lifted his hand to his side.

"Consul? Excuse me, Consul, but is there anything wrong?"

James winced at the lurch in his stomach, but Degaldon did not miss a step.

"Consul . . . ?"

The voice had become less querulous than commanding, and the room became silent, suddenly; perspiration broke beneath James's mask, and time began to move in nearly audible clicks. One for each pace, one for each breath.

"Consul, please."

Suddenly Degaldon spun to one side and his arms spread in pleading. "No!" he screamed as the colonel pulled his weapon free of his belt. James immediately darted between Consul and Justice, grabbing at the latter's robes and shoving him at Degaldon as he leaped for the 'tube. The Justice grunted, his papers flung into the air; Degaldon, trying an off-balance lunge for James, tripped over the man's leg, sprawled and rose just as the colonel fired, catching him just below his left knee. He screamed and went down, but James had already vanished into the 'tube, head and weapon up as he waited for the first face foolish enough to check his descent. He exited on the next level and raced to another 'tube, dropped four more, changed, and dropped until he judged his time short for a cutting of the power. He moved, then, through a maze of offices and cubicles, marching briskly, his weapon jammed out of sight in his waistband. No one stopped him, few even bothered to glance up at him; though the emergency had drawn most of the Service guards out of New Hill, James decided those who were left went about their business maintaining calm and the soporific of the status quo, and his Liaison patch would keep him from being asked questions about his assignment.

He passed the Hall of Representatives, then, and heard the commotion inside, imagined it ten times louder in the Senate Chamber, and grinned as he nodded to the brace of guards at the huge oaken doors.

A woman raised a hand as though to interrupt him. His silver mask glared at her, and her hand wavered back to her desk as he passed.

Finally, with a backward glance down a convoluted green corridor, he pushed aside a door leading to a stairwell, grabbed onto a polished brass railing and took the marble steps two at a time as he wound blackly down toward the sublevels where the war shelters and file vaults were maintained. He knew it would not take long for anyone to track his escape, but he was counting on the colonels' training and their implication in the coup to stifle their movements somewhat until one of them shook loose his stupor and came up a reason valid enough for pursuit, one to keep the regular Service from divining their guilt.

He lost track of the levels after several panting minutes, waiting only until he was positive he was below the plaza before sagging into a corner and letting reaction take over. And it was as he had expected: the trembling that made him feel chilled in spite of the perspiration, the dry surging of his stomach and the rasp in his throat as he tried to swallow, and a great wash of weariness that tempted him to sleep. He stripped off the mask and wiped a sleeve over his face, a hand roughly through his hair. His eyes lost focus for a moment, cleared, and he spotted a single door on the landing, emblazoned with a meter-high golden H. He stared at it dumbly for a moment, grinned and pushed himself from the wall. Though there was no guard on this side, he suspected the other and stood to one side when he set thumb to the oval plate on the frame. A hesitation, and the glossed blue metal slid into the wall while he nearly closed his eyes in anticipation of a confrontation. And when nothing happened but a gust of cool air, he stepped over the threshold and into the tunnel, seeing no one at all along its entire length.

A single laugh, then, and a gratefully deep breath.

Faux had just made his first serious mistake.

From ceiling to floor the slightly curved tunnel was tiled a faint luminescent white, the illumination blurring into a haze as it passed beneath the plaza. Behind him the end, and a lifttube wider than usual to allow for gurneys and diagmeds, attendants and powerchairs. There was a guardstation beside it–empty. When he checked, he saw this was the 'tube's last level, and he could hear no sounds of descent from the levels above. He searched quickly for a powerplate to immobilize the 'tube, but he could find nothing but wasted time and, after an ineffectual slam of a fist against the transparent wall, he turned, and he ran.

His footsteps harsh in the soft silence of the tunnel, his shadow crawling beside him, ahead of him, behind him, racing now with worry of discovery toward the haze that receded as he approached.

Slowing as the haze dispersed and he saw that the tunnel ended in a corridor branching left and right.

Again he slid on his mask, fastened the handgun to his beltclip, and smoothed palms over his uniform, his hair, each other. He moved around the corner and it was as though he had stepped through a curtain. Immediately there was noise. Quiet noise. Footsteps, murmurings, the sounds of muffled wheels on the trackless floor. He walked past several doors, opened to comfortable rooms whose mainstays were large beds and wall-sized diagmeds. They were all empty that he could see, and there was no one in any of the alcove guard cages beside each door. We have a healthy damned government, he thought, turned another corner and stopped.

There was a series of lifttubes scattered irregularly down the left wall of the corridor, all of them marked with nothing but color-codes. On the right wall a desk, but no attendant.

"Now what?" he muttered, and moved forward cautiously. For the moment safely out of the Hill, he realized that in his escape he had not given a thought to whom he would contact once safety had been achieved. And, as he stood in front of a 'tube marked in brown, he realized that there was, in fact, no one. Bendal was dead and because Alton was Usam, there was no other Consul from that Noram sector. Talle was dead, Shanlon surely so, and he was positive that by now the word had been delivered to Service and Blue that he was some sort of dangerous fugitive, not to be taken prisoner.

Again the chill, and he stepped into the 'tube, watched the levels pass, saw glimpses of white, of green, of doctors, of nurses, and finally, when his stomach could no longer stand the lifting, he stepped out into a corridor lined with beds, filled with patients, and nurses who turned to stare at him in undisguised amazement. He took a nervous step back, and a short and fat woman bustled around a diagmed, her hand raised to stop him.

"Yes?" he said, glad for the safety of the mask and his uniform.

"Are you looking for anyone special"–she glanced at his shoulder–"Captain? One of your men, is that right?"

He grinned, but nodded curtly. "That's correct. But it seems I've gotten myself onto the wrong floor. I'm sorry to have disturbed you." He turned to leave, but she took his arm lightly.

"They're all over the place, Captain, as you can well imagine," she said, almost apologetically. "In fact, the only patient we have on this floor who's not a civilian is a Blue. I gather he's something special or he wouldn't be here." She looked at him, waiting, then glanced around his arm and smiled. "Wait, there's Morag. Maybe she can help you find your man." She lowered her voice, then, and ducked her head. "But don't be too stiff with her, Captain. She's been on duty since the fighting started–as you have, I'll bet–and she's practically asleep on her feet. This isn't her wardfloor, but she seems to be in charge of that Blue." She grinned. "We don't dare ask, or she'll take our heads off. Just give her the name of the man you want. If anyone can help you in this . . . this Hell, she can."

James nodded helplessly as the nurse called to Morag, and frowned briefly when he saw the woman start and look to either side of her as though she were seeking some way to escape. He tried to think of some excuse to leave without causing comment, but his weariness dulled his thinking. Time, he realized, was what he needed; Faux would be furious, but not overly concerned. He must know, as James had already learned, that there was little the captain could do to jeopardize the revolution, in the Hill or out of it. He would bide his time, then, and James decided that he would play out the game, give himself room to think and to maneuver. He would be gentlemanly and anonymous and, as soon as he could, get out of the hospital and into the streets.

"What do you want?" Morag said, almost rudely, as soon as the fat nurse had lumbered away.

"I was looking for–"

"Did that general send you back here?" Her face was darker now, flushed with restrained anger. "He almost killed him the last time, you know, with all those fool questions. Why doesn't he let the man recover if he's so important?"

"Important? I'm afraid I don't understand what you're talking about, Mistress."

Morag's hands lifted in twin fists, then clasped at her waist in an odd strained primness. "Captain . . . no one sent you here?"

"No, ma'am. I was just looking for one of my men who was hurt in–"

"You didn't come to see Sergeant Caine?"

James became impatient. The woman was prattling.

"He thinks he's dead," she muttered.

Suddenly, James sensed that this nurse was somehow afraid. And as she turned half away, searching blindly down the hall, not meeting the glances of the other nurses or answering the calls of any of the patients, he wondered about that general, and the questions, and . . .

"Nurse," he said, "did the general come right at the start, when the fighting began, I mean?"

She nodded, almost absently.

"Nurse, listen to me." His voice was sharp and she looked back to him, startled. "Was the general's name Manquila?"

"I don't know," she snapped. "He was Cenam is all I know, and he was very rude."

James tapped a finger against the lower edge of his mask, took the nurse's arm and led her away from the 'tube. "Nurse, I'd like to see this man Caine, if that's all right. And you can believe me when I tell you that no general sent me here."

"They're called mice," Viller said with a smile that was bitter. "Usually women or small men who can pass as boys. They make the trip from nest to nest, like newshawks only they carry it all in their heads. The hardnests use them mostly, to see if the Blues have started one of their sweeps. The other nests don't usually bother, they have no use for citynews, they don't want it. Only the hards have to know if they're going to be swept. When I got out, see, I was picked up by a hard–only I didn't know it because I was new–he said later he was running from murder somewhere up north. He brought me to the nest because I could read and write and do things with a comunit when it broke down. I heard them talking–this was at least a year ago–about weapons and things, and then I realized they were planning something against one of the cities on the Big River. But even the hardnests don't keep rats who don't want to stay, so I got out after a few months and came east, found another nest and heard the same thing, only this time it was Wash they were after. Something about finding a nestheaven no one would take from them. It sounded good. A show of strength and purpose and shag like that. The hardnests would take the lead, see, and we would go in after, mess up a little and get out before we were flared. There was supposed to be creds, too, at the end of it, so I didn't mind much. I don't know what part of the city I went in on, I never been here before; but when I saw what the hards were doing to the Blues and even some of the people, I wasn't dumb enough to think it just a show of any strength. Not then. It was for real. See, there were others around, too, homs not rats, and when we got in there were normal people, and they came outside and they were cut down, burned, hacked, whatever they fell into. There was an explosion somewhere over my head–I was just making noise and faces with some rats I was with–and I got knocked down, stunned. My mind took a vacation, and when I came back I turned and ran. Shows are one thing, venner, but blood's something else."

"But you didn't go through the Fringe."

"Under, under. Cityfolk forget a lot, venner. They don't have to remember. The transtunnels used to come out this way, see, but they were closed off when the Fringes went up. Lots of nests in the parts that didn't fall down. Those hards that were moving us, they dug through, big enough for 'cats and landcars. It was when we came up that the fighting started. This head on this rat knows where it's going, never gets lost, not in the dark, not in the sun. Like a star I can follow even in the light. I ran with a couple of others and we got out. Real rats we were. Once in the trees we forked. I don't know where they went, I don't know if they got where they were going. Me . . . I got lucky."

"You did, Viller. From the sounds of it, the Service is finally making the move to clean."

"Listen, Viller, did you ever hear anything about taking New Hill?"

"You mean the government thing, Mistress? No, no, no one said that. In, fight, out, only the fighting was worse. How could we, anyway? There weren't enough rats to fill a Fringe, not a city. In and out, Mistress, that's all it was supposed to be."

"Then . . . you can get back in?"

"Sure, venner, no problem. Viller never gets lost, remember? I got a star in my head."

"Then you'll take us, won't you. Because if you don't, you can wish your star good morning."

Eight

The flotilla massed, merged, turned afternoon to night and vanquished the heat. Along the Fringe Kilometer, the wind slammed shards of charred clothing against charred walls, pinned and flapping and looking for shadows. At sporadic intervals, Blue patrols replaced Service, and the Service vanished into the black of the suburbs behind the whine of 'Dogs taking them to their units. In doorways, then, and against the buildings, the Blues huddled with shoulders hunched and lips tight, their weaponed dark cloaks slapping their thighs, their collars pressed to their necks. Many of them crouched to squat on their heels while officers paced into the open and stared through goggles into the wind, turned their backs and paced again.

In the windows above them there was light that was warm; and in the sky lightning that spat, curled, walked over the rooftops and once in a while shattered venthoods and brickcorners and snapped out the lights behind the timid warm windows.

When it rained, there was no spattering of drops to serve as a warning. There was nothing but the wind and the lightning and the cannonade of thunder—and then there was rain, hard and cold and merging into black rivers that gushed toward the drains, were caught, were swirled, were backed up into lakes when a body here and a stained cloak there stoppered the gaps that led down to the tunnels.

In the middle of New Hill Plaza a young tree barely leafed buckled, fell, was torn out of its plot and shoved in gusted strides until it came to a trembling rest against the broad marble steps that led to the public Hill chamber.

In the hospital, the contrast of warmth within and the brittle cold of the storm made patients and nurses rub at their arms, their palms, the backs of their necks. Shudder. Whimper. Look away to their wounds.

In the hills rats died, Service died, and their blood was washed pink, washed away, and staring blind eyes reflected harsh blue-white flares.

Shanlon listened and, for the second time in as many minutes, pressed a hand to the grimy wall behind him as though waiting for hints of its collapse or warnings of flood. He had no idea how long they had been wandering . . . not wandering, he corrected himself with fingers crossed at his side, but following the rat Viller toward the center of the city. The tunnel's mouth, once spotted, had not been easy to loose—a huge oval hood that had once been ornated with figures of gods and figures of people and a few that were mixed and looked like beasts. They lay crumpled and dusted at the base of the hood, and barriers of steel and wooden beams had stoppered the mouth. He had cursed, then, and lifted a hand to beat at the rat, but Viller only grinned and shoved a beam aside. They'd crawled in and followed, in the dark, in the damp, until Shanlon had called enough and slumped to the floor.

There had been no talking or speculation, but Shanlon had made sure he was the first behind Viller, less than an arm's length away, blade in its sheath ready to spit, handgun in his palm ready to hiss. Caro behind him and Ty at the rear, stumbling, falling once and groaning but refusing to stop until Shanlon made the call.

"There'll be a light up ahead, soon," Viller promised, and his voice had once again taken on the whine, as if he had forgotten.

Caro sighed relief and Yenkin echoed, but Shanlon only poked at the wall behind him and waited for collapse.

"Shan," Caro said, "are you all right?"

"Thinking," he muttered. "Catching my breath."

Thinking: he was a fool for leading these people back into hell, and more a fool for needing their company and their voices. Yet he could not have done it alone, and knew too that he would have done it regardless. Pushed around by more than the past two days, he was pushing back—and if everything worked out at least until they arrived at the hospital, no one would know him well enough to resist. It had come to him forcefully when he had entered the tunnel and left the storm and its light behind: he was no longer fighting for himself not to be killed, but for himself not to die—a difference, he thought. To be killed would end it all abruptly and in darkness; but to die and still live . . . like a Viller rat, but alone. It would be someone else in his clothes, doing his magic, sleeping his dreams. Someone else. Not Shanlon. He raised both hands and touched at his face until every curve had been examined and he knew . . . who he was.

James, he thought suddenly, I've sold all my gods.

"All right," he said loudly, "move it, Viller. Let's see that light."

Stumbling then, and the tunnel floor became less littered with debris of collapse and forgetting, reaching out and brushing at the rat's back to be sure of his presence, as Caro did to his, and Ty to hers. And round several bends before he saw in the immeasurable distance a faint green light.

"Welcome to the Fringe," Viller said.

The wind was louder, colder, snatching for their hair and clothes. When they passed the double gaps in the road above for entrance and exit they were sprayed with gusts of rain; when they came to a light that still functioned, though dimly, they stopped and looked to check on the familiar, and on Yenkin's wound.

Twice it had reopened, and the dark dried stain had spread over the makeshift bandage. The last time they looked, Caro had torn her sleeves off, thrown Shanlon's away and bound the old man again as he smiled, an old man's smile patiently waiting, as though the specter of his passing was holding his free hand. When Caro saw the look, she had to bite hard on her lips to keep from crying, averted her face to glare at the rat.

The wind slackened, picked up, and twice they detoured into tunnels the rat would not have chosen to escape the lingering odor of gas, and the small puddles of acid that clung to the floor.

"All right," Shanlon said. "Here's another, Caro."

She released her hold on Ty's wrist and scrambled up a ramp, pressing close to the wall, her face turned from the rain that slanted and drenched her. Carefully, until she vanished into the storm-laced air and returned again a few moments later.

"I'm not sure," she said. "I've never seen it before."

Shanlon scowled. He dared not leave Viller alone, but he ached to get one simple look at the outside world.

"It's not Fringe any more, though," she said, whispering and glancing up at the opening. "Keylofts and a couple of shops. I'm sorry, Shan. I just don't know."

He shook his head to hide his indecision. "Ridiculous. We could be going all around Prime and not even know it."

"Why don't we just walk up there?" Yenkin said.

"You want to try?" Shanlon asked. "The storm, patrols, the rats and fighting. There's no one walking outside now, Ty. Do you want to take the chance on some kid Blue not wanting a medal?"

"Well, one of us has to go," he insisted. "I'm not . . ." and his hand went to his head and he sagged too quickly for Caro to catch him. She knelt in front of him, Shanlon beside her as he put a hand to the old man's shoulder.

"Ty," he said.

"All right, you priest," Ty said.

Shanlon nodded and gave his handgun to Caro. That gave her two, and when he was sure she knew how to aim, how to press, he grabbed Viller and sat him against the wall, directly under a swinging green light.

"You don't trust me, hom," the rat said, no hurt in his voice.

"No," he admitted. "But you're in just as much danger as I am, see, and I wouldn't put it past you to bolt back to the trees. But you can't, you see, because I need what you know."

"You said that already, hom, and–"

"Yes, but this is something different." He put a fist against the rat's chest and pushed, just enough. "Stay," he said quietly. "Mistress Talle is just nervous enough to kill us all."

Then he scrambled up the ramp, wiping the rain from his face continually to keep from being blinded and, without looking, vaulted over the lip, the railing, and pressed himself against the nearest wall. As far as he could see the street was deserted. Most of the overhead lights were out, but he could see no patrols, or peds, or 'Dogs. He moved quickly to the corner and ducked around it, racing close to the buildings to the next intersection, the next, and the next. He'd ignored the cold, the slashing rain on his head and bare arms, the ache the thunder brought when it exploded in his ears. And at the fourth corner, stopping and grabbing at the pain in his side, he looked out and saw, several blocks distant, a faint fog of illumination that marked the first sections of City Prime.

He grinned, raced back to the ramp and slid down, smiling broadly and almost whistling until he reached the bottom and saw that he was alone.

Alton gladly gave up his seat behind the desk and moved to the window, the better to hide the flashes of hope that eased the sagging tension in his face. He had almost shouted when a gray-haired colonel had careened into the office with news of Thrush's escape, and had not quite hidden his pleasure when Degaldon had been brought in a few moments later, his leg bandaged, to lie groaning on the cushion-bed the captain had arranged for Consul Bendal.

Chips and splinters, he thought; little by little it was, at last, falling apart. So he hoped. So he prayed as he looked through the sheet of rain to the hospital, ignoring the lightning but wincing at the thunder.

"We can't trust them," Faux was saying to Manquila. "They'll start to ask questions."

"Not if I'm in charge."

"Don't be a fool! A general to chase a captain?"

"Then we'll say he attacked the Premier. Fatally wounded him. It will have to be done anyway."

Alton stiffened in the ensuing silence.

"No. We have enough going to keep the people wondering. If he goes, everything will fly off . . . and there'll be war no matter what we do."

"We're wasting time, Consul!"

Alton turned to see the general lean on the desk, his face a handsbreadth from Faux's; but the Consul only leaned back slightly, disdainfully, until Manquila straightened and looked to Torre, who shrugged, seemingly enjoying the Serviceman's discomfort.

"Time," Manquila repeated.

"Is what we still have," Faux said confidently. "What can he do, eh? We're on the screen constantly, we talk to Sens and Reps and anyone else . . . what's he going to say that anyone will believe him? Let him run. There's no place he can go."

Manquila pounded fist into palm, fighting the logic, glaring about the room until finally, with almost a groan of disgust, he turned on his heel and made for the door. "I'll look anyway. In the building, anyway. Maybe there's someone . . ."

"General," Torre said, not moving from in front of the door. "Stay with us for a while."

Faux rose and came around the desk, then stopped to stare at

Alton. The Premier managed a small mocking smile and leaned back against the sill. "All right," he said, without looking away. "Go ahead. But don't take any Service, General. You know you can't trust them."

"He'll have to trust someone," Alton said, quietly.

"He has officers," Faux said, his anger narrowing his eyes. He turned finally, but Manquila had already gone, the door still open, the antechamber empty. Degaldon groaned behind the screen.

"Someone gave him a popper," Torre said to Faux's look. "It won't put him to sleep, but it'll keep him from screaming."

"That's not good enough! Send one of those . . . no, no, take that tunnel down below and go to the hospital. Get a nurse or someone like that, no doctors, and have them bring something to bind and sleep him. I'm not going to listen to that whimpering until nightfall."

Torre hesitated, nearly ran when Faux waved an impatient hand at him, and when the door was closed, Premier and Consul faced each other across the room.

"And you," Faux said. "Are you planning something too?"

Alton watched him blink nervously at a fist of lightning striking down into the plaza, could not help but jump himself at the rip of thunder that seemed to crack open the dome above them. And the Consul was right in one respect: there was indeed little that Thrush could do except run for his life. But Faux seemed to miss what Alton thought was an important point–that James was, in fact, out. Out, and free. And as long as he was, it was something to wait for, to daydream about while he went about his business.

"No," he said. "I'm not going anywhere. There's a near war on, in case you'd forgotten. That, I think, needs me more than it needs you. No, I'm safe for a while longer, I think."

"You're sure?"

For the first time, then, since he had been told by the Consuls what had actually been behind the rebellion, he was. And when he smiled as he walked to his desk, the hatred in Faux's expression was only a ghost away from palpable.

"Get me Frazier from Eurecom again," he ordered. "He's a little wild, but maybe he can speed things up an hour or so. Then let me see that Meditcom fool. But this time, Faux, try not to have them see each other, all right?" He glanced at the timepieces, frowning. "We have two hours until the meeting. And I think you're pessimistic, Faux. I expect we'll know, not tomorrow morning, but before . . . well, I think we'll know by no later than nine, our time."

"You're cutting hours off your own life, Mordan," the Consul said stiffly; but Alton only smiled at the tremor in the man's voice.

Shanlon raced a dozen meters to his left, skidded to a halt and ran back past the ramp. He shouted. He listened. And heard only the storm.

"I want that man out of here as soon as possible, nurse," the doctor said, barely keeping his rage from exploding into yelling. "He's dirty, he's Service and he's disturbing the other patients."

Morag nodded dutifully as the doctor left her, but did not move. She stood at the ward doors and watched the captain kneeling by Delan's bed. They'd been talking for nearly twenty minutes, and she'd been unable to hear any of it because of the demands on her services. He had said little to her when she'd brought him to the Blue, and she said nothing after once looking up and seeing the blurs of white reflect across his mask. He frightened her in spite of his reassurances, and when he stood at last and moved down the aisle toward her, she wanted to turn, to run, to get out into the rain and head for her loft, her Key and the neutral warmth of her bed.

"Morag," he said, using her name for the first time, "do you have an office, someplace where we can talk?"

She nodded, signaled for a replacement and took him two levels up and into the narrow room. He moved at once to the window and stared out at New Hill, turned and talked to her. His voice was calm, his words were not, and when he spoke of shooting the Cenam Consul, she groped for a chair and sat, heavily. Relaxing only slightly when he took off the mask and rubbed a hand over his face.

And when he had done, she said, "I knew it."

"What do you mean?"

She looked for the newsheet, remembered she had trashed it, and took the lightpen from its holder and saw herself as she had been, a hundred years before, trying to decide what to put on Delan's form.

"Shan," she said. "I knew he couldn't have done anything like that."

Thrush fairly leaped from the window to her side, kneeling and taking her hands tightly in his. "Shan? You know Shan, Shanlon Raille?"

"Well . . ." She fought for the trust Delan apparently already had, but could not help seeing in Thrush's face the angered features of the general who would have been a murderer. "Yes, sort of."

"You're not . . . pacted?"

She almost laughed. "Not quite, Captain. I'm close to a dozen years older than he is. No, we just liked to talk. He'd come over from the Hill once in a while and we'd solve the problems of the universe during my breaks. We never bedded, if that's what you wanted to know. I was more like . . . more like a replacement, if you–"

"Yes," Thrush said. "All right, I know. Yes, I know." He drummed his fingers on her knee, took the lightpen absently from her hand and poked at his chin with it. "You've been here since the fighting broke out that nurse told me."

She nodded.

"Shan. Was he . . . I mean, did you ever . . ."

"The ashers were out, still are for all I know," she said bluntly. "If he was caught, he's been flared."

Thrush got to his feet slowly, and for the first time she saw the few highlights of gray in his hair, the slight sag of skin at the sides of his neck. A clattering of rain filled the room.

"He was my nephew," he said softly. "I wish I had been around long enough to be his father."

"You're mourning."

His shoulders lost their military rigidity.

"Don't," she said. "There's something–" She stopped and turned suddenly when a nurse walked into the office, flustered that Morag was not alone. When she tried stammering out a message, Morag took her wrist and led her to the door. "What?" she said, not bothering to conceal her anger, not caring if her breach of hospital decorum was reported to a doctor, or a Panel, or to the Hill itself. Suddenly, in Thrush's shadow and despite Delan's living, she felt alone, and cold, and not caring for anything.

"Downstairs," the young girl said finally, pulling at her wrist but unable to free it. "They want to see you downstairs."

Caro's shoulders ached under the weight. She wanted to cry, she wanted to find a dark shadow and lose herself in it, but the scraping of Ty's boots on the tunnel floor rasped her nerves, and she only hoped it was loud enough for Shan to hear.

Not five minutes after he'd vanished into the outside, Yenkin had let out a moaning yell and fell over, unconscious, his face contorted by pain and the running of blood macabre in the green light's glow. Panicked, she'd forgotten about the rat and tore at her blouse, staunching the flow with the once white cloth but knowing that time would soon become vampiric. Viller had left his place and had sat beside her, concern evident, but indecision, too. She had dropped both her weapons and he'd picked up one, holding it loosely in one hand, tapping the muzzle against his chin. Then, with a grunt that she thought was angry, he stuffed the weapon into one of his pockets and told her to grab the old man's arm.

Ignoring the sound of pain that broke from Ty's pale lips, they lifted him. One arm over his shoulder, one arm over hers: not the most effective way to carry a wounded man, but the only way they could manage.

"Where?" she gasped.

"Docs and 'meds," he said. "No sense in staying. We keep moving in."

The wind raised a rash of bumps on her arms and back, pushed at her hair until it fell over her eyes. They sloshed through puddles, rested on islands, all the while listening for Shanlon to come. She tried to imagine him outside, timing him as he ran (hoping he would run) from one corner to the next, looking for something, anything, that would tell him where they were. Then running back, descending, finding them gone. She thought of his rage, and his fear, and wondered where the hesitation would come: in returning to the outside, in heading back toward the trees, or in following. How many mistakes in turnings would he make? How many seconds would he waste choosing right hand or left?

Her foot struck something wooden, and the pain was a brace that stiffened her leg. She heard Viller muttering to himself under most of Ty's weight. They stopped under a light and she checked Ty's bandage, wishing she had something to wipe off his face.

And when she heard the footsteps and the shouting, she waited for a lull in the storm before screaming, stopping, letting the rat take Yenkin while she ran back into the dark, still yelling, her arms outstretched, one hand scraping along the wall through the grime and the damp until they closed around Shanlon, nearly knocking him over.

He held her, squinting over her shoulder at Viller, who was kneeling over a fallen Yenkin, holding the old man's head clear of the slime with his hands. Rocking. Crooning. Looking up only once and grinning, with a shrug.

And Caro. Her hair darkly wet and clotted with dirt, the bare skin of her back gritty and cold. He stripped off what was left of his shirt and draped it awkwardly over her shoulders, grinning at her protests, then staring at the exposed straps and springs and long blade case. Shaking his head he took it all off and stuffed it into his pockets rather than discarding it. Then he led the girl back, looked down at Ty and sucked his lips in between his teeth.

He pointed to the right-hand branch of a fork straight ahead.

"Prime," he said. "The hospital will be just a few stops further on."

"I don't think he can do it, hom," the rat said.

Caro grabbed at Shanlon's hand. He took hers, then without knowing why, kissed it lightly.

"Just a few stops more," he insisted.

"People," Caro said nervously. "What if there's a patrol or something down here, or up at the mouth?"

Shanlon looked pointedly at her, at Viller, at Ty still unconscious. "Victims," he said simply, took Yenkin's arm and lifted him, his hands under the shoulders and clasped across the chest; the rat took the ankles, and they walked. Faster. Shanlon tensing his stomach muscles at each thump of Ty's head. It wasn't going to work, he thought; Ty was too far gone with too little blood. But to leave him behind once he had come this far would be far worse in nightmares than arriving with him dead.

Twice they stopped and Shanlon checked up the ramp, and the third time he came down grinning.

"Just down the block," he said, and went over again the story they would tell, listening for anything in Viller's voice that would sound out betrayal, anything in Caro's that would raise any objection. Then, with a curt nod and a swallow of something that lodged in his throat, they struggled up the ramp and into the rain.

Delan stared at the ceiling, but he saw nothing but the white caps of Denver's mountains and the contrast they would have with Morag's black hair. He had to think of that; not to would mean thinking of the captain and the voice behind the mask, the careful questions, the assurance that Morag had taken the diagmed's tapes and had hidden their diagnosis away for safekeeping. And in the past hour someone in the ward, or someone passing through, had heard details on the news of impending war. The rumors had spread faster than contagion, and speculation among those still able to talk bordered on the gruesome and the horrid and the intensely patriotic.

Think then of Morag, he'd ordered himself. And he did, while waiting for the pain to leave him, and for her to return.

"One hour," Faux said. "And where in hell is Manquila?"

The hospital's emergency entrance opened onto a forty-meter-square room now jammed with white-and-red islands of civilians in various states of injuries, the major already weeded out, the minor waiting for a nurse to be free, a doctor to pop from a 'tube and cure them, send them home, away from the screams.

A woman holding a young man whose face was raw with two-score scratches; a pair of children sitting at the bleeding feet of their mother; a man lying on a cot, unconscious, a transparent tube dangling from his mouth; another man, beside the first, covered and waiting for the asher that hovered ominously beyond a side door.

Nearly one hundred, Morag estimated as she stepped from the wide-mouthed 'tube and was assailed with the mingling odors of sweet blood and sweeter antiseptics. She could see only five harried nurses to attend to them all, and a single doctor who stood against one wall trying to calm a screaming woman who held a mangled hand in front of his face. One of the nurses was near the entrance and, when their gazes locked, waved furiously, and kept on waving until Morag wound through the islands of white and red. It was, she saw, Arley, and standing almost protectively in front of a motley group of people, two men and a woman, with a third man lying on a gurney between them. She nodded again in answer to Arley's now frantic signals, pushed away a hand that groped for her leg, and . . . stopped.

The short man standing by the wounded man's head. He was staring at her intently, bare-chested and cut in half a dozen places.

"Mistress," he said before Arley could stop him, "I've brought your father here right away. Rats came to our loft only a while ago. I knew you'd want to see him."

Arley frowned. "Father? I thought he died years ago. What is this, Morag?"

"Get me a 'med," she ordered sharply, so surprisingly that Arley hurried away before she could protest.

"He's lost a lot of blood," the red-haired girl said.

Morag was busy at wrist and throat, not daring to do more than glance at Shanlon; and when Arley returned she put the diagmed on the ledge in front of the gurney and cut on the fans. The slab table lifted to waist height after a shudder, the extrusions from the 'med already clamped to the proper places.

A man leaped up in the middle of the room, tearing at the white robe he'd been given, blood bubbling from his mouth.

"Go to him," Morag ordered Arley, who hesitated, heard the doctor bellowing and darted away. "This way," she said to Shanlon and the others, and led them around the perimeter of the room to the wide-mouthed 'tube. Once in, they rose to the tenth, Morag's, level and she handed Yenkin over to one of the younger nurses, shoved the rest into the office and closed the door, leaning against it and frowning, smiling, when Captain Thrush turned away from the window.

"If he says magic," Caro said, "believe him."

"Consul," Alton said, "you're making me nervous."

Faux laughed and, once started, was unable to stop. He leaned against the window sill and held one hand to his chest, shaking his head, sagging until he was almost kneeling. The center of the storm had passed overhead, and now there was only the drumming of rain, and some few jogs of lightning. He put a hand to the window, sobered and stood, and Alton almost lost the confidence he had gained since the captain had fled.

Degaldon whimpered.

Alton swiveled round in his chair. The screens were all blank, Faux's only concession, and he tried to imagine what the fighting would be like as the storm died down. He shook his head, turned back and took note of the time. The room was silent, and suddenly he feared that Faux, after all, would slide through untouched. He left his seat slowly, one hand on the desk, and sat on one corner, staring at the map. Looking at the colors, at the lines, at the water. Hearing Faux pacing behind him again. He looked down at his hands, clenched them, spread his fingers wide and wondered how much strength there was left in them, or in his arms, or in his legs. If he had the nerve, would he be able to grapple with Faux, grapple and win and save himself that way? Or, failing that, try to position himself by the door so that, when Torre or Manquila returned, he would grab for their weapons?

He turned his hands over to look at his palms.

Dropped them to his knees, and sighed.

"You won't be dishonored," Faux said, his voice suspiciously sympathetic. "It won't be as if we'll flare you in an asher."

"You might as well," Alton said. "I'm not going to be heroic, if that's what you want."

He followed the Consul's footsteps to the door and back.

"It's a dream, you know," Faux said. "I don't think anyone really believed we could actually do it. Bendal . . . until the last minute he was working out alternatives. Plebiscites, referendums, spiriting you away with only a false will left behind. Ridiculous. I think he even tried to warn Talle, there at the end. Perhaps he should have gone then, I don't know. It was dangerous enough. Someone could have seen me."

Alton did not want to listen to a madman's blather, but there was nothing he could concentrate on long enough to divert him.

"Just think of what it will mean, Mordan, to hear the name Canada again."

"It will mean . . . blesséd priest, who gives a damn."

"You sound tired, old friend."

Alton looked over his shoulder at the Consul framed by the rain. "We were never friends, Consul. Your name is more than apt."

"Shall we exchange little jokes at the end? Is that the way you want to be remembered?"

Faux tented his fingers, his eyes raised to the ceiling in mockery of thought, and Alton pushed himself away from the desk, took two strides across the floor . . . and stopped. Shook his head. Shrugged.

"I think," he said, "the general likes his nurses more than you."

Shanlon's eyes adjusted slowly to the dim light of the room. A desk on his left with a goose-necked compscreen, beyond it two chairs; on the right a row of shoulder-high lockers, and above them portraits of the Premiers and Directors of Hospital. There was no excitement left in him, no capacity for surprise; he was . . . drained, and the promise of sleep would make him a slave to whoever offered, and produced, and allowed him. The nurse, Morag, had closed the door and opaqued it, telling a colleague outside she had had enough, finally, and needed her rest. The other nurse agreed and promised to pass the word. And when it was done and they were alone, the two women took the chairs, he the desk, James the window sill, and the rat crouched on the floor in front of the door.

One at a time, then, they filled in the gaps. The words, first fast, dislodged themselves painfully, and no one looked to Shanlon when Thrush finally finished.

He tapped on the compscreen with his finger, the clicking of his nail like hail on the window. He had come this far, could perhaps go farther, but as he held the last piece, reluctant to place it, he knew there was nothing left he could do to clear his name. He allowed himself no pride for the guesses he had made correctly—they were secondary now to the damning facts.

He was alone.

Shanlon Raille, venner, magician . . . alone.

He could see—and knew the others did, too, though they would not say it—that word of the coup had to be kept back, from the Noram Community as well as the world. War, internal and globe-wide, was the alternative, as well as the loss of Noram prestige and leadership. The spacefacs would go begging as the medievalists chipped at foundations laid by men like Alton; unity on the ultimate scale would become a utopian definition in a dreamer's lexicon.

There was, then, only one chance to give dawn to a hope—reverse Faux's progress.

And keep it all silent.

With Shanlon the villain.

He licked at his lips and rubbed a fist over his chin, blew out a breath and stared at the ceiling. His vision blurred for a moment, and he blamed it on the light, an overcast gray as the rain slackened in the wake of the thunder. He whistled silently. He wished someone would speak. And when Caro did, he swallowed.

"Shan," she said from her near black corner, "we don't have much time."

They had been given fresh clothes from hospital stores, and he flexed his left arm, then his right, and slid off the desk to his feet. He pressed a finger against the hidden blade. He watched James stand away from the sill and slip on his mask. Viller rose and plucked bemusedly at his new dress, stroked what was left of his hair after Morag had shorn it.

I should be the Premier, Shan thought, for the choice I have to make.

"So," he said. "It's over, and it begins." He looked to his uncle, who nodded, once. "There's only one way we can get inside. We'll have to use the tunnel. From what James says, no one expects us to dare to try. So we'll dare."

They left the office quickly, not touching, not smiling, and took the first 'tube down to the tunnel level. The corridors were still as James led the way, but when they reached the tunnel itself, he stopped them with a wave and pressed back against the wall. Shanlon came up beside him and cocked an ear.

"Torre," James said. "He and a doctor, I think. They're heading back. It must be for Degaldon, unless Faux has already done something to Alton."

Shanlon stared at the opposite wall, considering, then stepped around the corner and looked down the tunnel. Torre and a doctor, heads bent toward each other, neither apparently in any great hurry. There were no guards that he could see, nor could he see that the Consul was carrying a weapon. He checked his own handgun and suddenly began to run, hearing and grinning at James's muttered oath behind him. His footsteps were as soft as he could make them, but long before he reached the pair, the doctor turned, hesitated, and Torre followed suit.

Shanlon waved.

The Consul's right hand lifted in reaction, then froze as his eyes widened and he took a step back. His left hand slapped to his waist and Shanlon dove forward, firing, watching the Consul snap back as though slapped, then buckle at the knees and fall face down. The doctor, young and bulky, immediately dropped the portmed in his hands and raised his arms as he sidled back until he was stopped by the wall. The others had entered the tunnel at a run, and as they passed, Viller clipped the doctor with the butt of his weapon, paused only long enough to be sure he was still breathing, then raced to catch up with Thrush and Raille, who were already at the door to the stairwell, and waiting.

Faux pushed away from the desk and stood, walked carefully to the wallmap and punched a fist against the Eurepac/Meditcom border. "Here," he said. "Right here, and there's nothing I can do about it."

"You can wait," Alton said. He had checked behind the screen, but Degaldon was still unconscious. Sooner or later he'll wake up, the Premier thought, and I'll kill him if he starts screaming.

"That, by the way," Faux said, waving at the comunit on the desk, "was the general. He says there's a captain in the Service wandering around the hospital."

"It's a big place," was all Alton could say to the smug grin on Faux's face as he turned back to the map.

"Right now," the Consul said, "they're in the halls, talking, probably making deals already we'll never hear about. Some of them will be at the table behind their papers. The others will come in all at the same time. Protocol. If the doors are wide enough." He looked back over his shoulder, his smile satisfied and relaxed. "They're not stupid, Mordan. They won't fight."

"Are you praying, and telling me something you wish you knew?"

"I think," Faux said, "I've had enough of talking to you." He strode angrily to the door, opened it and left, and Alton heard him summoning the conspiring officers from the reception chamber below. I wish, he thought with a trace of regret, that I were as effective with the rest of his people.

Caro listened as the two men argued and the rat leaned against the wall, staring idly down the tunnel. She wished, then, that Morag had come with them, but exactly why she could not say.

She only knew, however, that she herself would not be left behind. It was not a crusade nor a drive for vengeance—or so she hoped when she allowed herself to think about it—but rather a keeping together of something Shanlon had started. An indefinable something that linked them without words, without pacts, without the formalities of the legal. Her weapon weighed heavily in her hand, and she let her arm hang loosely in imitation of the rat. Why Viller came she still could not understand. Shan had made it clear that he would be necessary in letting the people know the true make-up of the rebels, yet Shan had allowed him to jeopardize his life.

And Ty. Ty. Brought immediately to an intensive care level as soon as Morag had read the diagmed's initial report. There wasn't much left of him, and little for him to look forward to; nevertheless, he was . . . Ty. And she did not want him dead.

"All right," James snapped. "Damnit, Shan, have it your own way."

"One more time," Raille said as Caro broke through her woolgathering and leaned closer to listen.

"I said all right, didn't I?"

"Blesséd priest, James, it'll take us forever to climb all those stairs. The whole thing could be over before we ever get there!"

"And if we use the 'tube, we can only go so far. Then it's one at a time, and we can be picked off. Idiot, is that what you came this far to have done?"

Shanlon turned to her in exasperation. "Caro, does not that 'tube over there go as far as the Chamber levels?"

"It has to," she said. "Otherwise, why bother?"

"Right," Shanlon said as though that proved his point.

"But it does not go as far as we need it to, Shan," James said, his voice tight to keep from yelling.

"It must," Shanlon insisted. "Suppose Alton gets sick, all right? What are they going to do, snake him down those alternate 'tubes you told me about? Upend him on a stretcher and let him drop? It doesn't make sense!"

Caro sighed and paced slowly across the mouth of the lifttube, listening as they went round and round for the fourth or fifth time, their voices rising and falling in harsh, grated whispers. She wanted to shout herself, to shut them up and get them moving, and she looked to Viller for support, found nothing but a blank and amused stare, and leaned against the wall, unwillingly letting her gaze travel down the floor to the dark still figure of the dead Consul. Beyond him the doctor still slumped against the wall. And beyond that point, the fall of the lights' haze that blocked the other end.

Suddenly James clapped his hands and she jumped, looked, and saw him frown in concentrated thought.

"If you didn't yell so much," he muttered.

"What yell? You want a yell, I'll give you a yell, idiot. Now what's going on in there?" and Shanlon snapped a finger against James's mask.

"There's a room," James said, "behind the Premier's office. We were stuck in there on the second night. On the wall there's a small comunit, barely large enough to look at without eyestrain. I wondered about that but didn't say anything at the time because how do I know what Alton likes? Anyway, next to that there's a part of the wall that juts out into the room. It's covered with some curious mural, and Alton called it his escape hatch. I thought he meant the painting. He didn't. He meant it was a cover for . . . for this 'tube."

"Then why the hell didn't you use it?"

"Well, *I* didn't know about it, and he couldn't even if he wanted to. He had a near war on his hands, if you recall. Still does, for that matter. If he dropped out of sight and ran, all hell would have broken loose, here *and* there. Besides . . ." and James closed his eyes to bring back a scene. "Besides, there's a lock and latch on it, top and bottom. I suspect Faux has the key."

Caro nodded as James talked, then looked back over her shoulder. Frowned. Listened. Once it was quiet, she could hear voices from the hospital end. She turned to warn Shanlon, but the venner had heard them too and was pushing James into the 'tube ahead of him, grabbing at Caro's arm and scowling at the rat, who was the last to climb in.

Her stomach lurched. Her vision distorted. She clasped both hands tightly around her weapon and pressed it to her chest. She knew it wasn't the 'tube or the lifting; it was what would come after, and she wasn't sure she could do it if she had to.

Morag and a doctor stood at the foot of his bed, conferring quietly and angering him with their secretiveness. She had just finished telling him what had happened not twenty minutes before in her office when the doctor, demanding to know what the Blue was doing on his floor, began without permission a ruthlessly efficient examination. Caine said nothing except when asked, his eyes refusing to leave Morag's face as she was reprimanded and threatened and then ordered into conference.

He was patient for several minutes, then tried to lift himself onto his elbows to interrupt when he saw the Service officer come through the doors at the other end of the ward. He stared and fell back, but the general had stopped in his headlong walk, grabbed at the arm of a colonel beside him and pointed.

No, Delan thought, and groaned loudly.

The doctor scowled; Morag glanced, saw his wide eyes and followed their gaze.

"Doctor," she began, but the general had already pushed his man back through the doors and was gone.

Delan breathed. Deeply. Once. And wondered how long he would have until it was over.

The space between the 'tube's lip and the false wall was something less than a meter, little enough room for them all to stand much less exert any meaningful pressure on the locks they knew were there.

"Burn it," Viller said.

Shanlon nodded. "Have to."

"It'll smell like hell," James said, doubt heavy, then suddenly clearing. "But there's no sense in wondering what will happen, is there? If there's no one in there, we're safe. For a while."

He knelt as best he could, and Shanlon averted his face when the gun's red tongue struck the wall, charred it, bored it and met the metal on the other side. James was right, the stench was horrid, and more . . . before he had taken all the latch through, his handgun lost its charge and he had to take the rat's. Within moments he had finished, stood and had started on the highest point. And again the charge weakened, and Shanlon reluctantly handed over his own.

Caro's hand found its way to his wrist, and he covered it, squeezed it, released it when James grunted and pushed and the door fell out to the floor with a thunderous crash that had them all on their hands and knees, waiting, and . . . waiting.

Then James ran for the door with Shanlon beside him, pressed an ear to it, looked down at him and shrugged. Shanlon pointed to the handgun; James indicated it still had a charge. Then he turned and motioned to Caro, who gave him hers.

"All right," he whispered, and he went through the door before it had opened completely, dropping to his right as James dropped to his left, Caro and the rat ducking straight in and running for the desk and the cover it offered.

"Captain," the Premier said, turning from the window. Then, "Blesséd priest, Shanlon Raille!"

Shanlon acknowledged Alton with a quick nod as he hurried across the room to the outer door. He heard voices beyond it, several of them, and waved frantically to James, who was trying to explain and heed the warning at the same time.

Suddenly, the door opened and Shanlon, not taking time to think, reached out and grabbed at Faux's tunic, yanked him in across the threshold and cast him to one side. Raised his handgun and aimed it very carefully at the nearest Service officer and shook his head. The others, four in all, were too amazed to move quickly, and before they could recover, James had added his weapon to Shanlon's.

Faux groaned and pushed himself to his feet.

The colonels dropped face down, arms stretched wide, at James's silent order, and Viller ran past them to pluck at their weapons, grinning, whistling, poking at them with a finger when they tried to lift their heads.

Shanlon watched it all carefully, then turned around and saw Caro walk up to Faux, her arms stiff at her sides, ignoring the inaudible words of the Premier. Faux sneered, and she slapped him, twice, bringing blood to his mouth and a great red welt that stained his cheek.

Done, he thought, dropped his arm and left the officers to James and the rat. He walked quickly to the windowwall and slid a portion of it aside, stepped out onto the terrace and dropped his gun to grip the railing. The wind had not died, nor had the rain, but he could do nothing more than stare out over the city. So long in coming, the end had come too fast, and he was unable to accept it just yet, not for a while. He turned and watched as James herded the officers into Alton's office; most likely, he thought, to bind them and cell them with poor Consul Faux. The captain was taking no chances in letting any of them out of his sight while he told the Premier everything.

Shanlon supposed he should be in there, too, to receive the thanks of the nation and of its Premier, but he did not want to hear any more about it until he had done some thinking on his own.

And while he was watching, he saw a movement in the lifttube, a glimmer of a uniform, and General Manquila stepped out, took one look into the office and turned, saw Raille . . . and walked slowly toward him.

Shanlon tensed, looked up and down the terrace, then relaxed as he decided it was fruitless to run.

Manquila stepped carelessly through the door and moved to lean against the railing some three meters away; too far to jump for him, close enough to fire that gun before Shanlon had taken two steps.

"Nice night," Shanlon said into the rain.

The general grunted and toyed with his weapon. "I'll have to leave the city," he said. "A shame. It could have been mine."

"Not quite," Shanlon said.

"If you're thinking about Faux, don't. He probably thought he was very clever, pushing Bendal into dying, thinking he would have two of the three while Torre and I and Degaldon fought over the third. He wanted it all. And we knew it. He wouldn't have gotten any of it, you know. Shag, but it would have been a nice city to have."

Shanlon readied to flex his arm, hoping the rain wouldn't make his hand too slippery to hold the blade. He eased himself away from the wall in hopes he would have room, and Manquila straightened then and lifted his gun.

"Right there," the general said. "Stop right there."

A shadow on Shanlon's right. He did not look.

"Why bother to kill me now?" he said. "You're wasting your time. You could have been halfway to the suburbs by now if you hurry."

"You won't feel a thing," the general said, gripped his gun wrist with his free hand, spread his legs, and . . . the shadow moved. Into a blur. Into a dark yelling figure that wrapped itself around the general's torso while it lifted the gun to fire harmlessly into the storm. The momentum of Viller's leap thrust them both against the railing, lifted them, balanced them, and as Shanlon moved to grab at something to stop them, he thought he saw the general's left foot push off the terrace floor.

They fell, soundlessly, into the rain.

Shanlon had hoped for something degrees more dramatic. Dawn. A fresh clear sky. A cleansing breeze that ruffled the young trees in the plaza and brought out the citizenry in gay celebration.

But it was noon when Alton had finished making the arrangements for him, and the slate of the storm still hung over the city. He was in the back room of Alton's office, Caro beside him and saying nothing.

Finally, when he had made up his mind with a short sharp nod, he turned away from the window and looked at her hair, her face, the nervous twisting of her hands.

"I have a magic trick for you," he said with a smile.

"Shanlon, I don't ever want to hear that word again."

He laughed and with two fingers on her chin made her look at him. "Just one," he said, "and I promise no more. Now please watch me carefully, very carefully, and you'll be sure that my hands are completely empty."

"Shan," she said, in spite of herself watching his hands weave, and dart, and reach out for her ear. "Shan, are you really going to the Colonies?"

"Keep watching. I have to. There isn't a person in the country outside these two rooms, except for Morag and Delan, who don't think I led the rats in their rebellion. I have no place else to go, Caro. And please, keep watching."

"Do you want to go?"

His smile wavered. "No. Because I don't like leaving what I know so well. But yes, because for someone like me the Colonies will give me a chance to practice my art."

"Which? The magic, or the talking?"

He snapped his fingers and pulled from behind her ear a small white fan he opened and placed in her hands. Then he stepped back and watched her examine it, turning it round, then staring.

"There's nothing on it," she said.

"I told you I only made the pictures. I didn't have time for one. But Morag makes the fans, and I took one from her desk just before we came over."

"Can I go with you?"

"Mistress–"

"Ty's dead, Shanlon, he died last night. What do I have any more than you?"

"There won't be a war now, or so it seems. You can have dozens of things right here. Your father . . . you could probably have his seat if you wanted."

Caro lifted the fan to cover the lower part of her face, her brow creased, her eyes laughing. "Does this look like a Senator to you?"

"It's a long way to fly, Caro," he said.

"If I get tired, I'll use my wiles and have you carry me."

"We'll be going farther than the moon."

She lay the fan into his open palm. "I know what picture I want on here."

"Caro–"

"Shanlon, if you say one more word . . . and spoil my moment . . . I promise you now that you'll live to regret it."

Shanlon closed the fan.

And grinned.